THE COMPLEAT WEREWOLF

ANTHONY BOUCHER

Carroll & Graf Publishers, Inc.
New York

First Carroll & Graf edition 1990

Published by arrangement with Curtis Brown, Ltd

ACKNOWLEDGMENTS

"The Compleat Werewolf," originally published in *Unknown Worlds*,
April, 1942, copyright 1942 by Street & Smith Publications, Inc. Reprinted
by permission of The Condé Nast Publications, Inc.

"The Pink Caterpillar," originally published in *Adventure Magazine*,
copyright 1945 by Anthony Boucher.

"Q.U.R.," originally published in *Unknown Worlds*, 1942, copyright
1942 by Street & Smith Publications, Inc. Reprinted by permission of
The Condé Nast Publications, Inc.

"Robinc," originally published in *Astounding Science Fiction*,
September, 1943, copyright 1943 by Street & Smith Publications, Inc.
Reprinted by permission of The Condé Nast Publications, Inc.

"Snulbug," originally published in *Unknown Worlds*, December, 1941,
copyright 1941 by Street & Smith Publications, Inc. Reprinted by permission
of The Condé Nast Publications, Inc.

"Mr. Lupescu," originally published in *Weird Tales Magazine*,
September, 1945, copyright 1945 by Anthony Boucher.

"They Bite," originally published in *Unknown Worlds*, June, 1942,
copyright 1942 by Street & Smith Publications, Inc. Reprinted by permission
of The Condé Nast Publications, Inc.

"Expedition," originally published in *Thrilling Wonder Stories*, August,
1943, copyright 1943 by Anthony Boucher.

"We Print the Truth," originally published in *Astounding Science
Fiction*, 1943, copyright 1943 by Street & Smith Publications, Inc.
Reprinted by permission of The Condé Nast Publications, Inc.

"The Ghost of Me," originally published in *Astounding Science Fiction*,
June, 1942, copyright 1942 by Street & Smith Publications, Inc. Reprinted
by permission of The Condé Nast Publications, Inc.

Carroll & Graf Publishers, Inc.
260 Fifth Avenue
New York, NY 10001

ISBN: 0-88184-557-4

Manufactured in the United States of America

Contents

THE COMPLEAT WEREWOLF

Anthony Boucher was long known as an important book critic and editor, music scholar, master of languages and successful novelist. He was also a superb short-story writer of science fiction and fantasy: inventive, prolific—and always entertaining.

The stories and novelettes in this collection were chosen for the sheer virtuosity of their themes, moods, backgrounds; for their technical brilliance; for their insights; for their laughter.

They were wonderfully peopled by moth-eaten little demons, grim interplanetary predators, rebellious androids and doppelgangers; by humans with otherworld talents; and finally, not least, by one very special werewolf.

The Complete Werewolf is a memorable volume, representing as it does a rich display of a fine author's creativeness and craftsmanship.

The Compleat Werewolf

*T*he professor glanced at the note:

Don't be silly—Gloria.

Wolfe Wolf crumpled the sheet of paper into a yellow ball and hurled it out the window into the sunshine of the bright campus spring. He made several choice and profane remarks in fluent Middle High German.

Emily looked up from typing the proposed budget for the departmental library. "I'm afraid I didn't understand that, Professor Wolf. I'm weak on Middle High."

"Just improvising," said Wolf, and sent a copy of the *Journal of English and Germanic Philology* to follow the telegram.

Emily rose from the typewriter. "There's something the matter. Did the committee reject your monograph on Hager?"

"That monumental contribution to human knowledge? Oh, no. Nothing so important as that."

· "But you're so upset—"

"The office wife!" Wolf snorted. "And pretty damned polyandrous at that, with the whole department on your hands. Go away."

Emily's dark little face lit up with a flame of righteous anger that removed any trace of plainness. "Don't talk to me like that, Mr. Wolf. I'm simply trying to help you. And it isn't the whole department. It's—"

Professor Wolf picked up an inkwell, looked after the tele-gram and the *Journal,* then set the glass pot down again. "No. There are better ways of going to pieces. Sorrows drown easier than they smash. Get Herbrecht to take my two-o'clock, will you?"

"Where are you going?"

"To hell in sectors. So long."

"Wait. Maybe I can help you. Remember when the dean jumped you for serving drinks to students? Maybe I can—"

Wolf stood in the doorway and extended one arm impres-sively, pointing with that curious index which was as long as the middle finger. "Madam, academically you are indispensa-ble. You are the prop and stay of the existence of this depart-ment. But at the moment this department can go to hell, where it will doubtless continue to need your invaluable services."

"But don't you see—" Emily's voice shook. "No. Of course not. You wouldn't see. You're just a man—no, not even a man. You're just Professor Wolf. You're Woof-woof."

Wolf staggered. "I'm what?"

"Woof-woof. That's what everybody calls you because your name's Wolfe Wolf. All your students, everybody. But you wouldn't notice a thing like that. Oh, no. Woof-woof, that's what you are."

"This," said Wolfe Wolf, "is the crowning blow. My heart is breaking, my world is shattered, I've got to walk a mile from the campus to find a bar; but all this isn't enough. I've got to be called Woof-woof. Goodbye!"

He turned, and in the doorway caromed into a vast and yielding bulk, which gave out with a noise that might have been either a greeting of "Wolf!" or more probably an in-evitable grunt of "Oof!"

Wolf backed into the room and admitted Professor Fearing, paunch, pince-nez, cane and all. The older man waddled over to his desk, plumped himself down, and exhaled a long breath. "My dear boy," he gasped. "Such impetuosity."

"Sorry, Oscar."

"Ah, youth—" Professor Fearing fumbled about for a handkerchief, found none, and proceeded to polish his pince-nez on his somewhat stringy necktie. "But why such haste to depart? And why is Emily crying?"

"Is she?"

"You see?" said Emily hopelessly, and muttered "Woof-woof" into her damp handkerchief.

"And why do copies of the JEGP fly about my head as I harmlessly cross the campus? Do we have teleportation on our hands?"

"Sorry," Wolf repeated curtly. "Temper. Couldn't stand that ridiculous argument of Glocke's. Goodbye."

"One moment." Professor Fearing fished into one of his unnumbered handkerchiefless pockets and produced a sheet of yellow paper. "I believe this is yours?"

Wolf snatched at it and quickly converted it into confetti.

Fearing chuckled. "How well I remember when Gloria was a student here! I was thinking of it only last night when I saw her in *Moonbeams and Melody*. How she did upset this whole department! Heavens, my boy, if I'd been a younger man myself—"

"I'm going. You'll see about Herbrecht, Emily?"

Emily sniffled and nodded.

"Come, Wolfe." Fearing's voice had grown more serious. "I didn't mean to plague you. But you mustn't take these things too hard. There are better ways of finding consolation than in losing your temper or getting drunk."

"Who said anything about—"

"Did you need to say it? No, my boy, if you were to— You're not a religious man, are you?"

"Good God, no," said Wolf contradictorily.

"If only you were. . . . If I might make a suggestion, Wolfe, why don't you come over to the Temple tonight? We're having very special services. They might take your mind off Glo— off your troubles."

"Thanks, no. I've always meant to visit your Temple—I've heard the damnedest rumors about it—but not tonight. Some other time."

"Tonight would be especially interesting."

"Why? What's so special of a feast day about April thirtieth?"

Fearing shook his gray head. "It is shocking how ignorant a scholar can be outside of his chosen field. . . . But you know the place, Wolfe; I'll hope to see you there tonight."

"Thanks. But my troubles don't need any supernatural solutions. A couple of zombies will do nicely, and I do *not* mean serviceable stiffs. Goodbye, Oscar." He was halfway through the door before he added as an afterthought, " 'Bye, Emily."

"Such rashness," Fearing murmured. "Such impetuosity. Youth is a wonderful thing to enjoy, is it not, Emily?"

Emily said nothing, but plunged into typing the proposed budget as though all the fiends of hell were after her, as indeed many of them were.

The sun was setting, and Wolf's tragic account of his troubles had laid an egg, too. The bartender had polished every glass in the joint and still the repetitive tale kept pouring forth. He was torn between a boredom new even in his experience and a professional admiration for a customer who could consume zombies indefinitely.

"Did I tell you about the time she flunked the mid-term?" Wolf demanded truculently.

"Only three times," said the bartender.

"All right, then; I'll tell you. Yunnerstand, I don't do things like this. Profeshical ethons, that's what's I've got. But this was different. This wasn't like somebody that doesn't know just because she doesn't know; this was a girl that didn't know because she wasn't the kind of girl that has to know the kind of things a girl has to know if she's the kind of girl that ought to know that kind of things. Yunnerstand?"

The bartender cast a calculating glance at the plump little man who sat alone at the end of the deserted bar, carefully nursing his gin-and-tonic.

"She made me see that. She made me see lossa things and I can still see the things she made me see the things. It wasn't just like a professor falls for a coed, yunnerstand? This was different. This was wunnaful. This was like a whole new life, like."

The bartender sidled down to the end of the bar. "Brother," he whispered softly.

The little man with the odd beard looked up from his gin-and-tonic. "Yes, colleague?"

"If I listen to that potted professor another five minutes, I'm going to start smashing up the joint. How's about slipping down there and standing in for me, huh?"

The little man looked Wolf over and fixed his gaze especially on the hand that clenched the tall zombie glass. "Gladly, colleague," he nodded.

The bartender sighed a gust of relief.

"She was Youth," Wolf was saying intently to where the bartender had stood. "But it wasn't just that. This was different. She was Life and Excitement and Joy and Ecstasy and stuff. Yunner—" He broke off and stared at the empty space. "*Uh*-mazing!" he observed. "Right before my very eyes. *Uh*-mazing!"

"You were saying, colleague?" the plump little man prompted from the adjacent stool.

Wolf turned. "So there you are. Did I tell you about the time I went to her house to check her term paper?"

"No. But I have a feeling you will."

"Howja know? Well, this night—"

The little man drank slowly; but his glass was empty by the time Wolf had finished the account of an evening of point-lessly tentative flirtation. Other customers were drifting in, and the bar was now about a third full.

"—and ever since then—" Wolf broke off sharply. "That isn't you," he objected.

"I think it is, colleague."

"But you're a bartender and *you* aren't a bartender."

"No. I'm a magician."

"Oh. That explains it. Now, like I was telling you— Hey! Your bald is beard."

"I beg your pardon?"

"Your bald is beard. Just like your head. It's all jussa fringe running around."

"I like it that way."

"And your glass is empty."

"That's all right too."

"Oh, no it isn't. It isn't every night you get to drink with a man that proposed to Gloria Garton and got turned down. This is an occasion for celebration." Wolf thumped loudly on the bar and held up his first two fingers.

The little man regarded their equal length. "No," he said softly. "I think I'd better not. I know my capacity. If I have another—well, things might start happening."

"Lettemappen!"

"No. Please, colleague. I'd rather—"

The bartender brought the drinks. "Go on, brother," he whispered. "Keep him quiet. I'll do you a favor sometime."

Reluctantly the little man sipped at his fresh gin-and-tonic.

The professor took a gulp of his nth zombie. "My name's Woof-woof," he proclaimed. "Lots of people call me Wolfe Wolf. They think that's funny. But it's really Woof-woof. Wazoors?"

The other paused a moment to decipher that Arabic-sounding word, then said, "Mine's Ozymandias the Great."

"That's a funny name."

"I told you, I'm a magician. Only I haven't worked for a long time. Theatrical managers are peculiar, colleague. They don't want a real magician. They won't even let me show 'em my best stuff. Why, I remember one night in Darjeeling—"

"Glad to meet you, Mr. . . . Mr.—"

"You can call me Ozzy. Most people do."

"Glad to meet you, Ozzy. Now, about this girl. This Gloria. Yunnerstand, donya?"

"Sure, colleague."

"She thinks being a professor of German is nothing. She wants something glamorous. She says if I was an actor, now, or a G-man— Yunnerstand?"

Ozymandias the Great nodded.

"Awright, then! So yunnerstand. Fine. But whatddayou want to keep talking about it for? Yunnerstand. That's that. To hell with it."

Ozymandias' round and fringed face brightened. "Sure," he said, and added recklessly, "Let's drink to that."

They clinked glasses and drank. Wolf carelessly tossed off a toast in Old Low Frankish, with an unpardonable error in the use of the genitive.

The two men next to them began singing "My Wild Irish Rose," but trailed off disconsolately. "What we need," said the one with the derby, "is a tenor."

"What I need," Wolf muttered, "is a cigarette."

"Sure," said Ozymandias the Great. The bartender was drawing beer directly in front of them. Ozymandias reached across the bar, removed a lighted cigarette from the barkeep's ear, and handed it to his companion.

"Where'd that come from?"

"I don't quite know. All I know is how to get them. I told you I was a magician."

"Oh. I see. Pressajijijation."

"No. Not a prestidigitator; I said a magician. Oh, blast it! I've done it again. More than one gin-and-tonic and I start showing off."

"I don't believe you," said Wolf flatly. "No such thing as magicians. That's just as silly as Oscar Fearing and his Temple and what's so special about April thirtieth anyway?"

The bearded man frowned. "Please, colleague. Let's forget it."

"No. I don't believe you. You pressajijijated that cigarette. You didn't magic it." His voice began to rise. "You're a fake."

"Please, brother," the barkeep whispered. "Keep him quiet."

"All right," said Ozymandias wearily. "I'll show you something that can't be prestidigitation." The couple adjoining had begun to sing again. "They need a tenor. All right; listen!"

And the sweetest, most ineffably Irish tenor ever heard

joined in on the duet. The singers didn't worry about the source; they simply accepted the new voice gladly and were spurred on to their very best, with the result that the bar knew the finest harmony it had heard since the night the Glee Club was suspended en masse.

Wolf looked impressed, but shook his head. "That's not magic either. That's ventrocolism."

"As a matter of strict fact, that was a street singer who was killed in the Easter Rebellion. Fine fellow, too; never heard a better voice, unless it was that night in Darjeeling when—"

"Fake!" said Wolfe Wolf loudly and belligerently.

Ozymandias once more contemplated that long index finger. He looked at the professor's dark brows that met in a straight line over his nose. He picked his companion's limpish hand off the bar and scrutinized the palm. The growth of hair was not marked, but it was perceptible.

The magician chortled. "And you sneer at magic!"

"Whasso funny about me sneering at magic?"

Ozymandias lowered his voice. "Because, my fine furry friend, you are a werewolf."

The Irish martyr had begun "Rose of Tralee," and the two mortals were joining in valiantly.

"I'm what?"

"A werewolf."

"But there isn't any such thing. Any fool knows that."

"Fools," said Ozymandias, "know a great deal which the wise do not. There are werewolves. There always have been, and quite probably always will be." He spoke as calmly and assuredly as though he were mentioning that the earth was round. "And there are three infallible physical signs: the meeting of eyebrows, the long index finger, the hairy palms. You have all three. And even your name is an indication. Family names do not come from nowhere. Every Smith has an ancestor somewhere who was a smith. Every Fisher comes from a family that once fished. And your name is Wolf."

The statement was so quiet, so plausible, that Wolf faltered.

"But a werewolf is a man that changes into a wolf. I've never done that. Honest I haven't."

"A mammal," said Ozymandias, "is an animal that bears its young alive and suckles them. A virgin is nonetheless a mammal. Because you have never changed does not make you any the less a werewolf."

"But a werewolf—" Suddenly Wolf's eyes lit up. "A were-wolf! But that's even better than a G-man! Now I can show Gloria!"

"What on earth do you mean, colleague?"

Wolf was climbing down from his stool. The intense excitement of this brilliant new idea seemed to have sobered him. He grabbed the little man by the sleeve. "Come on. We're going to find a nice quiet place. And you're going to prove you're a magician."

"But how?"

"You're going to show me how to change!"

Ozymandias finished his gin-and-tonic, and with it drowned his last regretful hesitation. "Colleague," he announced, "you're on!"

Professor Oscar Fearing, standing behind the curiously carved lectern of the Temple of the Dark Truth, concluded the reading of the prayer with mumbling sonority. "And on this night of all nights, in the name of the black light that glows in the darkness, we give thanks!" He closed the parchment-bound book and faced the small congregation, calling out with fierce intensity, "Who wishes to give his thanks to the Lower Lord?"

A cushioned dowager rose. "I give thanks!" she shrilled excitedly. "My Ming Choy was sick, even unto death. I took of her blood and offered it to the Lower Lord, and he had mercy and restored her to me!"

Behind the altar an electrician checked his switches and spat disgustedly. "Bugs! Every last one of 'em!"

The man who was struggling into a grotesque and horrible costume paused and shrugged. "They pay good money. What's it to us if they're bugs?"

A tall, thin old man had risen uncertainly to his feet. "I give thanks!" he cried. "I give thanks to the Lower Lord that I have finished my great work. My protective screen against magnetic bombs is a tried and proven success, to the glory of our country and science and the Lord."

"Crackpot," the electrician muttered.

The man in costume peered around the altar. "Crackpot, hell! That's Chiswick from the physics department. Think of a man like that falling for this stuff! And listen to him: He's even telling about the government's plans for installation. You know, I'll bet you one of these fifth columnists could pick up something around here."

There was silence in the Temple when the congregation had finished its thanksgiving. Professor Fearing leaned over the lectern and spoke quietly and impressively. "As you know, brothers in Darkness, tonight is May Eve, the thirtieth of April, the night consecrated by the Church to that martyr missionary St. Walpurgis, and by us to other and deeper purposes. It is on this night, and this night only, that we may directly give our thanks to the Lower Lord himself. Not in wanton orgy and obscenity, as the Middle Ages misconceived his desires, but in praise and in the deep, dark joy that issues forth from Blackness."

"Hold your hats, boys," said the man in the costume. "Here I go again."

"*Eka!*" Fearing thundered. "*Dva tri chatur! Pancha! Shas sapta! Ashta nava dasha ekadasha!*" He paused. There was always the danger that at this moment some scholar in this university town might recognize that the invocation, though perfect Sanskrit, consisted solely of the numbers from one to eleven. But no one stirred, and he launched forth in more apposite Latin: "*Per vota nostra ipse nunc surgat nobis dicatus Baal Zebub!*"

"Baal Zebub!" the congregation chorused.

"Cue," said the electrician, and pulled a switch.

The lights flickered and went out. Lightning played across the sanctuary. Suddenly out of the darkness came a sharp bark, a yelp of pain, and a long-drawn howl of triumph.

A blue light now began to glow dimly. In its faint reflection, the electrician was amazed to see his costumed friend at his side, nursing his bleeding hand.

"What the hell—" the electrician whispered.

"Hanged if I know. I go out there on cue, all ready to make my terrifying appearance, and what happens? Great big hell of a dog up and nips my hand. Why didn't they tell me they'd switched the script?"

In the glow of the blue light the congregation reverently contemplated the plump little man with the fringe of beard and the splendid gray wolf that stood beside him. "Hail, O Lower Lord!" resounded the chorus, drowning out one spinster's murmur of "But my *dear*, I swear he was *much* handsomer last year."

"Colleagues!" said Ozymandias the Great, and there was utter silence, a dread hush awaiting the momentous words of the Lower Lord. Ozymandias took one step forward, placed his tongue carefully between his lips, uttered the ripest, juiciest raspberry of his career, and vanished, wolf and all.

Wolfe Wolf opened his eyes and shut them again hastily. He had never expected the quiet and sedate Berkeley Inn to install centrifugal rooms. It wasn't fair. He lay in darkness, waiting for the whirling to stop and trying to reconstruct the past night.

He remembered the bar all right, and the zombies. And the bartender. Very sympathetic chap that, up until he suddenly changed into a little man with a fringe of beard. That was where things began getting strange. There was something about a cigarette and an Irish tenor and a werewolf. Fantastic idea, that. Any fool knows—

Wolf sat up suddenly. He *was* the werewolf. He threw back the bedclothes and stared down at his legs. Then he sighed relief. They were long legs. They were hairy enough. They were brown from much tennis. But they were indisputably human.

He got up, resolutely stifling his qualms, and began to pick up the clothing that was scattered nonchalantly about the floor. A crew of gnomes was excavating his skull, but he hoped they might go away if he didn't pay too much attention to them. One thing was certain: he was going to be good from now on. Gloria or no Gloria, heartbreak or no heartbreak, drowning your sorrows wasn't good enough. If you felt like this and could imagine you'd been a werewolf—

But why should he have imagined it in such detail? So many fragmentary memories seemed to come back as he dressed. Going up Strawberry Canyon with the fringed beard, finding a desolate and isolated spot for magic, learning the words—

Hell, he could even remember the words. The word that changed you and the one that changed you back.

Had he made up those words, too, in his drunken imaginings? And had he made up what he could only barely recall—the wonderful, magical freedom of changing, the single, sharp pang of alteration and then the boundless happiness of being lithe and fleet and free?

He surveyed himself in the mirror. Save for the unwonted wrinkles in his conservative single-breasted gray suit, he looked exactly what he was: a quiet academician; a little better built, a little more impulsive, a little more romantic than most, perhaps, but still just that—Professor Wolf.

The rest was nonsense. But there was, that impulsive side of him suggested, only one way of proving the fact. And that was to say The Word.

"All right," said Wolfe Wolf to his reflection. "I'll show you." And he said it.

The pang was sharper and stronger than he'd remembered. Alcohol numbs you to pain. It tore him for a moment with an anguish like the descriptions of childbirth. Then it was gone, and he flexed his limbs in happy amazement. But he was not a lithe, fleet, free beast. He was a helplessly trapped wolf, irrevocably entangled in a conservative single-breasted gray suit.

He tried to rise and walk, but the long sleeves and legs tripped him over flat on his muzzle. He kicked with his paws, trying to tear his way out, and then stopped. Werewolf or no werewolf, he was likewise still Professor Wolf, and this suit had cost thirty-five dollars. There must be some cheaper way of securing freedom than tearing the suit to shreds.

He used several good, round Low German expletives. This was a complication that wasn't in any of the werewolf legends he'd ever read. There, people just—boom!—became wolves or —bang!—became men again. When they were men, they wore clothes; when they were wolves, they wore fur. Just like Hyperman becoming Bark Lent again on top of the Empire State Building and finding his street clothes right there. Most misleading. He began to remember now how Ozymandias the Great had made him strip before teaching him the words—

The words! That was it. All he had to do was say the word that changed you back—*Absarka!*—and he'd be a man again, comfortably fitted inside his suit. Then he could strip and play what games he wished. You see? Reason solves all. "*Absarka!*" he said.

Or thought he said. He went through all the proper mental processes for saying *Absarka!* but all that came out of his muzzle was a sort of clicking whine. And he was still a conservatively dressed and helpless wolf.

This was worse than the clothes problem. If he could be released only by saying *Absarka!* and if, being a wolf, he could say nothing, why, there he was. Indefinitely. He could go find Ozzy and ask—but how could a wolf wrapped up in a gray suit get safely out of a hotel and set out hunting for an unknown address?

He was trapped. He was lost. He was—

"*Absarka!*"

Professor Wolfe Wolf stood up in his grievously rumpled gray suit and beamed on the beard-fringed face of Ozymandias the Great.

"You see, colleague," the little magician explained, "I figured you'd want to try it again as soon as you got up, and I knew darned well you'd have your troubles. Thought I'd come over and straighten things out for you."

Wolf lit a cigarette in silence and handed the pack to Ozymandias. "When you came in just now," he said at last, "what did you see?"

"You as a wolf."

"Then it really— I actually—"

"Sure. You're a full-fledged werewolf, all right."

Wolf sat down on the rumpled bed. "I guess," he ventured slowly, "I've got to believe it. And if I believe that— But it means I've got to believe everything I've always scorned. I've got to believe in gods and devils and hells and—"

"You needn't be so pluralistic. But there is a God." Ozymandias said this as calmly and convincingly as he had stated last night that there were werewolves.

"And if there's a God, then I've got a soul?"

"Sure."

"And if I'm a werewolf— Hey!"

"What's the trouble, colleague?"

"All right, Ozzy. You know everything. Tell me this: Am I damned?"

"For what? Just for being a werewolf? Shucks, no; let me explain. There's two kinds of werewolves. There's the cursed kind that can't help themselves, that just go turning into wolves without any say in the matter; and there's the voluntary kind like you. Now, most of the voluntary kind are damned, sure, because they're wicked men who lust for blood and eat innocent people. But they aren't damnably wicked because they're werewolves; they became werewolves because they are damnably wicked. Now, you changed yourself just for the hell of it and because it looked like a good way to impress a gal; that's an innocent-enough motive, and being a werewolf doesn't make it any less so. Werewolves don't have to be monsters; it's just that we hear about only the ones that are."

"But how can I be voluntary when you told me I was a werewolf before I ever changed?"

"Not everybody can change. It's like being able to roll your tongue or wiggle your ears. You can, or you can't; and that's that. And as with those abilities, there's probably a genetic factor involved, though nobody's done any serious research on it. You were a werewolf *in posse;* now you're one *in esse.*"

"Then it's all right? I can be a werewolf just for having fun, and it's safe?"

"Absolutely."

Wolf chortled. "Will I show Gloria! Dull and unglamorous indeed! Anybody can marry an actor or a G-man; but a werewolf—"

"Your children probably will be, too," said Ozymandias cheerfully.

Wolf shut his eyes dreamily, then opened them with a start. "You know what?"

"What?"

"I haven't got a hangover anymore! This is marvelous. This is— Why, this is practical. At last the perfect hangover cure. Shuffle yourself into a wolf and back and— Oh, that reminds me. How do I get back?"

"*Absarka.*"

"I know. But when I'm a wolf I can't say it."

"That," said Ozymandias sadly, "is the curse of being a white magician. You keep having to use the second-best form of spells, because the best would be black. Sure, a black-magic werebeast can turn himself back whenever he wants to. I remember in Darjeeling—"

"But how about me?"

"That's the trouble. You have to have somebody to say *Absarka!* for you. That's what I did last night, or do you remember? After we broke up the party at your friend's Temple—Tell you what. I'm retired now, and I've got enough to live on modestly because I can always magic up a little— Are you going to take up werewolfing seriously?"

"For a while, anyway. Till I get Gloria."

"Then why shouldn't I come and live here in your hotel? Then I'll always be handy to *Absarka!* you. After you get the girl, you can teach her."

Wolf extended his hand. "Noble of you. Shake." And then

his eye caught his wrist watch. "Good Lord! I've missed two classes this morning. Werewolfing's all very well, but a man's got to work for his living."

"Most men." Ozymandias calmly reached his hand into the air and plucked a coin. He looked at it ruefully; it was a gold moidore. "Hang these spirits; I simply cannot explain to them about gold being illegal."

From Los Angeles, Wolf thought, with the habitual contempt of the northern Californian, as he surveyed the careless sport coat and the bright-yellow shirt of his visitor.

This young man rose politely as the professor entered the office. His green eyes gleamed cordially and his red hair glowed in the spring sunlight. "Professor Wolf?" he asked.

Wolf glanced impatiently at his desk. "Yes."

"O'Breen's the name. I'd like to talk to you a minute."

"My office hours are from three to four Tuesdays and Thursdays. I'm afraid I'm rather busy now."

"This isn't faculty business. And it's important." The young man's attitude was affable and casual, but he managed nonetheless to convey a sense of urgency that piqued Wolf's curiosity. The all-important letter to Gloria had waited while he took two classes; it could wait another five minutes.

"Very well, Mr. O'Breen."

"And alone, if you please."

Wolf himself hadn't noticed that Emily was in the room. He now turned to the secretary and said, "All right. If you don't mind, Emily—"

Emily shrugged and went out.

"Now, sir. What is this important and secret business?"

"Just a question or two. To start with, how well do you know Gloria Garton?"

Wolf paused. You could hardly say, "Young man, I am about to repropose to her in view of my becoming a werewolf." Instead he simply said—the truth, if not the whole truth—"She was a pupil of mine a few years ago."

"I said *do*, not *did*. How well do you know her now?"

"And why should I bother to answer such a question?"

The young man handed over a card. Wolf read:

FERGUS O'BREEN
Private Inquiry Agent
Licensed by the State of California

Wolf smiled. "And what does this mean? Divorce evidence? Isn't that the usual field of private inquiry agents?"

"Miss Garton isn't married, as you probably know very well. I'm just asking if you've been in touch with her much lately."

"And I'm simply asking why you should want to know."

O'Breen rose and began to pace around the office. "We don't seem to be getting very far, do we? I'm to take it that you refuse to state the nature of your relations with Gloria Garton?"

"I see no reason why I should do otherwise." Wolf was beginning to be annoyed.

To his surprise, the detective relaxed into a broad grin. "OK. Let it ride. Tell me about your department. How long have the various faculty members been here?"

"Instructors and all?"

"Just the professors."

"I've been here for seven years. All the others at least a good ten, probably more. If you want exact figures, you can probably get them from the dean, unless, as I hope"—Wolf smiled cordially—"he throws you out flat on your red pate."

O'Breen laughed. "Professor, I think we could get on. One more question, and you can do some pate-tossing yourself. Are you an American citizen?"

"Of course."

"And the rest of the department?"

"All of them. And now would you have the common decency to give me some explanation of this fantastic farrago of questions?"

"No," said O'Breen casually. "Goodbye, professor." His

alert green eyes had been roaming about the room, sharply noticing everything. Now, as he left, they rested on Wolf's long index finger, moved up to his heavy meeting eyebrows, and returned to the finger. There was a suspicion of a startled realization in those eyes as he left the office.

But that was nonsense, Wolf told himself. A private detective, no matter how shrewd his eyes, no matter how apparently meaningless his inquiries, would surely be the last man on earth to notice the signs of lycanthropy.

Funny. "Werewolf" was a word you could accept. You could say, "I'm a werewolf," and it was all right. But say "I am a lycanthrope" and your flesh crawled. Odd. Possibly material for a paper on the influence of etymology on connotation for one of the learned periodicals.

But, hell! Wolfe Wolf was no longer primarily a scholar. He was a werewolf now, a white-magic werewolf, a werewolf-for-fun; and fun he was going to have. He lit his pipe, stared at the blank paper on his desk, and tried desperately to draft a letter to Gloria. It should hint at just enough to fascinate her and hold her interest until he could go south when the term ended and reveal to her the whole wonderful new truth. It—

Professor Oscar Fearing grunted his ponderous way into the office. "Good afternoon, Wolfe. Hard at it, my boy?"

"Afternoon," Wolf replied distractedly, and continued to stare at the paper.

"Great events coming, eh? Are you looking forward to seeing the glorious Gloria?"

Wolf started. "How— What do you mean?"

Fearing handed him a folded newspaper. "You hadn't heard?"

Wolf read with growing amazement and delight:

GLORIA GARTON TO ARRIVE FRIDAY
Local Girl Returns to Berkeley

As part of the most spectacular talent hunt since the search for Scarlett O'Hara, Gloria Garton, glamorous Metropolis starlet, will visit Berkeley Friday.

Friday afternoon at the Campus Theater, Berkeley canines will have their chance to compete in the nation-wide quest for a dog to play Tookah the wolf dog in the great Metropolis epic "Fangs of the Forest," and Gloria Garton herself will be present at the auditions.

"I owe so much to Berkeley," Miss Garton said. "It will mean so much to me to see the campus and the city again." Miss Garton has the starring human role in "Fangs of the Forest."

Miss Garton was a student at the University of California when she received her first chance in films. She is a member of Mask and Dagger, honorary dramatic society, and Rho Rho Rho Sorority.

Wolfe Wolf glowed. This was perfect. No need now to wait till term was over. He could see Gloria now and claim her in all his wolfish vigor. Friday—today was Wednesday; that gave him two nights to practice and perfect the technique of werewolfry. And then—

He noticed the dejected look on the older professor's face, and a small remorse smote him. "How did things go last night, Oscar?" he asked sympathetically. "How were your big Walpurgis Night services?"

Fearing regarded him oddly. "You know that now? Yesterday April thirtieth meant nothing to you."

"I got curious and looked it up. But how did it go?"

"Well enough," Fearing lied feebly. "Do you know, Wolfe," he demanded after a moment's silence, "what is the real curse of every man interested in the occult?"

"No. What?"

"That true power is never enough. Enough for yourself, perhaps, but never enough for others. So that no matter what your true abilities, you must forge on beyond them into charlatanry to convince the others. Look at St. Germain. Look at Francis Stuart. Look at Cagliostro. But the worst tragedy is the next stage: when you realize that your powers were greater than you supposed and that the charlatanry was needless. When you realize that you have no notion of the extent of your powers. Then—"

"Then, Oscar?"

"Then, my boy, you are a badly frightened man."

Wolf wanted to say something consoling. He wanted to say, "Look, Oscar. It was just me. Go back to your halfhearted charlatanry and be happy." But he couldn't do that. Only Ozzy could know the truth of that splendid gray wolf. Only Ozzy and Gloria.

The moon was bright on that hidden spot in the canyon. The night was still. And Wolfe Wolf had a severe case of stage fright. Now that it came to the real thing—for this morning's clothes-complicated fiasco hardly counted and last night he could not truly remember—he was afraid to plunge cleanly into wolfdom and anxious to stall and talk as long as possible.

"Do you think," he asked the magician nervously, "that I could teach Gloria to change, too?"

Ozymandias pondered. "Maybe, colleague. It'd depend. She might have the natural ability, and she might not. And, of course, there's no telling what she might change into."

"You mean she wouldn't necessarily be a wolf?"

"Of course not. The people who can change, change into all sorts of things. And every folk knows best the kind that most interests it. We've got an English and Central European tradition, so we know mostly about werewolves. But take Scandinavia and you'll hear chiefly about werebears, only they call 'em berserkers. And Orientals, now, they're apt to know about weretigers. Trouble is, we've thought so much about were*wolves* that that's all we know the signs for; I wouldn't know how to spot a weretiger just offhand."

"Then there's no telling what might happen if I taught her The Word?"

"Not the least. Of course, there's some werethings that just aren't much use being. Take like being a wereant. You change and somebody steps on you and that's that. Or like a fella I knew once in Madagascar. Taught him The Word, and know what? Hanged if he wasn't a werediplodocus. Shattered the whole house into little pieces when he changed and damned near trampled me under hoof before I could say *Absarka!* He decided not to make a career of it. Or then there was that time in Darjeeling— But, look, colleague, are you going to stand around here naked all night?"

"No," said Wolf. "I'm going to change now. You'll take my clothes back to the hotel?"

"Sure. They'll be there for you. And I've put a very small spell on the night clerk, just enough for him not to notice wolves wandering in. Oh, and by the way—anything missing from your room?"

"Not that I noticed. Why?"

"Because I thought I saw somebody come out of it this afternoon. Couldn't be sure, but I think he came from there. Young fella with red hair and Hollywood clothes."

Wolfe Wolf frowned. That didn't make sense. Pointless questions from a detective were bad enough, but searching your hotel room— But what were detectives to a full-fledged werewolf? He grinned, nodded a friendly goodbye to Ozymandias the Great, and said The Word.

The pain wasn't so sharp as this morning, though still quite bad enough. But it passed almost at once, and his whole body filled with a sense of limitless freedom. He lifted his snout and sniffed deep at the keen freshness of this night air. A whole new realm of pleasure opened up for him through this acute new nose alone. He wagged his tail amicably at Ozzy and set off up the canyon on a long, easy lope.

For hours, loping was enough—simply and purely enjoying one's wolfness was the finest pleasure one could ask. Wolf left the canyon and turned up into the hills, past the Big C and on into noble wildness that seemed far remote from all campus civilization. His brave new legs were stanch and tireless, his wind seemingly inexhaustible. Every turning brought fresh and vivid scents of soil and leaves and air, and life was shimmering and beautiful.

But a few hours of this, and Wolf realized that he was damned lonely. All this grand exhilaration was very well, but if his mate Gloria were loping by his side— And what fun was it to be something as splendid as a wolf if no one admired you? He began to want people, and he turned back to the city.

Berkeley goes to bed early. The streets were deserted. Here and there a light burned in a rooming house where some solid grind was plodding on his almost-due term paper. Wolf had done that himself. He couldn't laugh in this shape, but his tail twitched with amusement at the thought.

He paused along the tree-lined street. There was a fresh human scent here, though the street seemed empty. Then he heard a soft whimpering, and trotted off toward the noise.

Behind the shrubbery fronting an apartment house sat a disconsolate two-year-old, shivering in his sunsuit and obviously lost for hours on hours. Wolf put a paw on the child's shoulder and shook him gently.

The boy looked around and was not in the least afraid. "He'o," he said, brightening up.

Wolf growled a cordial greeting, and wagged his tail and pawed at the ground to indicate that he'd take the lost infant wherever it wanted to go.

The child stood up and wiped away its tears with a dirty fist which left wide black smudges. "Tootootootoo!" he said.

Games, thought Wolf. He wants to play choo-choo. He took the child by the sleeve and tugged gently.

"Tootootootoo!" the boy repeated firmly. "Die way."

The sound of a railway whistle, to be sure, does die away; but this seemed a poetic expression for such a toddler. Wolf thought, and then abruptly would have snapped his fingers if he'd had them. The child was saying "2222 Dwight Way," having been carefully brought up to tell his address when lost. Wolf glanced up at the street sign. Bowditch and Hillegas; 2222 Dwight would be just a couple of blocks.

Wolf tried to nod his head, but the muscles didn't seem to work that way. Instead he wagged his tail in what he hoped indicated comprehension, and started off leading the child.

The infant beamed and said, "Nice woof-woof."

For an instant Wolf felt like a spy suddenly addressed by his right name, then realized that if some say "bow-wow" others might well say "woof-woof."

He led the child for two blocks without event. It felt good, having an innocent human being like this. There was something about children; he hoped Gloria felt the same. He wondered what would happen if he could teach this confiding infant The Word. It would be swell to have a pup that would—

He paused. His nose twitched and the hair on the back of his neck rose. Ahead of them stood a dog: a huge mongrel, seemingly a mixture of St. Bernard and Husky. But the growl that issued from his throat indicated that carrying brandy kegs or rushing serum was not for him. He was a bandit, an outlaw, an enemy of man and dog. And they had to pass him.

Wolf had no desire to fight. He was as big as this monster and certainly, with his human brain, much cleverer; but scars from a dog fight would not look well on the human body of Professor Wolf, and there was, moreover, the danger of hurting the toddler in the fracas. It would be wiser to cross the street. But before he could steer the child that way, the mongrel brute had charged at them, yapping and snarling.

Wolf placed himself in front of the boy, poised and ready to leap in defense. The scar problem was secondary to the fact that this baby had trusted him. He was ready to face this cur and teach him a lesson, at whatever cost to his own human body. But halfway to him the huge dog stopped. His growls died away to a piteous whimper. His great flanks trembled in the moonlight. His tail curled craven between his legs. And abruptly he turned and fled.

The child crowed delightedly. "Bad woof-woof go away." He put his little arms around Wolf's neck. "*Nice* woof-woof." Then he straightened up and said insistently, "Tootootootoo. Die way," and Wolf led on, his strong wolf's heart pounding as it had never pounded at the embrace of a woman.

"Tootootootoo" was a small frame house set back from the street in a large yard. The lights were still on, and even from the sidewalk Wolf could hear a woman's shrill voice.

"—since five o'clock this afternoon, and you've got to find him, Officer. You simply must. We've hunted all over the neighborhood and—"

Wolf stood up against the wall on his hind legs and rang the doorbell with his front right paw.

"Oh! Maybe that's somebody now. The neighbors said they'd— Come, Officer, and let's see— Oh!"

At the same moment Wolf barked politely, the toddler yelled "Mamma!" and his thin and worn-looking young mother let out a scream—half delight at finding her child and half terror of this large gray canine shape that loomed behind him. She snatched up the infant protectively and turned to the large man in uniform. "Officer! Look! That big dreadful thing! It stole my Robby!"

"No," Robby protested firmly. "Nice woof-woof."

The officer laughed. "The lad's probably right, ma'am. It *is* a nice woof-woof. Found your boy wandering around and helped him home. You haven't maybe got a bone for him?"

"Let that big, nasty brute into my home? Never! Come on, Robby."

"Want my nice woof-woof."

"I'll woof-woof you, staying out till all hours and giving your father and me the fright of our lives. Just wait till your father sees you, young man; he'll—Oh, good night, Officer!" And she shut the door on the yowls of Robby.

The policeman patted Wolf's head. "Never mind about the bone, Rover. She didn't so much as offer me a glass of beer, either. My, you're a husky specimen, aren't you, boy? Look almost like a wolf. Who do you belong to, and what are you doing wandering about alone? Huh?" He turned on his flash and bent over to look at the nonexistent collar.

He straightened up and whistled. "No license. Rover, that's bad. You know what I ought to do? I ought to turn you in. If you weren't a hero that just got cheated out of his bone, I'd— Hell, I ought to do it, anyway. Laws are laws, even for heroes. Come on, Rover. We're going for a walk."

Wolf thought quickly. The pound was the last place on earth he wanted to wind up. Even Ozzy would never think of looking for him there. Nobody'd claim him, nobody'd say *Absarka!* and in the end a dose of chloroform— He wrenched loose from the officer's grasp on his hair and with one prodigious leap cleared the yard, landed on the sidewalk, and started hell for leather up the street. But the instant he was out of the officer's sight he stopped dead and slipped behind a hedge.

He scented the policeman's approach even before he heard it. The man was running with the lumbering haste of two hundred pounds. But opposite the hedge, he too stopped. For a moment Wolf wondered if his ruse had failed; but the officer had paused only to scratch his head and mutter, "Say! There's something screwy here. *Who rang that doorbell?* The kid couldn't reach it, and the dog— Oh, well," he concluded. "Nuts," and seemed to find in that monosyllabic summation the solution to all his problems.

As his footsteps and smell died away, Wolf became aware of another scent. He had only just identified it as cat when someone said, "You're were, aren't you?"

Wolf started up, lips drawn back and muscles tense. There was nothing human in sight, but someone had spoken to him. Unthinkingly, he tried to say "Where are you?" but all that came out was a growl.

"Right behind you. Here in the shadows. You can scent me, can't you?"

"But you're a cat," Wolf thought in his snarls. "And you're talking."

"Of course. But I'm not talking human language. It's just

your brain that takes it that way. If you had your human body, you'd think I was just going *meowrr*. But you are were, aren't you?"

"How do you . . . why do you think so?"

"Because you didn't try to jump me, as any normal dog would have. And besides, unless Confucius taught me all wrong, you're a wolf, not a dog; and we don't have wolves around here unless they're were."

"How do you know all this? Are you—"

"Oh, no. I'm just a cat. But I used to live next door to a werechow named Confucius. He taught me things."

Wolf was amazed. "You mean he was a man who changed to chow and stayed that way? Lived as a pet?"

"Certainly. This was back at the worst of the depression. He said a dog was more apt to be fed and looked after than a man. I thought it was a smart idea."

"But how terrible! Could a man so debase himself as—"

"Men don't debase themselves. They debase each other. That's the way of most weres. Some change to keep from being debased, others to do a little more effective debasing. Which are you?"

"Why, you see, I—"

"*Sh!* Look. This is going to be fun. Holdup."

Wolf peered around the hedge. A well-dressed, middle-aged man was walking along briskly, apparently enjoying a night constitutional. Behind him moved a thin, silent figure. Even as Wolf watched, the figure caught up with him and whispered harshly, "Up with 'em, buddy!"

The quiet pomposity of the stroller melted away. He was ashen and aspen as the figure slipped a hand around into his breast pocket and removed an impressive wallet.

And what, thought Wolf, was the good of his fine, vigorous body if it merely crouched behind hedges as a spectator? In one fine bound, to the shocked amazement of the were-wise cat, he had crossed the hedge and landed with his forepaws full in the figure's face. It went over backward with him on top, and then there came a loud noise, a flash of light, and a frightful sharp smell. For a moment Wolf felt an acute pang in his shoulder, like the jab of a long needle, and then the pain was gone.

But his momentary recoil had been enough to let the figure get to its feet. "Missed you, huh?" it muttered. "Let's see how you like a slug in the belly, you interfering—" and he applied an epithet that would have been purely literal description if Wolf had not been were.

There were three quick shots in succession even as Wolf sprang. For a second he experienced the most acute stomach-ache of his life. Then he landed again. The figure's head hit the concrete sidewalk and he was still.

Lights were leaping into brightness everywhere. Among all the confused noises, Wolf could hear the shrill complaints of Robby's mother, and among all the compounded smells, he could distinguish scent of the policeman who wanted to impound him. That meant getting the hell out, and quick.

The city meant trouble, Wolf decided as he loped off. He could endure loneliness while he practiced his wolfry, until he had Gloria. Though just as a precaution he must arrange with Ozzy about a plausible-looking collar, and—

The most astounding realization yet suddenly struck him! He had received four bullets, three of them square in the stomach, and he hadn't a wound to show for it! Being a werewolf certainly offered its practical advantages. Think what a criminal could do with such bullet-proofing. Or— But no. He was a werewolf for fun, and that was that.

But even for a werewolf, being shot, though relatively painless, is tiring. A great deal of nervous energy is absorbed in the magical and instantaneous knitting of those wounds. And when Wolfe Wolf reached the peace and calm of the uncivilized hills, he no longer felt like reveling in freedom. Instead he stretched out to his full length, nuzzled his head down between his forepaws, and slept.

"Now, the essence of magic," said Heliophagus of Smyrna, "is deceit; and that deceit is of two kinds. By magic, the magician deceives others; but magic deceives the magician himself."

So far the lycanthropic magic of Wolfe Wolf had worked smoothly and pleasantly, but now it was to show him the second trickery that lurks behind every magic trick. And the first step was that he slept.

He woke in confusion. His dreams had been human—and of Gloria—despite the body in which he dreamed them, and it took several full minutes for him to reconstruct just how he happened to be in that body. For a moment the dream, even that episode in which he and Gloria had been eating blueberry waffles on a roller coaster, seemed more sanely plausible than the reality.

But he readjusted quickly, and glanced up at the sky. The sun looked as though it had been up at least an hour, which meant in May that the time was somewhere between six and seven. Today was Thursday, which meant that he was saddled with an eight-o'clock class. That left plenty of time to change back, shave, dress, breakfast, and resume the normal life of Professor Wolf—which was, after all, important if he intended to support a wife.

He tried, as he trotted through the streets, to look as tame and unwolflike as possible, and apparently succeeded. No one paid him any mind save children, who wanted to play, and dogs, who began by snarling and ended by cowering away terrified. His friend the cat might be curiously tolerant of weres, but not so dogs.

He trotted up the steps of the Berkeley Inn confidently. The clerk was under a slight spell and would not notice wolves. There was nothing to do but rouse Ozzy, be *Absarka!*'d, and—

"Hey! Where are you going? Get out of here! Shoo!"

It was the clerk, a stanch and brawny young man, who straddled the stairway and vigorously waved him off.

"No dogs in here! Go on now. Scoot!"

Quite obviously this man was under no spell, and equally

obviously there was no way of getting up that staircase short of using a wolf's strength to tear the clerk apart. For a second Wolf hesitated. He had to get changed back. It would be a damnable pity to use his powers to injure another human being. If only he had not slept, and arrived before this un-magicked day clerk came on duty; but necessity knows no—

Then the solution hit him. Wolf turned and loped off just as the clerk hurled an ash tray at him. Bullets may be relatively painless, but even a werewolf's rump, he learned promptly, is sensitive to flying glass.

The solution was foolproof. The only trouble was that it meant an hour's wait, and he was hungry. Damnably hungry. He found himself even displaying a certain shocking interest in the plump occupant of a baby carriage. You do get different appetites with a different body. He could understand how some originally well-intentioned werewolves might in time become monsters. But he was stronger in will, and much smarter. His stomach could hold out until this plan worked.

The janitor had already opened the front door of Wheeler Hall, but the building was deserted. Wolf had no trouble reaching the second floor unnoticed or finding his classroom. He had a little more trouble holding the chalk between his teeth and a slight tendency to gag on the dust; but by balancing his forepaws on the eraser trough, he could man-age quite nicely. It took three springs to catch the ring of the chart in his teeth, but once that was pulled down there was nothing to do but crouch under the desk and pray that he would not starve quite to death.

The students of German 31B, as they assembled reluctantly for their eight-o'clock, were a little puzzled at being con-fronted by a chart dealing with the influence of the gold standard on world economy, but they decided simply that the janitor had been forgetful.

The wolf under the desk listened unseen to their gathering murmurs, overheard that cute blonde in the front row make dates with three different men for that same night, and finally decided that enough had assembled to make his chances plausible. He slipped out from under the desk far enough to reach the ring of the chart, tugged at it, and let go.

The chart flew up with a rolling crash. The students broke off their chatter, looked up at the blackboard, and beheld in a huge and shaky scrawl the mysterious letters

A B S A R K A

It worked. With enough people, it was an almost mathematical certainty that one of them in his puzzlement—for the race of subtitle readers, though handicapped by the talkies, still exists—would read the mysterious word aloud. It was the much-bedated blonde who did it.

"*Absarka*," she said wonderingly.

And there was Professor Wolfe Wolf, beaming cordially at his class.

The only flaw was this: He had forgotten that he was only a werewolf, and not Hyperman. His clothes were still at the Berkeley Inn, and here on the lecture platform he was stark naked.

Two of his best pupils screamed and one fainted. The blonde only giggled appreciatively.

Emily was incredulous but pitying.
Professor Fearing was sympathetic but reserved.
The chairman of the department was cool.
The dean of letters was chilly.
The president of the university was frigid.
Wolfe Wolf was unemployed.
And Heliophagus of Smyrna was right. "The essence of magic is deceit."

"But what can I do?" Wolf moaned into his zombie glass. "I'm stuck. I'm stymied. Gloria arrives in Berkeley tomorrow, and here I am—nothing. Nothing but a futile, worthless werewolf. You can't support a wife on that. You can't raise a family. You can't— Hell, you can't even propose. . . . I want another. Sure you won't have one?"

Ozymandias the Great shook his round, fringed head. "The last time I took two drinks I started all this. I've got to behave if I want to stop it. But you're an able-bodied, strapping young man; surely, colleague, you can get work?"

"Where? All I'm trained for is academic work, and this scandal has put the kibosh on that forever. What university is going to hire a man who showed up naked in front of his class without even the excuse of being drunk? And supposing I try something else—say one of these jobs in defense that all my students seem to be getting—I'd have to give references, say something about what I'd been doing with my thirty-odd years. And once these references were checked— Ozzy, I'm a lost man."

"Never despair, colleague. I've learned that magic gets you into some tight squeezes, but there's always a way of getting out. Now, take that time in Darjeeling—"

"But what can I do? I'll wind up like Confucius the were-chow and live off charity, if you'll find me somebody who wants a pet wolf."

"You know," Ozymandias reflected, "you may have something there, colleague."

"Nuts! That was a joke. I can at least retain my self-respect, even if I go on relief doing it. And I'll bet they don't like naked men on relief, either."

"No. I don't mean just being a pet wolf. But look at it this way: What are your assets? You have only two outstanding abilities. One of them is to teach German, and that is now completely out."

"Check."

"And the other is to change yourself into a wolf. All right, colleague. There must be some commercial possibilities in that. Let's look into them."

"Nonsense."

"Not quite. For every kind of merchandise there's a market. The trick is to find it. And you, colleague, are going to be the first practical commercial werewolf on record."

"I could— They say Ripley's Odditorium pays good money. Supposing I changed six times a day regular for delighted audiences?"

Ozymandias shook his head sorrowfully. "It's no good. People don't want to see real magic. It makes 'em uncomfortable —starts 'em wondering what else might be loose in the world. They've got to feel sure it's all done with mirrors. I know. I had to quit vaudeville because I wasn't smart enough at faking it; all I could do was the real thing."

"I could be a Seeing Eye dog, maybe?"

"They have to be female."

"When I'm changed I can understand animal language. Maybe I could be a dog trainer and— No, that's out. I forgot: they're scared to death of me."

But Ozymandias' pale-blue eyes had lit up at the suggestion. "Colleague, you're warm. Oh, are you warm! Tell me: why did you say your fabulous Gloria was coming to Berkeley?"

"Publicity for a talent hunt."

"For what?"

"A dog to star in *Fangs of the Forest*."

"And what kind of a dog?"

"A—" Wolf's eyes widened and his jaw sagged. "A wolf dog," he said softly.

And the two men looked at each other with a wild surmise—silent, beside a bar in Berkeley.

"It's all the fault of that damned Disney dog," the trainer complained. "Pluto does anything. Everything. So our poor mutts are expected to do likewise. Listen to that dope! 'The dog should come into the room, give one paw to the baby, indicate that he recognizes the hero in his Eskimo disguise, go over to the table, find the bone, and clap his paws gleefully!' Now, who's got a set of signals to cover stuff like that? Pluto!" he snorted.

Gloria Garton said, "Oh." By that one sound she managed to convey that she sympathized deeply, that the trainer was a nice-looking young man whom she'd just as soon see again, and that no dog star was going to steal *Fangs of the Forest* from her. She adjusted her skirt slightly, leaned back, and made the plain wooden chair on the bare theater stage seem more than ever like a throne.

"All right." The man in the violet beret waved away the last unsuccessful applicant and read from a card: "'Dog: Wopsy. Owner: Mrs. Channing Galbraith. Trainer: Luther Newby.' Bring it in."

An assistant scurried offstage, and there was a sound of whines and whimpers as a door opened.

"What's got into those dogs today?" the man in the violet beret demanded. "They all seem scared to death and beyond."

"I think," said Fergus O'Breen, "that it's that big, gray wolf dog. Somehow, the others just don't like him."

Gloria Garton lowered her bepurpled lids and cast a queenly stare of suspicion on the young detective. There was nothing wrong with his being there. His sister was head of publicity for Metropolis, and he'd handled several confidential cases for the studio; even one for her, that time her chauffeur had decided to try his hand at blackmail. Fergus O'Breen was a Metropolis fixture; but still it bothered her.

The assistant brought in Mrs. Galbraith's Wopsy. The man in the violet beret took one look and screamed. The scream bounced back from every wall of the theater in the ensuing minute of silence. At last he found words. "A wolf dog! Tookah is the greatest role ever written for a wolf dog! And what do they bring us? A terrier, yet! So if we wanted a terrier we could cast Asta!"

"But if you'd only let us show you—" Wopsy's tall young trainer started to protest.

"Get out!" the man in the violet beret shrieked. "Get out before I lose my temper!"

Wopsy and her trainer slunk off.

"In El Paso," the casting director lamented, "they bring me a Mexican hairless. In St. Louis it's a Pekinese yet! And if I do find a wolf dog, it sits in a corner and waits for somebody to bring it a sled to pull."

"Maybe," said Fergus, "you should try a real wolf."

"Wolf, *schmolf!* We'll end up wrapping John Barrymore in a wolfskin." He picked up the next card. " 'Dog: Yoggoth. Owner and trainer: Mr. O. Z. Manders.' Bring it in."

The whining noise offstage ceased as Yoggoth was brought out to be tested. The man in the violet beret hardly glanced at the fringe-bearded owner and trainer. He had eyes only for that splendid gray wolf. "If you can only act . . ." he prayed, with the same fervor with which many a man has thought, If you could only cook . . .

He pulled the beret to an even more unlikely angle and snapped, "All right, Mr. Manders. The dog should come into the room, give one paw to the baby, indicate that he recognizes the hero in his Eskimo disguise, go over to the table, find the bone, and clap his paws joyfully. Baby here, hero here, table here. Got that?"

Mr. Manders looked at his wolf dog and repeated, "Got that?"

Yoggoth wagged his tail.

"Very well, colleague," said Mr. Manders. "Do it."

Yoggoth did it.

The violet beret sailed into the flies, on the wings of its owner's triumphal scream of joy. "He did it!" he kept burbling. "He did it!"

"Of course, colleague," said Mr. Manders calmly.

The trainer who hated Pluto had a face as blank as a vampire's mirror. Fergus O'Breen was speechless with wonderment. Even Gloria Garton permitted surprise and interest to cross her regal mask.

"You mean he can do anything?" gurgled the man who used to have a violet beret.

"Anything," said Mr. Manders.

"Can he— Let's see, in the dance-hall sequence . . . can he knock a man down, roll him over, and frisk his back pocket?"

Even before Mr. Manders could say "Of course," Yoggoth had demonstrated, using Fergus O'Breen as a convenient dummy.

"Peace!" the casting director sighed. "Peace. . . . Charley!" he yelled to his assistant. "Send 'em all away. No more tryouts. We've found Tookah! It's wonderful."

The trainer stepped up to Mr. Manders. "It's more than that, sir. It's positively superhuman. I'll swear I couldn't detect the slightest signal, and for such complicated operations, too. Tell me, Mr. Manders, what system do you use?"

Mr. Manders made a Hoople-ish *kaff-kaff* noise. "Professional secret, you understand, young man. I'm planning on opening a school when I retire, but obviously until then—"

"Of course, sir. I understand. But I've never seen anything like it in all my born days."

"I wonder," Fergus O'Breen observed abstractly from the floor, "if your marvel dog can get off of people, too?"

Mr. Manders stifled a grin. "Of course! Yoggoth!"

Fergus picked himself up and dusted from his clothes the grime of the stage, which is the most clinging grime on earth. "I'd swear," he muttered, "that beast of yours enjoyed that."

"No hard feelings, I trust, Mr.—"

"O'Breen. None at all. In fact, I'd suggest a little celebration in honor of this great event. I know you can't buy a drink this near the campus, so I brought along a bottle just in case."

"Oh," said Gloria Garton, implying that carousals were ordinarily beneath her; that this, however, was a special occasion; and that possibly there was something to be said for the green-eyed detective after all.

This was all too easy, Wolfe Wolf–Yoggoth kept thinking. There was a catch to it somewhere. This was certainly the ideal solution to the problem of how to earn money as a werewolf. Bring an understanding of human speech and instructions into a fine animal body, and you are the answer to a director's prayer. It was perfect as long as it lasted; and if *Fangs of the Forest* was a smash hit, there were bound to be other Yoggoth pictures. Look at Rin-Tin-Tin. But it was too easy. . . .

His ears caught a familiar "Oh," and his attention reverted

to Gloria. This "Oh" had meant that she really shouldn't have another drink, but since liquor didn't affect her anyway and this was a special occasion, she might as well.

She was even more beautiful than he had remembered. Her golden hair was shoulder-length now, and flowed with such rippling perfection that it was all he could do to keep from reaching out a paw to it. Her body had ripened, too; was even more warm and promising than his memories of her. And in his new shape he found her greatest charm in something he had not been able to appreciate fully as a human being: the deep, heady scent of her flesh.

"To *Fangs of the Forest!*" Fergus O'Breen was toasting. "And may that pretty-boy hero of yours get a worse mauling than I did."

Wolf-Yoggoth grinned to himself. That had been fun. That'd teach the detective to go crawling around hotel rooms.

"And while we're celebrating, colleagues," said Ozymandias the Great, "why should we neglect our star? Here, Yoggoth." And he held out the bottle.

"He drinks, yet!" the casting director exclaimed delightedly.

"Sure. He was weaned on it."

Wolf took a sizable gulp. It felt good. Warm and rich— almost the way Gloria smelled.

"But how about you, Mr. Manders?" the detective insisted for the fifth time. "It's your celebration really. The poor beast won't get the four-figure checks from Metropolis. And you've taken only one drink."

"Never take two, colleague. I know my danger point. Two drinks in me and things start happening."

"More should happen yet than training miracle dogs? Go on, O'Breen. Make him drink. We should see what happens."

Fergus took another long drink himself. "Go on. There's another bottle in the car, and I've gone far enough to be re-solved not to leave here sober. And I don't want sober companions, either." His green eyes were already beginning to glow with a new wildness.

"No, thank you, colleague."

Gloria Garton left her throne, walked over to the plump

man, and stood close, her soft hand resting on his arm. "Oh," she said, implying that dogs were dogs, but still that the party was unquestionably in her honor and his refusal to drink was a personal insult.

Ozymandias the Great looked at Gloria, sighed, shrugged, resigned himself to fate, and drank.

"Have you trained many dogs?" the casting director asked.

"Sorry, colleague. This is my first."

"All the more wonderful! But what's your profession otherwise?"

"Well, you see, I'm a magician."

"Oh," said Gloria Garton, implying delight, and went so far as to add, "I have a friend who does black magic."

"I'm afraid, ma'am, mine's simply white. That's tricky enough. With the black you're in for some real dangers."

"Hold on!" Fergus interposed. "You mean really a magician? Not just presti . . . sleight of hand?"

"Of course, colleague."

"Good theater," said the casting director. "Never let 'em see the mirrors."

"Uh-huh," Fergus nodded. "But look, Mr. Manders. What can you do, for instance?"

"Well, I can change—"

Yoggoth barked loudly.

"Oh, no," Ozymandias covered hastily, "that's really a little beyond me. But I can—"

"Can you do the Indian rope trick?" Gloria asked languidly. "My friend says that's terribly hard."

"Hard? Why, ma'am, there's nothing to it. I can remember that time in Darjeeling—"

Fergus took another long drink. "I," he announced defiantly, "want to see the Indian rope trick. I have met people who've met people who've met people who've seen it, but that's as close as I ever get. And I don't believe it."

"But, colleague, it's so simple."

"I don't believe it."

Ozymandias the Great drew himself up to his full lack of height. "Colleague, you are about to see it!" Yoggoth tugged

warningly at his coattails. "Leave me alone, Wolf. An asper-
sion has been cast!"

Fergus returned from the wings dragging a soiled length of
rope. "This do?"

"Admirably."

"What goes?" the casting director demanded.

"*Shh!*" said Gloria. "Oh—"

She beamed worshipfully on Ozymandias, whose chest
swelled to the point of threatening the security of his buttons.
"Ladies and gentlemen!" he announced, in the manner of one
prepared to fill a vast amphitheater with his voice. "You are
about to behold Ozymandias the Great in—The Indian Rope
Trick! Of course," he added conversationally, "I haven't got a
small boy to chop into mincemeat, unless perhaps one of
you— No? Well, we'll try it without. Not quite so impressive,
though. And will you stop yapping, Wolf?"

"I thought his name was Yogi," said Fergus.

"Yoggoth. But since he's part wolf on his mother's side—
Now, quiet, all of you!"

He had been coiling the rope as he spoke. Now he placed
the coil in the center of the stage, where it lurked like a
threatening rattler. He stood beside it and deftly, professionally, went through a series of passes and mumblings so rapidly
that even the superhumanly sharp eyes and ears of Wolf-
Yoggoth could not follow them.

The end of the rope detached itself from the coil, reared in
the air, turned for a moment like a head uncertain where to
strike, then shot straight up until all the rope was uncoiled.
The lower end rested a good inch above the stage.

Gloria gasped. The casting director drank hurriedly. Fergus,
for some reason, stared curiously at the wolf.

"And now, ladies and gentlemen—oh, hang it, I do wish I
had a boy to carve—Ozymandias the Great will ascend this
rope into that land which only the users of the rope may
know. Onward and upward! Be right back," he added reas-
suringly to Wolf.

His plump hands grasped the rope above his head and gave

a little jerk. His knees swung up and clasped about the hempen pillar. And up he went, like a monkey on a stick, up and up and up—until suddenly he was gone.

Just gone. That was all there was to it. Gloria was beyond even saying "Oh." The casting director sat his beautiful flannels down on the filthy floor and gaped. Fergus swore softly and melodiously. And Wolf felt a premonitory prickling in his spine.

The stage door opened, admitting two men in denim pants and work shirts. "Hey!" said the first. "Where do you think you are?"

"We're from Metropolis Pictures," the casting director started to explain, scrambling to his feet.

"I don't care if you're from Washington, we gotta clear this stage. There's movies here tonight. Come on, Joe, help me get 'em out. And that pooch, too."

"You can't, Fred," said Joe reverently, and pointed. His voice sank to an awed whisper. "That's Gloria Garton—"

"So it is. Hi, Miss Garton. Cripes, wasn't that last one of yours a stinkeroo!"

"Your public, darling," Fergus murmured.

"Come on!" Fred shouted. "Out of here. We gotta clean up. And you, Joe! Strike that rope!"

Before Fergus could move, before Wolf could leap to the rescue, the efficient stagehand had struck the rope and was coiling it up.

Wolf stared up into the flies. There was nothing up there. Nothing at all. Someplace beyond the end of that rope was the only man on earth he could trust to say *Absarka!* for him; and the way down was cut off forever.

Wolfe Wolf sprawled on the floor of Gloria Garton's boudoir and watched that vision of volupty change into her most fetching negligee.

The situation was perfect. It was the fulfillment of all his dearest dreams. The only flaw was that he was still in a wolf's body.

Gloria turned, leaned over, and chucked him under the snout. "Wuzzum a cute wolf dog, wuzzum?"

Wolf could not restrain a snarl.

"Doesn't um like Gloria to talk baby talk? Um was a naughty wolf, yes, um was."

It was torture. Here you are in your best-beloved's hotel room, all her beauty revealed to your hungry eyes, and she talks baby talk to you! Wolf had been happy at first when Gloria suggested that she might take over the care of her co-star pending the reappearance of his trainer—for none of them was quite willing to admit that "Mr. O. Z. Manders" might truly and definitely have vanished—but he was beginning to realize that the situation might bring on more torment than pleasure.

"Wolves are funny," Gloria observed. She was more talkative when alone, with no need to be cryptically fascinating. "I knew a Wolfe once, only that was his name. He was a man. And he was a funny one."

Wolf felt his heart beating fast under his gray fur. To hear his own name on Gloria's warm lips . . . But before she could go on to tell her pet how funny Wolfe was, her maid rapped on the door.

"A Mr. O'Breen to see you, madam."

"Tell him to go 'way."

"He says it's important, and he does look, madam, as though he might make trouble."

"Oh, all right." Gloria rose and wrapped her negligee more respectably about her. "Come on, Yog— No, that's a silly name. I'm going to call you Wolfie. That's cute. Come on, Wolfie, and protect me from the big, bad detective."

Fergus O'Breen was pacing the sitting room with a certain vicious deliberateness in his strides. He broke off and stood still as Gloria and the wolf entered.

"So?" he observed tersely. "Reinforcements?"

"Will I need them?" Gloria cooed.

"Look, light of my love life." The glint in the green eyes was cold and deadly. "You've been playing games, and whatever their nature, there's one thing they're not. And that's cricket."

Gloria gave him a languid smile. "You're amusing, Fergus."

"Thanks. I doubt, however, if your activities are."

"You're still a little boy playing cops and robbers. And what boogyman are you after now?"

"Ha-ha," said Fergus politely. "And you know the answer to that question better than I do. That's why I'm here."

Wolf was puzzled. This conversation meant nothing to him. And yet he sensed a tension of danger in the air as clearly as though he could smell it.

"Go on," Gloria snapped impatiently. "And remember how dearly Metropolis Pictures will thank you for annoying one of its best box-office attractions."

"Some things, my sweeting, are more important than pictures, though you mightn't think it where you come from. One of them is a certain federation of forty-eight units. Another is an abstract concept called democracy."

"And so?"

"And so I want to ask you one question: Why did you come to Berkeley?"

"For publicity on *Fangs,* of course. It was your sister's idea."

"You've gone temperamental and turned down better ones. Why leap at this?"

"You don't haunt publicity stunts yourself, Fergus. Why are *you* here?"

Fergus was pacing again. "And why was your first act in Berkeley a visit to the office of the German department?"

"Isn't that natural enough? I used to be a student here."

"Majoring in dramatics, and you didn't go near the Little Theater. Why the German department?" He paused and stood straight in front of her, fixing her with his green gaze.

Gloria assumed the attitude of a captured queen defying the barbarian conqueror. "Very well. If you must know—I went to the German department to see the man I love."

Wolf held his breath, and tried to keep his tail from thrashing.

"Yes," she went on impassionedly, "you strip the last veil from me, and force me to confess to you what he alone should have heard first. This man proposed to me by mail. I foolishly rejected his proposal. But I thought and thought—and at last I knew. When I came to Berkeley I had to see him—"

"And did you?"

"The little mouse of a secretary told me he wasn't there. But I shall see him yet. And when I do—"

Fergus bowed stiffly. "My congratulations to you both, my sweeting. And the name of this more than fortunate gentleman?"

"Professor Wolfe Wolf."

"Who is doubtless the individual referred to in this?" He whipped a piece of paper from his sport coat and thrust it at Gloria. She paled and was silent. But Wolfe Wolf did not wait for her reply. He did not care. He knew the solution to his problem now, and he was streaking unobserved for her boudoir.

Gloria Garton entered the boudoir a minute later, a shaken and wretched woman. She unstoppered one of the delicate perfume bottles on her dresser and poured herself a stiff tot of whiskey. Then her eyebrows lifted in surprise as she stared at her mirror. Scrawlingly lettered across the glass in her own deep-crimson lipstick was the mysterious word

ABSARKA

Frowning, she said it aloud. "*Absarka—*"

From behind a screen stepped Professor Wolfe Wolf, incongruously wrapped in one of Gloria's lushest dressing robes. "Gloria dearest—" he cried.

"Wolfe!" she exclaimed. "What on earth are you doing here in my room?"

"I love you. I've always loved you since you couldn't tell a strong from a weak verb. And now that I know that you love me—"

"This is terrible. Please get out of here!"

"Gloria—"

"Get out of here, or I'll sick my dog on you. Wolfie—
Here, nice Wolfie!"

"I'm sorry, Gloria. But Wolfie won't answer you."

"Oh, you beast! Have you hurt Wolfie? Have you—"

"I wouldn't touch a hair on his pelt. Because, you see,
Gloria darling, I am Wolfie."

"What on earth do you—" Gloria stared around the room.
It was undeniable that there was no trace of the presence of a
wolf dog. And here was a man dressed only in one of her robes
and no sign of his own clothes. And after that funny little
man and the rope . . .

"You thought I was drab and dull," Wolf went on. "You
thought I'd sunk into an academic rut. You'd sooner have an
actor or a G-man. But I, Gloria, am something more exciting
than you've ever dreamed of. There's not another soul on
earth I'd tell this to, but I, Gloria, am a werewolf."

Gloria gasped. "That isn't possible! But it does all fit in.
What I heard about you on campus, and your friend with the
funny beard and how he vanished, and, of course, it explains
how you did tricks that any real dog couldn't possibly do—"

"Don't you believe me, darling?"

Gloria rose from the dresser chair and went into his arms.
"I believe you, dear. And it's wonderful! I'll bet there's not
another woman in all Hollywood that was ever married to a
werewolf!"

"Then you will—"

"But of course, dear. We can work it out beautifully. We'll
hire a stooge to be your trainer on the lot. You can work day-
times, and come home at night and I'll say that word for you.
It'll be perfect."

"Gloria . . ." Wolf murmured with tender reverence.

"One thing, dear. Just a little thing. Would you do Gloria
a favor?"

"Anything!"

"Show me how you change. Change for me now. Then I'll
change you back right away."

Wolf said The Word. He was in such ecstatic bliss that he

hardly felt the pang this time. He capered about the room with all the litheness of his fine wolfish legs, and ended up before Gloria, wagging his tail and looking for approval.

Gloria patted his head. "Good boy, Wolfie. And now, darling, you can just damned well stay that way."

Wolf let out a yelp of amazement.

"You heard me, Wolfie. You're staying that way. You didn't happen to believe any of that guff I was feeding the detective, did you? Love you? I should waste my time! But this way you can be very useful to me. With your trainer gone, I can take charge of you and pick up an extra thousand a week or so. I won't mind that. And Professor Wolfe Wolf will have vanished forever, which fits right in with my plans."

Wolf snarled.

"Now, don't try to get nasty, Wolfie darling. Um wouldn't threaten ums darling Gloria, would ums? Remember what I can do for you. I'm the only person that can turn you into a man again. You wouldn't dare teach anyone else that. You wouldn't dare let people know what you really are. An ignorant person would kill you. A smart one would have you locked up as a lunatic."

Wolf still advanced threateningly.

"Oh, no. You can't hurt me. Because all I'd have to do would be to say the word on the mirror. Then you wouldn't be a dangerous wolf any more. You'd just be a man here in my room, and I'd scream. And after what happened on the campus yesterday, how long do you think you'd stay out of the madhouse?"

Wolf backed away and let his tail droop.

"You see, Wolfie darling? Gloria has ums just where she wants ums. And ums is damned well going to be a good boy."

There was a rap on the boudoir door, and Gloria called, "Come in."

"A gentleman to see you, madam," the maid announced. "A Professor Fearing."

Gloria smiled her best cruel and queenly smile. "Come along, Wolfie. This may interest you."

Professor Oscar Fearing, overflowing one of the graceful chairs of the sitting room, beamed benevolently as Gloria and the wolf entered. "Ah, my dear! A new pet. Touching."

"And what a pet, Oscar. Wait till you hear."

Professor Fearing buffed his pince-nez against his sleeve. "And wait, my dear, until you hear all that I have learned. Chiswick has perfected his protective screen against magnetic bombs, and the official trial is set for next week. And Farnsworth has all but completed his researches on a new process for obtaining osmium. Gas warfare may start any day, and the power that can command a plentiful supply of—"

"Fine, Oscar," Gloria broke in. "But we can go over all this later. We've got other worries right now."

"What do you mean, my dear?"

"Have you run onto a red-headed young Irishman in a yellow shirt?"

"No, I— Why, yes. I did see such an individual leaving the office yesterday. I believe he had been to see Wolfe."

"He's on to us. He's a detective from Los Angeles, and he's tracking us down. Someplace he got hold of a scrap of record that should have been destroyed. He knows I'm in it, and he knows I'm tied up with somebody here in the German department."

Professor Fearing scrutinized his pince-nez, approved of their cleanness, and set them on his nose. "Not so much excitement, my dear. No hysteria. Let us approach this calmly. Does he know about the Temple of the Dark Truth?"

"Not yet. Nor about you. He just knows it's somebody in the department."

"Then what could be simpler? You have heard of the strange conduct of Wolfe Wolf?"

"Have I!" Gloria laughed harshly.

"Everyone knows of Wolfe's infatuation with you. Throw the blame onto him. It should be easy to clear yourself and make you appear an innocent tool. Direct all attention to him and the organization will be safe. The Temple of the Dark Truth can go its mystic way and extract even more invaluable information from weary scientists who need the emotional release of a false religion."

"That's what I've tried to do. I gave O'Breen a long song and dance about my devotion to Wolfe, so obviously phony he'd be bound to think it was a cover-up for something else. And I think he bit. But the situation's a damned sight trickier than you guess. Do you know where Wolfe Wolf is?"

"No one knows. After the president . . . ah . . . rebuked him, he seems to have vanished."

Gloria laughed again. "He's right here. In this room."

"My dear! Secret panels and such? You take your espionage too seriously. Where?"

"There!"

Professor Fearing gaped. "Are you serious?"

"As serious as you are about the future of Fascism. That is Wolfe Wolf."

Fearing approached the wolf incredulously and extended his hand.

"He might bite," Gloria warned him a second too late.

Fearing stared at his bleeding hand. "That, at least," he observed, "is undeniably true." And he raised his foot to deliver a sharp kick.

"No, Oscar! Don't! Leave him alone. And you'll have to take my word for it—it's way too complicated. But the wolf is Wolfe Wolf, and I've got him absolutely under control. He's perfectly in our hands. We'll switch suspicion to him, and I'll keep him this way while Fergus and his friends the G-men go off hotfoot on his trail."

"My dear!" Fearing ejaculated. "You're mad. You're more hopelessly mad than the devout members of the Temple." He took off his pince-nez and stared again at the wolf. "And yet Tuesday night— Tell me one thing: From whom did you get this . . . this wolf dog?"

"From a funny plump little man with a fringy beard."

Fearing gasped. Obviously he remembered the furor in the Temple, and the wolf and the fringe-beard. "Very well, my dear. I believe you. Don't ask me why, but I believe you. And now—"

"Now, it's all set, isn't it? We keep him here helpless, and we use him to—"

"The wolf as scapegoat. Yes. Very pretty."

"Oh! One thing—" She was suddenly frightened.

Wolfe Wolf was considering the possibilities of a sudden attack on Fearing. He could probably get out of the room before Gloria could say *Absarka!* But after that? Whom could he trust to restore him? Especially if G-men were to be set on his trail . . .

"What is it?" Fearing asked.

"That secretary. That little mouse in the department office. She knows it was you I asked for, not Wolf. Fergus can't have talked to her yet, because he swallowed my story; but he will. He's thorough."

"Hm-m-m. Then, in that case—"

"Yes, Oscar?"

"She must be attended to." Professor Oscar Fearing beamed genially and reached for the phone.

Wolf acted instantly, on inspiration and impulse. His teeth were strong, quite strong enough to jerk the phone cord from the wall. That took only a second, and in the next second he was out of the room and into the hall before Gloria could open her mouth to speak that word that would convert him from a powerful and dangerous wolf to a futile man.

There were shrill screams and a shout or two of "Mad dog!" as he dashed through the hotel lobby, but he paid no heed to them. The main thing was to reach Emily's house before she could be "attended to." Her evidence was essential. That could swing the balance, show Fergus and his G-men where the true guilt lay. And, besides, he admitted to himself, Emily was a damned nice kid. . . .

His rate of collision was about one point six six per block, and the curses heaped upon him, if theologically valid, would have been more than enough to damn him forever. But he was making time, and that was all that counted. He dashed through traffic signals, cut into the path of trucks, swerved from under streetcars, and once even leaped over a stalled car that was obstructing him. Everything was going fine, he was halfway there, when two hundred pounds of human flesh landed on him in a flying tackle.

He looked up through the brilliant lighting effects of smashing his head on the sidewalk and saw his old nemesis, the policeman who had been cheated of his beer.

"So, Rover!" said the officer. "Got you at last, did I? Now we'll see if you'll wear a proper license tag. Didn't know I used to play football, did you?"

The officer's grip on his hair was painfully tight. A gleeful crowd was gathering and heckling the policeman with fantastic advice.

"Get along, boys," he admonished. "This is a private matter between me and Rover here. Come on," and he tugged even harder.

Wolf left a large tuft of fur and skin in the officer's grasp and felt the blood ooze out of the bare patch on his neck. He heard a ripe oath and a pistol shot simultaneously, and felt the needlelike sting through his shoulder. The awestruck crowd thawed before him. Two more bullets hied after him, but he was gone, leaving the most dazed policeman in Berkeley.

"I hit him," the officer kept muttering blankly. "I hit the—"

Wolfe Wolf coursed along Dwight Way. Two more blocks and he'd be at the little bungalow that Emily shared with a teaching assistant in something or other. Ripping out that telephone had stopped Fearing only momentarily; the orders would have been given by now, the henchmen would be on their way. But he was almost there. . . .

"He'o!" a child's light voice called to him. "Nice woof-woof come back!"

Across the street was the modest frame dwelling of Robby and his shrewish mother. The child had been playing on the sidewalk. Now he saw his idol and deliverer and started across the street at a lurching toddle. "Nice woof-woof!" he kept calling. "Wait for Robby!"

Wolf kept on. This was no time for playing games with

even the most delightful of cubs. And then he saw the car. It was an ancient jalopy, plastered with wisecracks even older than itself; and the high school youth driving was obviously showing his girl friend how it could make time on this deserted residential street. The girl was a cute dish, and who could be bothered watching out for children?

Robby was directly in front of the car. Wolf leaped straight as a bullet. His trajectory carried him so close to the car that he could feel the heat of the radiator on his flank. His forepaws struck Robby and thrust him out of danger. They fell to the ground together, just as the car ground over the last of Wolf's caudal vertebrae.

The cute dish screamed. "Homer! Did we hit them?"

Homer said nothing, and the jalopy zoomed on.

Robby's screams were louder. "You hurt me! You hurt me! *Baaaaad* woof-woof!"

His mother appeared on the porch and joined in with her own howls of rage. The cacophony was terrific. Wolf let out one wailing yelp of his own, to make it perfect and to lament his crushed tail, and dashed on. This was no time to clear up misunderstandings.

But the two delays had been enough. Robby and the policeman had proved the perfect unwitting tools of Oscar Fearing. As Wolf approached Emily's little bungalow, he saw a gray sedan drive off. In the rear was a small, slim girl, and she was struggling.

Even a werewolf's lithe speed cannot equal that of a motor car. After a block of pursuit, Wolf gave up and sat back on his haunches panting. It felt funny, he thought even in that tense moment, not to be able to sweat, to have to open your mouth and stick out your tongue and . . .

"Trouble?" inquired a solicitous voice.

This time Wolf recognized the cat. "Heavens, yes," he assented wholeheartedly. "More than you ever dreamed of."

"Food shortage?" the cat asked. "But that toddler back there is nice and plump."

"Shut up," Wolf snarled.

"Sorry; I was just judging from what Confucius told me about werewolves. You don't mean to tell me that you're an altruistic were?"

"I guess I am. I know werewolves are supposed to go around slaughtering, but right now I've got to save a life."

"You expect me to believe that?"

"It's the truth."

"Ah," the cat reflected philosophically. "Truth is a dark and deceitful thing."

Wolfe Wolf was on his feet. "Thanks," he barked. "You've done it."

"Done what?"

"See you later." And Wolf was off at top speed for the Temple of the Dark Truth.

That was the best chance. That was Fearing's headquarters. The odds were at least even that when it wasn't being used for services it was the hangout of his ring, especially since the consulate had been closed in San Francisco. Again the wild running and leaping, the narrow escapes; and where Wolf had not taken these too seriously before, he knew now that he might be immune to bullets, but certainly not to being run over. His tail still stung and ached tormentingly. But he had to get there. He had to clear his own reputation, he kept reminding himself; but what he really thought was, I have to save Emily.

A block from the Temple he heard the crackle of gunfire. Pistol shots and, he'd swear, machine guns, too. He couldn't figure what it meant, but he pressed on. Then a bright-yellow roadster passed him and a vivid flash came from its window. Instinctively he ducked. You might be immune to bullets, but you still didn't just stand still for them.

The roadster was gone and he was about to follow when a glint of bright metal caught his eye. The bullet that had missed him had hit a brick wall and ricocheted back onto the sidewalk. It glittered there in front of him—pure silver!

This, he realized abruptly, meant the end of his immunity. Fearing had believed Gloria's story, and with his smattering of occult lore he had known the successful counterweapon. A bullet, from now on, might mean no more needle sting, but instant death.

And so Wolfe Wolf went straight on.

He approached the Temple cautiously, lurking behind shrubbery. And he was not the only lurker. Before the Temple, crouching in the shelter of a car every window of which was shattered, were Fergus O'Breen and a moonfaced giant. Each held an automatic, and they were taking pot shots at the steeple.

Wolf's keen lupine hearing could catch their words even above the firing. "Gabe's around back," Moonface was explaining. "But it's no use. Know what that damned steeple is? It's a revolving machine-gun turret. They've been ready for something like this. Only two men in there, far as we can tell, but that turret covers all the approaches."

"Only two?" Fergus muttered.

"And the girl. They brought a girl here with them. If she's still alive."

Fergus took careful aim at the steeple, fired, and ducked back behind the car as a bullet missed him by millimeters. "Missed him again! By all the kings that ever ruled Tara, Moon, there's got to be a way in there. How about tear gas?"

Moon snorted. "Think you can reach the firing gap in that armored turret at this angle?"

"That girl . . ." said Fergus.

Wolf waited no longer. As he sprang forward, the gunner noticed him and shifted his fire. It was like a needle shower in which all the spray is solid steel. Wolf's nerves ached with the pain of reknitting. But at least machine guns apparently didn't fire silver.

The front door was locked, but the force of his drive carried him through and added a throbbing ache in his shoulder to his other comforts. The lower-floor guard, a pasty-faced individual with a jutting Adam's apple, sprang up, pistol in hand. Behind him, in the midst of the litter of the cult, ceremonial robes, incense burners, curious books, even a Ouija board, lay Emily.

Pasty-face fired. The bullet struck Wolf full in the chest and for an instant he expected death. But this, too, was lead, and he jumped forward. It was not his usual powerful leap. His strength was almost spent by now. He needed to lie on cool earth and let his nerves knit. And this spring was only enough to grapple with his foe, not to throw him.

The man reversed his useless automatic and brought its butt thudding down on the beast's skull. Wolf reeled back, lost his balance, and fell to the floor. For a moment he could not rise. The temptation was so strong just to lie there and . . .

The girl moved. Her bound hands grasped a corner of the Ouija board. Somehow, she stumbled to her rope-tied feet and raised her arms. Just as Pasty-face rushed for the prostrate wolf, she brought the heavy board down.

Wolf was on his feet now. There was an instant of temptation. His eyes fixed themselves to the jut of that Adam's apple, and his long tongue licked his jowls. Then he heard the machine-gun fire from the turret, and tore himself from Pasty-face's unconscious form.

Ladders are hard on a wolf, damned near impossible. But if you use your jaws to grasp the rung above you and pull up, it can be done. He was halfway up the ladder when the gunner heard him. The firing stopped, and Wolf heard a rich German oath in what he automatically recognized as an East Prussian dialect with possible Lithuanian influences. Then he saw the man himself, a broken-nosed blond, staring down the ladder well.

The other man's bullets had been lead. So this must be the one with the silver. But it was too late to turn back now. Wolf bit the next rung and hauled up as the bullet struck his snout and stung through. The blond's eyes widened as he fired again and Wolf climbed another rung. After the third shot he withdrew precipitately from the opening.

Shots still sounded from below, but the gunner did not return them. He stood frozen against the wall of the turret watching in horror as the wolf emerged from the well. Wolf halted and tried to get his breath. He was dead with fatigue and stress, but this man must be vanquished.

The blond raised his pistol, sighted carefully, and fired once more. He stood for one terrible instant, gazing at this death-less wolf and knowing from his grandmother's stories what it must be. Then deliberately he clamped his teeth on the muzzle of the automatic and fired again.

Wolf had not yet eaten in his wolf's body, but food must have been transferred from the human stomach to the lupine. There was at least enough for him to be extensively sick.

Getting down the ladder was impossible. He jumped. He had never heard anything about a wolf's landing on its feet, but it seemed to work. He dragged his weary and bruised body along to where Emily sat by the still unconscious Pasty-face, his discarded pistol in her hand. She wavered as the wolf approached her, as though uncertain yet as to whether he was friend or foe.

Time was short. With the machine gun silenced, Fergus and his companions would be invading the Temple at any minute. Wolf hurriedly nosed about and found the planchette of the Ouija board. He pushed the heart-shaped bit of wood onto the board and began to shove it around with his paw.

Emily watched, intent and puzzled. "A," she said aloud. "B—S—"

Wolf finished the word and edged around so that he stood directly beside one of the ceremonial robes. "Are you trying to say something?" Emily frowned.

Wolf wagged his tail in vehement affirmation and began again.

"A—" Emily repeated. "B—S—A—R—"

He could already hear approaching footsteps.

"—K—A— What on earth does that mean? *Absarka*—"

Ex-professor Wolfe Wolf hastily wrapped his naked human body in the cloak of the Dark Truth. Before either he or Emily knew quite what was happening, he had folded her in his arms, kissed her in a most thorough expression of gratitude, and fainted.

Even Wolf's human nose could tell, when he awakened, that he was in a hospital. His body was still limp and exhausted. The bare patch on his neck, where the policeman had pulled out the hair, still stung, and there was a lump where the butt of the automatic had connected. His tail, or where his tail had been, sent twinges through him if he moved. But the sheets were cool and he was at rest and Emily was safe.

"I don't know how you got in there, Mr. Wolf, or what you did; but I want you to know you've done your country a signal service." It was the moonfaced giant speaking.

Fergus O'Breen was sitting beside the bed too. "Congratulations, Wolf. And I don't know if the doctor would approve, but here."

Wolfe Wolf drank the whiskey gratefully and looked a question at the huge man.

"This is Moon Lafferty," said Fergus. "FBI man. He's been helping me track down this ring of spies ever since I first got wind of them."

"You got them—all?" Wolf asked.

"Picked up Fearing and Garton at the hotel," Lafferty rumbled.

"But how— I thought—"

"You thought we were out for you?" Fergus answered. "That was the Garton's idea, but I didn't quite tumble. You see, I'd already talked to your secretary. I knew it was Fearing she'd wanted to see. And when I asked around about Fearing, and learned of the Temple and the defense researches of some of its members, the whole picture cleared up."

"Wonderful work, Mr. Wolf," said Lafferty. "Any time we can do anything for you— And how you got into that machine-gun turret— Well, O'Breen, I'll see you later. Got to check up on the rest of this roundup. Pleasant convalescence to you, Wolf."

Fergus waited until the G-man had left the room. Then he leaned over the bed and asked confidentially, "How about it, Wolf? Going back to your acting career?"

Wolf gasped. "What acting career?"

"Still going to play Tookah? If Metropolis makes *Fangs* with Miss Garton in a Federal prison."

Wolf fumbled for words. "What sort of nonsense—"

"Come on, Wolf. It's pretty clear I know that much. Might as well tell me the whole story."

Still dazed, Wolf told it. "But how in heaven's name did you know it?" he concluded.

Fergus grinned. "Look. Dorothy Sayers said someplace that in a detective story the supernatural may be introduced only to be dispelled. Sure, that's swell. Only in real life there come times when it won't be dispelled. And this was one. There was too damned much. There were your eyebrows and fingers, there were the obviously real magical powers of your friend, there were the tricks which no dog could possibly do without signals, there was the way the other dogs whimpered and cringed— I'm pretty hardheaded, Wolf, but I'm Irish. I'll string along only so far with the materialistic, but too much coincidence is too much."

"Fearing believed it too," Wolf reflected. "But one thing that worries me: if they used a silver bullet on me once, why were all the rest of them lead? Why was I safe from then on?"

"Well," said Fergus, "I'll tell you. Because it wasn't 'they' who fired the silver bullet. You see, Wolf, up till the last minute I thought you were on 'their' side. I somehow didn't associate good will with a werewolf. So I got a mold from a gunsmith and paid a visit to a jeweler and— I'm damned glad I missed," he added sincerely.

"*You're* glad!"

"But look. Previous question stands. Are you going back to acting? Because if not, I've got a suggestion."

"Which is?"

"You say you fretted about how to be a practical, commercial werewolf. All right. You're strong and fast. You can terrify people even to commit suicide. You can overhear conversations that no human being could get in on. You're invulnerable to bullets. Can you tell me better qualifications for a G-man?"

Wolf goggled. "Me? A G-man?"

"Moon's been telling me how badly they need new men.

They've changed the qualifications lately so that your language knowledge'll do instead of the law or accounting they used to require. And after what you did today, there won't be any trouble about a little academic scandal in your past. Moon's pretty sold on you."

Wolf was speechless. Only three days ago he had been in torment because he was not an actor or a G-man. Now—

"Think it over," said Fergus.

"I will. Indeed I will. Oh, and one other thing. Has there been any trace of Ozzy?"

"Nary a sign."

"I like that man. I've got to try to find him and—"

"If he's the magician I think he is, he's staying up there only because he's decided he likes it."

"I don't know. Magic's tricky. Heavens knows I've learned that. I'm going to try to do my damnedest for that fringe-bearded old colleague."

"Wish you luck. Shall I send in your other guest?"

"Who's that?"

"Your secretary. Here on business, no doubt."

Fergus disappeared discreetly as he admitted Emily. She walked over to the bed and took Wolf's hand. His eyes drank in her quiet, charming simplicity, and his mind wondered what freak of belated adolescence had made him succumb to the blatant glamour of Gloria.

They were silent for a long time. Then at once they both said, "How can I thank you? You saved my life."

Wolf laughed. "Let's not argue. Let's say we saved our life."

"You mean that?" Emily asked gravely.

Wolf pressed her hand. "Aren't you tired of being an office wife?"

In the bazaar of Darjeeling, Chulundra Lingasuta stared at his rope in numb amazement. Young Ali had climbed up only five minutes ago, but now as he descended he was a hundred pounds heavier and wore a curious fringe of beard.

The Pink Caterpillar

"*A*nd their medicine men can do time travel, too," Norm Harker said. "At least, that's the firm belief everywhere on the island: a *tualala* can go forward in time and bring you back any single item you specify, for a price. We used to spend the night watches speculating on what would be the one best thing to order."

Norman hadn't told us the name of the island. The stripe and a half on his sleeve lent him discretion, and Tokyo hadn't earned yet what secret installations the Navy had been busy with on that minute portion of the South Pacific. He couldn't talk about the installations, of course; but the island had provided him with plenty of other matters to keep us entertained, sitting up there in the Top of the Mark.

"What would you order, Tony," he asked, "with a carte blanche like that on the future?"

"How far future?"

"They say a *tualala* goes to one hundred years from date: no more, no less."

"Money wouldn't work," I mused. "Jewels maybe. Or a gadget—any gadget—and you could invent it as of now and make a fortune. But then it might depend on principles not yet worked out. . . . Or the *Gone with the Wind* of the twenty-first century—but publish it now and it might lay an egg. Can you imagine today's best sellers trying to compete with

Dickens? No . . . it's a tricky question. What did you try?"

"We finally settled on Hitler's tombstone. Think of the admission tickets we could sell to see that!"

"And—?"

"And nothing. We couldn't pay the *tualala's* price. For each article fetched through time he wanted one virgin from the neighboring island. We felt the staff somehow might not understand if we went collecting them. There's always a catch to magic," Norman concluded lightly.

Fergus said "Uh-huh" and nodded gravely. He hadn't been saying much all evening—just sitting there and looking out over the panorama of the bay by night, a glistening joy now that the dimout was over, and listening. I still don't know the sort of work he's been doing, but it's changing him, toning him down.

But even a toned-down Irishman can stand only so much silence, and there was obviously a story on his lips. Norm asked, "You've been running into magic too?"

"Not lately." He held his glass up to the light and watched his drink. "Damned if I know why writers call a highball an amber liquid," he observed. "Start a cliché and it sticks. . . Like about detectives being hardheaded realists. Didn't you ever stop to think that there's hardly another profession outside the clergy that's so apt to run up against the things beyond realism? Why do you call in a detective? Because something screwy's going on and you need an explanation. And if there isn't an explanation . . .

"This was back a ways. Back when I didn't have anything worse to deal with than murderers and, once, a werewolf. But he was a hell of a swell guy. The murderers I used to think were pretty thorough low-lifes, but now . . . Anyway, this was back then. I was down in Mexico putting the finishing touches on that wacky business of the Aztec Calendar when I heard from Dan Rafetti. I think you know him, Tony; he's an investigator for Southwest National Life Insurance, and he's thrown some business my way now and then, like the Solid Key case.

"This one sounded interesting. Nothing spectacular, you

understand, and probably no money to speak of. But the kind of crazy unexplained little detail that stirs up the O'Breen curiosity. Very simple: Southwest gets a claim from a beneficiary. One of their customers died down in Mexico and his sister wants the cash. They send to the Mexican authorities for a report on his death and it was heart failure and that's that. Only the policy is made out to Mr. Frank Miller and the Mexican report refers to him as *Dr.* F. Miller. They ask the sister and she's certain he hadn't any right to such a title. So I happen to be right near Tlichotl, where he died, and would I please kind of nose around and see was there anything phony, like maybe an imposture. Photographs and fingerprints, from a Civil Service application he once made, enclosed."

"Nice businesslike beginning," Norman said.

Fergus nodded. "That's the way it started: all very routine, yours-of-the-27th-*ult*. Prosaic, like. And Tlichotl was prosaic enough too. Maybe to a tourist it'd be picturesque, but I'd been kicking around these Mexican mountain towns long enough so one seemed as commonplace as another. Sort of a montage of flat houses and white trousers and dogs and children and an old church and an almost-as-old pulquería and one guy who plays a hell of a guitar on Saturday nights.

"Tlichotl wasn't much different. There was a mine near it, and just out of town was a bunch of drab new frame houses for the American engineers. Everybody in town worked in the mine—all pure Indians, with those chaste profiles straight off of the Aztec murals that begin to seem like the only right and normal human face when you've seen 'em long enough.

"I went to the doctor first. He was the government sanitation agent and health instructor, and the town looked like he was doing a good job. His English was better than my Spanish, and he was glad I liked tequila. Yes, he remembered Dr. Miller. He checked up his records and announced that Dr. M. died on November 2. It was January when I talked to him. Simple death: heart failure. He'd had several attacks in past weeks, and the doctor had expected him to go any day. All of a sudden a friend he hadn't seen in years showed up in town unannounced, and the shock did it. Any little thing might have.

"The doctor wasn't a stupid man, or a careless one. I was willing to take his word that the death had been natural. And maybe I ought to put in here, before your devious minds start getting ahead of me, that as far as I ever learned he was absolutely right. Common-or-garden heart failure, and that didn't fit into any picture of insurance fraud. But there was still the inconsistency of the title, and I went on, 'Must've been kind of nice for you to have a colleague here to talk with?'

"The doctor frowned a little at that. It seemed he'd been sort of hurt by Dr. Miller's attitude. Had tried to interest him in some researches he was doing with an endemic variant of undulant fever, which he'd practically succeeded in wiping out. But the North American 'doctor' just didn't give a damn. No fraternal spirit; no scientific curiosity; nothing.

"I gathered they hadn't been very friendly, my doctor and 'Dr.' Miller. In fact, Miller hadn't been intimate with anybody, not even the other North Americans at the mine. He liked the Indians and they liked him, though they were a little scared of him on account of the skeleton—apparently an anatomical specimen and the first thing I'd heard of to go with his assumed doctorate. He had a good short-wave radio, and he listened to music on that and sketched a little and read and went for short hikes. It sounded like a good life, if you like a lonely one. They might know a little more about him at the pulquería; he stopped there for a drink sometimes. And the widow Sánchez had kept house for him; she might know something.

"I tried the widow first. She wore a shapeless black dress that looked as though she'd started mourning Mr. Sánchez ten years before, but her youngest child wasn't quite walking yet. She'd liked her late employer, might he rest in peace. He had been a good man, and so little trouble. No, he never gave medicine to anybody; that was the job of the señor médico from Mexico City. No, he never did anything with bottles. No, he never received much mail and surely not with money in it, for she had often seen him open his few letters. But yes, indeed he was a médico; did he not have the bones, the *esquéleto*, to prove it?

"And if the señor interested himself so much for el doctor Miller, perhaps the señor would care to see his house? It was untouched, as he'd left it. No one lived there now. No, it was not haunted—at least, not that anyone knew, though no man knows about such things. It was only that no one new ever comes to live in Tlichotl, and an empty house stays empty.

"I looked the house over. It had two rooms and a kitchen and a tiny patio. 'Dr.' Miller's things were undisturbed; no one had claimed them and it was up to time and heat and insects to take care of them. There was the radio and beside it the sketching materials. One wall was a bookcase, well filled, mostly with sixteenth- and seventeenth-century literature in English and Spanish. The books had been faithfully read. There were a few recent volumes, mostly on travel or on Mexican Indian culture, and a few magazines. No medical books or periodicals.

"Food, cooking utensils, clothing, a pile of sketches (good enough so you'd feel all right when you'd done them and bad enough so you wouldn't feel urged to exhibit them), pipes and tobacco—these just about made up the inventory. No papers to speak of, just a few personal letters, mostly from his sister (and beneficiary). No instruments or medicines of any kind. Nothing whatsoever out of the way—not even the skeleton.

"I'd heard about that twice, so I asked what had become of it. The sons of the mining engineers, the young demons, had stolen it to celebrate a gringo holiday, which I gathered had been Halloween. They had built an enormous bonfire, and the skeleton had fallen in and been consumed. The doctor Miller had been very angry; he had suffered one of his attacks then, almost as bad as the one that gave him death, may the Lord hold him in His kindness. But now it was time for a mother to return and feed her brood; and her house was mine, and would the señor join in her poor supper?

"The beans were good and the tortillas wonderful; and the youngest children hadn't ever seen red hair before and had some pointed questions to ask me about mine. And in the middle of the meal something suddenly went *click* in my brain and I knew why Frank Miller had called himself 'doctor.'"

Fergus paused and beckoned to a waiter.

Norman said, "Is that all?"

"For the moment. I'm giving you boys a chance to scintillate. There you have all the factors up to that point. All right: *Why* was Miller calling himself 'doctor'?"

"He wasn't practicing," Norman said slowly. "And he wasn't even running a fake medical racket by mail, as people have done from Mexico to avoid the U.S. Post Office Department."

"And," I added, "he hadn't assumed the title to impress people, to attain social standing, because he had nothing to do with his neighbors. And he wasn't carrying on any experiments or research which he might have needed the title in writing up. So he gained nothing in cash or prestige. All right, what other reason is there for posing as a doctor?"

"Answer," said Fergus leisurely: "he wasn't posing as a doctor. Look; you might pose as a doctor with no props at all, thinking no one would come in your house but the housekeeper. Or you might stage an elaborate front complete with instrument cabinets and five-pound books. But you wouldn't try it with just one prop, an anatomical skeleton."

Norman and I looked at each other and nodded. It made sense. "Well then?" I asked.

The fresh drinks came, and Fergus said, "My round. Well then, the skeleton was not a prop for the medical pose. Quite the reverse. Turn it around and it makes sense. He called himself a doctor *to account for the skeleton.*"

I choked on my first sip, and Norman spluttered a little, too. Fergus went on eagerly, with that keen light in his green eyes, "You can't hide a skeleton in a tiny house. The housekeeper's bound to see it, and word gets around. Miller liked the Indians and he liked peace. He had to account for the skeleton. So he became a 'doctor.'"

"But that—" Norman objected. "That's no answer. That's just another question."

"I know," said Fergus. "But that's the first step in detection: to find the right question. And that's it: *Why does a man live with a skeleton?*"

We were silent for a bit. The Top of the Mark was full of glasses and smoke and uniforms; and despite the uniforms it seemed a room set aside that was not a part of a world at war —still less of a world in which a man might live with a skeleton.

"Of course you checked the obvious answer," I said at last.

Fergus nodded. "He couldn't very well have been a black magician, if that's what you mean, or white either. Not a book or a note in the whole place dealing with the subject. No wax, chalk, incense or what-have-you. The skeleton doesn't fit any more into a magical pattern than into a medical."

"The Dead Beloved?" Norman suggested, hesitantly uttering the phrase in mocking capitals. "Rose-for-Emily stuff? A bit grisly, but not inconceivable."

"The Mexican doctor saw the skeleton. It was a man's, and not a young one."

"Then he was planning an insurance fraud—burn the house down and let the bones be found while he vanished."

"A, you don't burn adobe. B, you don't let the skeleton be seen by the doctor who'll examine it later. C, it was that of a much shorter man than Miller."

"A writer?" I ventured wildly. "I've sometimes thought myself a skeleton might be useful in the study—check where to inflict skull wounds and such."

"With no typewriter, no manuscripts, and very little mail?"

Norman's face lit up. "You said he sketched. Maybe he was working on a modern *Totentanz*—Dance of Death allegory. Holbein and Dürer must have had a skeleton or two around."

"I saw his sketches. Landscapes only."

I lit my pipe and settled back. "All right. We've stooged and we don't know. Now tell us why a man keeps house with a set of bones." My tone was lighter than necessary.

Fergus said, "I won't go into all the details of my investigations. I saw damned near every adult in Tlichotl and most of the kids. And I pieced out what I think is the answer. But I think you can gather it from the evidence of four people.

"First, Jim Reilly, mining engineer. Witness deposeth and saith he was on the main street, if you can call it that, of Tlichotl on November 2. He saw a stranger, 'swarthy but not a Mex,' walk up to Miller and say, 'Frank!' Miller looked up and was astonished. The stranger said, 'Sorry for the delay. But it took me a little time to get here.' And he hadn't finished the sentence before Miller dropped dead. Queried about the stranger, witness says he gave his name as Humbert Targ; he stayed around town for a few days for the funeral and then left. Said he'd known Miller a long time ago— never clear quite where, but seemingly in the South Seas, as we used to say before we learned to call it the South Pacific. Asked for description, witness proved pretty useless: medium height, medium age, dark complexion . . . Only helpful details: stranger wore old clothes ('Shabby?' 'No, just old.' 'Out-of-date?' 'I guess so.' 'How long ago? What kind?' 'I don't know. Just old—funny-looking') and had only one foot ('One leg?' 'No, two legs, just one foot.' 'Wooden peg?' 'No, just empty trouser cuff. Walked with crutches').

"Second witness, Father Gonzaga, and it's a funny sensation to be talking to a priest who wears just a plain business suit. He hadn't known 'Dr.' Miller well, though he'd said a mass for his soul. But one night Miller had come from the pulquería and insisted on talking to him. He wanted to know how you could ever get right with God and yourself if you'd done someone a great wrong and there was no conceivable way you could make it up to him. The padre asked why, was the injured person dead? Miller hesitated and didn't answer. He's alive, then? Oh no, no! Restitution could surely be made to the next of kin if it were a money matter? No, it was . . . personal. Father's advice was to pray for the injured party's soul and for grace to avoid such temptation another time. I don't much see what else he could have suggested, but Miller wasn't satisfied."

I wasn't hearing the noise around us any more. Norman was

eaning forward too, and I saw in his eyes that he too was
eginning to feel the essential *wrong*ness of the case the detec-
ive had stumbled on.

"Third witness, the widow Sánchez. She told me about the
keleton when I came back for more beans and brought a
ottle of red wine to go with them—which it did, magnifi-
ently. 'Dr.' Miller had treasured his skeleton very highly. She
vas supposed not even to dust it. But once she forgot, and a
nger came off. This was in October. She thought he might
ot notice a missing finger, where she knew she'd catch it if
e found a loose one, so she burned the bones in the charcoal
razier over which she fried her tortillas. Two days later
he was serving the doctor his dinner when she saw a pink
aterpillar crawling near his place. She'd never seen a pink
aterpillar before. She flicked it away with a napkin; but not
efore the 'doctor' saw it. He jumped up from the table and
an to look at the skeleton and gave her a terrific bawling-
ut. After that she saw the caterpillar several times. It was
bout then that Miller started having those heart attacks.
Vhenever she saw the caterpillar it was crawling around the
loctor.' I looked at her a long time while she finished the
vine, and then I said, 'Was it a caterpillar?' She crossed herself
nd said 'No.' She said it very softly, and that was all she
aid that night."

I looked down at the table. My hand lay there, and the
ndex finger was tapping gently. We seemed to be sitting in
uite a draft, and I shuddered.

"Fourth witness, Timmy Reilly, twelve-year-old son to
im. He thought it was a great lark that they'd stolen the old
oy's bones for Halloween. Fun and games. These dopes
own here didn't know from nothin' about Halloween, but
im and the gang, they sure showed 'em. But I could see he
vas holding something back. I made a swap. He could wear
ny detective badge (which I've never worn yet) for a whole
ay if he'd tell me what else he knew. So he showed it to
ne: the foot that he'd rescued when the skeleton was burned
p. He'd tried to grab the bones as they toppled over and
ll he could reach was the heel. He had the whole foot, well

articulated and lousy with tarsals and stuff. So I made a
better deal: he could have the badge for keeps (with the
number scratched out a little) if he'd let me burn the foot
He let me."

Fergus paused, and it all began to click into place. The
pattern was clear, and it was a pattern that should not be

"You've got it now?" Fergus asked quietly. "All I needed
to make it perfect was Norm's story. There had to be such a
thing as *tualala,* with such powers as theirs. I'd deduced them
but it's satisfying to have them confirmed.

"Miller had had an enemy, many years before, a man who
had sworn to kill him. And Miller had known a *tualala*
back there in the South Seas. And when he'd asked himsel
what would be the best single item to bring back from the
future, he knew the answer: *his enemy's skeleton.*

It wasn't murder. He probably had scruples about that
He sounded like a good enough guy in a way, and maybe
his *tualala* asked a more possible price. The skeleton was the
skeleton that would exist a hundred years from now, no
matter how or when the enemy had died. But bring that
skeleton back here and the enemy can no longer exist. His
skeleton can't be two places at once. You've got the dry, dead
bones. What becomes of the live ones with flesh on them? You
don't know. You don't care. You're safe. You're free to lead
the peaceful life you want with Indians and mountain
scenery and your scratch pad and your radio. And your
skeleton.

"You've got to be careful of that skeleton. If it ceases to
exist in this time, the full-fleshed living skeleton might re
turn. You mustn't even take a chance on the destruction of
little piece. You lose a finger, and a finger returns—a pink
thing that crawls, and always toward you.

"Then the skeleton itself is destroyed. You're in mortal
terror, but nothing happens. Two days go by and it's No
vember 2. You know what the Second of November is in
Latin America? It's All Souls' Day in the Church, and the
call it the *Día de los difuntos*—the Day of the Dead. But i
isn't a sad day outside of church. You go to the cemetery and

it's a picnic. There are skeletons everywhere, same like Halloween—bright, funny skeletons that never hurt anybody. And there are skulls to wear and skulls to drink out of and bright white sugar skulls with pink and green trimmings to eat. All along every street are vendors with skulls and skeletons for every purpose, and every kid you see has a sugar skull to suck. Then at night you go to the theater to see *Don Juan Tenorio* where the graves open and the skeletons dance, while back home the kids are howling themselves to sleep because death is so indigestible.

"Of course, there's no theater in Tlichotl, but you can bet there'd be skulls and skeletons—some of them dressed up like Indian gods for the Christian feast, some of them dancing on wires, some of them vanishing down small gullets. And there you are in the midst of skeletons, skeletons everywhere, and your skeleton is gone and all your safety with it. And there on the street with all the skulls staring at you, you see him and he isn't a skull any more. He's Humbert Targ and he's explaining that it took him a little time to get here.

"Wouldn't *you* drop dead?" Fergus concluded simply.

My throat felt dry as I asked, "What did you tell the insurance company?"

"Much like Norm's theory. Man was an artist, had an anatomical model, gave out he was a doctor to keep the natives from conniption fits. Collected expenses, but no bonus: the prints they sent me fitted what I found in his home, and they had to pay the sister."

Norman cleared his throat. "I'm beginning to hope they don't send me back to the island."

"Afraid you might get too tempted by a *tualala*?"

"No. But on the island we really do have pink caterpillars. I'm not sure I could face them."

"There's one thing I still wonder," Fergus said reflectively. "Where was Humbert Targ while his skeleton hung at Miller's side? Or should I say, *when* was he? He said, 'It took a little time to get here.' From where? From when? And what kind of time?"

There are some questions you don't even try to answer.

Q. U. R.

It's got so the young sprouts nowadays seem never to have heard of androids. Oh, they look at them in museums and they read the references to them in the literature of the time, but they never seem to realize how essential a part of life androids once were, how our whole civilization, in fact, depended on them. And when you say you got your start in life as trouble shooter for an android factory, they look at you as though you'd worked in two-dimensional shows way back before the sollies, as though you ought to be in a museum yourself.

Now, I'll admit I'm no infant. I'll never see a hundred again. But I'm no antique either. And I think it's a crying shame that the rising generation is so completely out of touch with the last century. Not that I ever intended to be writing my memoirs; I didn't exactly construct my life to that end. But somebody's got to tell the real story of what androids meant and how they ceased to mean it. And I'm the man to tell it, because I'm the man who discovered Dugg Quinby.

Yes, I said Quinby. Dugglesmarther H. Quinby, the Q. in Q. U. R. The man who made your life run the way it does today. And I found him.

That summer was a hell of a season for a trouble shooter for androids. There was nothing but trouble. My five-hour day stretched to eight, and even ten and twelve, while I dashed all over New Washington checking on one android after another that had cracked up. And maybe you know how hot the Metropolitan District gets in summer—even worse than the rest of Oklahoma.

Because my job wasn't one that you could carry on comfortably in conditioned buildings and streets, it meant going outside and topside and everywhere that a robot might work. We called the androids robots then. We hadn't conceived of any kind of robot that wasn't an android, or at least a naturoid of some sort.

And these breakdowns were striking everywhere, hitting robots in every line of activity. Even the Martoids and Veneroids that some ex-colonists fancied for servants. It would be an arm that went limp or a leg that crumpled up or a tentacle that collapsed. Sometimes mental trouble, too: slight indications of a tendency toward insubordination, even a sort of mania that wasn't supposed to be in their make-up. And the thing kept spreading and getting worse. Any manifestation like this among living beings and you'd think of an epidemic. But what germ could attack tempered duralite?

The worst of it was there was nothing wrong with them. Nothing that I could find, and to me that meant plain nothing. You don't get to be head trouble shooter of Robinc if anything can get past you. And the second worst was that it was hitting my own staff. I had had six robots under me— plenty to cover the usual, normal amount of trouble. Now I had two, and I needed forty.

So all in all, I wasn't happy that afternoon. It didn't make me any happier to see a crowd in front of the Sunspot engaged in the merry pastime of Venusian-baiting. It was never safe for one of the little green fellows to venture out of the Venusian ghetto; this sport was way too common a spectacle.

They'd got his vapor inhalator away from him. That was all there was to the game, but that was enough. No extra-physical torment was needed. There the poor giller lay on the sidewalk, sprawled and gasping like a fish out of water, which he practically was. The men—factory executives mostly, and a few office foremen—made a circle around him and laughed. There was supposed to be something hilariously funny about the struggles of a giller drowning in air, though I never could see it myself.

Oh, they'd give him back his inhalator just in time. They never killed them off; the few Venusians around had their uses, particularly for repair work on the Veneroid robots that were used under water. But meanwhile there'd be some fun.

Despite the heat of the day, I shuddered a little. Then I crossed to the other side of the street. I couldn't watch the game. But I turned back when I heard one loud shout of fury.

That was when I found Dugg Quinby. That shout was the only sound he made. He was ragingly silent as he plowed through that mass of men, found the biggest of them, snatched the inhalator away from him, and restored it to its gasping owner. But there was noise enough from the others.

Ever try to take a bone from a dog? Or a cigar from a Martian mountaineer? Well, this was worse. Those boys objected to having their fun spoiled, and they expressed their objection forcibly.

I liked this young blond giant that had plowed in there. I liked him because his action had asked me what I was doing crossing over to the other side of the street, and I didn't have an answer. The only way even to try to answer was to cross back.

Androids or Q. U. R., single-drive space ships or modern multiples, one thing that doesn't change much is a brawl, and this was a good one. I don't know who delivered the right that met my chin as I waded in, and I don't know who it was meant for, but it was just what I needed. Not straight enough to do more than daze me for a minute, but just hard enough to rouse my fighting spirit to the point of the hell with anything but finding targets for my knuckles. I avenged the Venusian, I avenged the blond youth, I avenged the heat of the day and the plague of the robots. I avenged my job and my corns and the hangover I had two weeks ago.

The first detail that comes clear is sitting inside the Sunspot I don't know how much later. The blond boy was with me, and so was one of the factory men. We all seemed to be the best of friends, and there wasn't any telling whose blood was which.

Guzub was beaming at us. When you know your Martians pretty well you learn that that trick of shutting the middle eye is a beam. "You zure bolished 'em ub, boys," he gurgled.

The factory man felt of his neck and decided his head was still there. "Guzub," he declared, "I've learned me a lesson: From now on, any green giller is safe around me."

"That'z the zbird," Guzub glurked. "Avder all, we're all beings, ain'd we? Now, wad'll id be?"

Guzub was hurt when the blond youth ordered milk, but delighted when the factory man said he'd have a Three Planets with a double shot of margil. I'm no teetotaler, but I don't go for these strong drinks; I stuck to my usual straight whiskey.

We exchanged names while we waited. Mike Warren, the factory man was; and the other—but then I tipped that off already. That was Quinby. They both knew me by name.

"So you're with Robinc," Mike said. "I want to have a talk with you about that sometime. My brother-in-law's got a new use for a robot that could make somebody, including me, a pile of credits, and I can't get a hearing anyplace."

"Glad to," I said, not paying much attention. Everybody's got a new use for a robot, just like writers tell me everybody's got a swell idea for a solly.

Dugg Quinby had been staring straight ahead of him and not listening. Now he said, "What I don't see is why."

"Well," Mike began, "it seems like he was stuck once on the lunar desert and—"

"Uh-uh. Not that. What I don't see is why Venusians. Why we act that way about them, I mean. After all, they're more

or less like us. They're featherless bipeds, pretty much on
our general model. And we treat them like they weren't even
beings. While Martians are a different shape of life altogether, but we don't have ghettos for them, or Martian-
baiting."

"That's just it," said Mike. "The gillers are too much like
us. They're like a cartoon of us. We see them, and they're
like a dirty joke on humans, and we see red. I mean," he
added hastily, his hand rubbing his neck, "that's the way I
used to feel. I was just trying to explain."

"Nuts," I said. "It's all a matter of historical parallel. We
licked the pants—which they don't wear—off the Venusians
in the First War of Conquest, so we feel we can push 'em
around. The Second War of Conquest went sour on us and
damned near put an end to the Empire and the race to boot,
so we've got a healthy respect for the Martians." I looked over
at the bartender, his tentacles industriously plying an impressive array of bottles and a gleaming duralite shaker. "We
only persecute the ones it's safe to persecute."

Quinby frowned. "It's bad enough to do what no being
ought to do, but to do it only when you know you can get
away with it— I've been reading," he announced abruptly,
as though it was a challenge to another fight.

Mike grunted. "Sollies and telecasts are enough for a man,
I always say. You get to reading and you get mixed up."

"Do you think you aren't mixed up without it? Do you
think you aren't all mixed up? If people would only try to
look at things straight—"

"What have you been reading?" I asked.

"Old stuff. Dating, oh, I guess, a millennium or so back.
There were people then that used to write a lot about the
Brotherhood of Man. They said good things. And it all means
something to us now if you translate it into the Brotherhood
of Beings. Man is unified now, but what's the result? The doc-
trine of Terrene Supremacy."

Guzub brought the drinks and we forked out our credits.
When he heard the phrase "Terrene Supremacy," his left

eyelid went into that little quiver that is the Martian expression of polite incredulity, but he said nothing.

Quinby picked up his milk. "It's all because nobody looks at things straight. Everybody looks around the corners of his own prejudices. If you look at a problem straight, there isn't a problem. That's what I'm trying to do," he said with that earnestness you never come back to after youth. "I'm trying to train myself to look straight."

"So there isn't a problem. No problems at all." I thought of the day I'd had and the jobs still ahead of me and I snorted. And then I had an idea and calmly, between swallows of whiskey, changed the course of terrene civilization. "I've got problems," I asserted. "How'd you like to look straight at them? Are you working now?"

"I'm in my free-lance period," he said. "I've finished technical college and I'm not due for my final occupational analysis for another year."

"All right," I said. "How's about it?"

Slowly he nodded.

"If you can look," said Mike, wobbling his neck, "as straight as you can hit—"

I was back in my office when the call came from the space port. I'd seen Thuringer's face red before, but never purple. He had trouble speaking, but he finally spluttered out, "Somebody did a lousy job of sterilization on your new assistant's parents."

"What seems to be the trouble?" I asked in my soothingest manner.

"Trouble! The man's lunatic stock. Not a doubt. When you see what he's done to—" He shuddered. He reached out to switch the ike-range, but changed his mind. "Uh-uh. Come over here and see it for yourself. You wouldn't believe it. But come quick, before I go and apply for sterilization myself."

We had a special private tube to the space port; they used so many of our robots. It took me less than five minutes to get there. A robot parked my bus, and another robot took me up in the lift. It was a relief to see two in good working order, though I noticed that the second one showed signs o incipient limpness in his left arm. Since he ran the lift with his right, it didn't really matter, but Robinc had principles of perfection.

Thuringer's robot secretary said, "Tower room," and I went on up. The space-port manager scanned me and gave the click that meant the beam was on. The tower door opened as I walked in.

I don't know what I'd expected to see. I couldn't imagine what would get the hard-boiled Thuringer into such a blasting dither. This had been the first job that I'd tried Quinby out on, and a routine piece of work it was, or should have been. Routine, that is, in these damnable times. The robot that operated the signal tower had gone limp in the legs and one arm. He'd been quoted as saying some pretty strange things on the beam, too. Backsass to pilots and insubordinate mutterings.

The first thing I saw was a neat pile of scrap in the middle of the room. Some of it looked like robot parts. The next thing I saw was Thuringer, who had gone from purple to a kind of rosy black. "It's getting me!" he burst out. "I sit here and watch it and I'm going mad! Do something, man! Then go out and annihilate your assistant, but do something first!"

I looked where he pointed. I'd been in this tower control room before. The panel had a mike and an ike, a speaker and a viewer, and a set of directional lights. In front of it there used to be a chair where the robot sat, talking on the beam and watching the indicators.

Now there was no chair. And no robot. There was a table, and on the table was a box. And from that box there extended one arm, which was alive. That arm punched regularly and correctly at the lights, and out of the box there issued the familiar guiding voice.

I walked around and got a gander at the front of the box. It had eyes and a mouth and a couple of holes that it took me a minute to spot as ear holes. It was like a line with two dots above and two below it, so:

•   •

———————

•   •

It was like no face that ever was in nature, but it could obviously see and hear and talk.

Thuringer moaned. "And that's what you call a repair job! My beautiful robot! Your A-1-A Double Prime All-Utility Extra-Quality De Luxe Model! Nothing of him left but this"—he pointed at the box—"and this"—he gestured sadly at the scrap heap.

I looked a long time at the box and I scratched my head. "He works, doesn't he?"

"Works? What? Oh, works."

"You've been here watching him. He pushes the right lights? He gets messages right? He gives the right instructions?"

"Oh yes. I suppose so. Yes, he works all right. But damn it, man, he's not a robot any more. You've ruined him."

The box interrupted its beam work. "Ruined, hell," it said in the same toneless voice. "I never felt so good since I was animated. Thanks, boss."

Thuringer goggled. I started to leave the room.

"Where are you going? Are you going to make this right? I demand another A-1-A Double Prime at once, you understand. And I trust you'll kill that assistant."

"Kill him? I'm going to kiss him."

"Why, you—" He'd picked up quite a vocabulary when he ran the space port at Venusberg. "I'll see that you're fired from Robinc tomorrow!"

"I quit today," I said. "One minute ago."

That was the birth of Q. U. R.

I found Quinby at the next place on the list I'd given him. This was a job repairing a household servant—one of the

Class B androids with a pretty finish, but not up to commercial specifications.

I gawped when I saw the servant. Instead of two arms he had four tentacles, which he was flexing intently.

Quinby was packing away his repair kit. He looked up at me, smiling. "It was very simple," he said. "He'd seen Martoid robots at work, and he realized that flexible tentacles would be much more useful than jointed arms for housework. The more he brooded about it, the clumsier his arms got. But it's all right now, isn't it?"

"Fine, boss," said the servant. He seemed to be reveling in the free pleasure of those tentacles.

"There were some Martoid spares in the kit," Quinby explained, "and when I switched the circuit a little—"

"Have you stopped," I interposed, "to think what that housewife is going to say when she comes home and finds her servant waving Martoid tentacles at her?"

"Why, no. You think she'd—"

"Look at it straight," I said. "She's going to join the procession demanding that I be fired from Robinc. But don't let it worry you. Robinc's nothing to us. From now on we're ourselves. We're Us Incorporated. Come on back to the Sunspot and we'll thrash this out."

"Thanks, boss," the semi-Martoid called after us, happily writhing.

I recklessly ordered a Three Planets. This was an occasion. Quinby stuck to milk. Guzub shrugged—that is, he wrinkled his skin where shoulders might have been on his circular body—and said, "You loog abby, boys. Good news?"

I nodded. "Best yet, Guzub. You're dishing 'em up for a historic occasion. Make a note."

"Lazd dime you zelebrade izdorig oggazion," said Guzub resignedly, "you breag zevendy-vour glazzes. Wy zhould I maig a node?"

"This is different, Guz. Now," I said to Quinby, "tell me how you got this unbelievable idea of repair."

"Why, isn't it obvious?" he asked simply. "When Zwergenhaus invented the first robot, he wasn't thinking functionally. He was trying to make a mechanical man. He did, and he made a good job of it. But that's silly. Man isn't a functionally useful animal. There's very little he can do himself. What's made him top dog is that he can invent and use tools to do what needs doing. But why make his mechanical servants as helplessly constructed as he is?

"Almost every robot, except perhaps a few like farmhands, does only one or two things and does those things constantly. All right. Shape them so that they can best do just those things, with no parts left over. Give them a brain, eyes and ears to receive commands, and whatever organs they need for their work.

"There's the source of your whole robot epidemic. They were all burdened down with things they didn't need—legs when their job was a sedentary one, two arms when they used only one—or else, like my house servant, their organs were designed to imitate man's rather than to be ideally functional. Result: the unused waste parts atrophied, and the robots became physically sick, sometimes mentally as well because they were tortured by unrealized potentialities. It was simple enough, once you looked at it straight."

The drinks came. I went at the Three Planets cautiously. You know the formula: one part Terrene rum—170 proof—one part Venusian margil, and a dash or so of Martian vuzd. It's smooth and murderous. I'd never tasted one as smooth as this of Guzub's, and I feared it'd be that much the more murderous.

"You know something of the history of motor transportation?" Quinby went on. "Look at the twentieth-century models in the museum sometime. See how long they kept trying to make a horseless carriage look like a carriage for horses. We've been making the same mistake—trying to make a manless body look like the bodies of men."

"Son," I said—he was maybe five or ten years younger than I was—"there's something in this looking-straight business of yours. There's so much, in fact, that I wonder if even you

realize how much. Are you aware that if we go at this right
we can damned near wipe Robinc out of existence?"

He choked on his milk. "You mean," he ventured, slowly
and dreamily, "we could—"

"But it can't be done overnight. People are used to android
robots. It's the only kind they ever think of. They'll be scared
of your unhuman-looking contraptions, just like Thuringer
was scared. We've got to build into this gradually. Lots of
publicity. Lots of promotion. Articles, lectures, debates. Give
'em a name. A good name. Keep robots; that's common do-
main, I read somewhere, because it comes out of a play written
a long time ago in some dialect of Old Slavic. Quinby's
Something Robots—"

"Functionoid?"

"Sounds too much like fungoid. Don't like. Let me see—"
I took some more Three Planets. "I've got it. Usuform.
Quinby's Usuform Robots. Q. U. R."

Quinby grinned. "I like it. But shouldn't it have your name
too?"

"Me, I'll take a cut on the credits. I don't like my name
much. Now, what we ought to do is introduce it with a new
robot. One that can do something no android in the Robinc
stock can tackle—"

Guzub called my name. "Man ere looking vor you."

It was Mike. "Hi, mister," he said. "I was wondering did
you maybe have a minute to listen to my brother-in-law's
idea. You remember, about that new kind of robot—"

"Hey, Guzub," I yelled. "Two more Three Planets."

"Make it three," said Quinby quietly.

We talked the rest of that night. When the Sunspot closed at
twenty-three—we were going through one of our cyclic periods
of blue laws then—we moved to my apartment and kept at
it until we fell asleep from sheer exhaustion, scattered over
my furniture.

Quinby's one drink—he stopped there—was just enough
to stimulate him to seeing straighter than ever. He took some-

thing under one minute to visualize completely the possibilities of Mike's contribution.

This brother-in-law was a folklore hobbyist and had been reading up on the ancient notion of dowsing. He had realized at once that there could have been no particular virtue in the forked witch hazel rod that was supposed to locate water in the earth, but that certain individuals must have been able to perceive that water in some nth-sensory manner, communicating this reaction subconsciously to the rod in their hands.

To train that nth sense in a human being was probably impossible; it was most likely the result of a chance mutation. But you could attempt to develop it in a robot brain by experimentation with the patterns of the sense-perception tracks; and he had succeeded. He could equip a robot with a brain that would infallibly register the presence of water, and he was working on the further possibilities of oil and other mineral deposits. There wasn't any need to stress the invaluability of such a robot to an exploring party.

"All right," Quinby said. "What does such a robot need beside his brain and his sense organs? A means of locomotion and a means of marking the spots he finds. He'll be used chiefly in rough desert country, so a caterpillar tread will be far more useful to him than legs that can trip and stumble. The best kind of markers—lasting and easy to spot—would be metal spikes. He could, I suppose, carry those and have an arm designed as a pile driver; but . . . yes, look, this is best: Supposing he lays them?"

"Lays them?" I repeated vaguely.

"Yes. When his water sense registers maximum intensity— that is, when he's right over a hidden spring—there'll be a sort of sphincter reaction, and *plop,* he'll lay a sharp spike, driving it into the ground."

It was perfect. It would be a cheap robot to make—just a box on treads, the box containing the brain, the sense organs, and a supply of spikes. Maybe later in a more elaborate model he could be fed crude metal and make his own spikes. There'd be a decided demand for him, and nothing of

Robinc's could compete. An exploring party could simply send him out for the day, then later go over the clear track left by his treads and drill wherever he had laid a spike. And his pure functionalism would be the first step in our campaign to accustom the public to Quinby's Usuform Robots.

Then the ideas came thick and fast. We had among us figured out at least seventy-three applications in which usuforms could beat androids, before our eyes inevitably folded up on us.

I woke up with three sensations: First, a firm resolve to stick to whiskey and leave Three Planets to the Martians that invented them. Second, and practically obliterating this discomfort, a thrill of anticipation at the wonders that lay ahead of us, like a kid that wakes up and knows today's his birthday. But third, and uncomfortably gnawing at the back of this pleasure, the thought that there was something wrong, something we'd overlooked.

Quinby was fixing up a real cooked breakfast. He insisted that this was an occasion too noble for swallowing a few concentrates, and he'd rummaged in my freezing storeroom to find what he called "honest food." It was good eating, but this gnawing thought kept pestering me. At last I excused myself and went into the library. I found the book I wanted: *Planetary Civil Code. Volume 34. Robots.* I put it in the projector and ran it rapidly over the screen till I located the paragraph I half remembered.

That gnawing was all too well founded. I remembered now. The theory'd always been that this paragraph went into the Code because only Robinc controlled the use of the factor that guaranteed the robots against endangering any intelligent beings, but I've always suspected that there were other elements at work. Even Council Members get their paws greased sometimes.

The paragraph read:

> 259: All robots except those in military employ
> of the Empire shall be constructed according to the

patents held by Robots Inc., sometimes known as Robinc. Any robot constructed in violation of this section shall be destroyed at once, and all those concerned in constructing him shall be sterilized and segregated.

I read this aloud to the breakfast party. It didn't add to the cheer of the occasion.

"I knew it was too good to be true," Mike grunted. "I can just see Robinc leasing its patents to the boys that'll put it out of business."

"But our being great business successes isn't what's important," Quinby protested. "Do we really want . . . could any being of good will really want to become like the heads of Robinc?"

"I do," said Mike honestly.

"What's important is what this can do: Cure this present robot epidemic, conserve raw materials in robot building, make possible a new and simpler and more sensible life for everybody. Why can't we let Robinc take over the idea?"

"Look," I said patiently. "Quite aside from the unworthy ambitions that Mike and I may hold, what'll happen if we do? What has always happened when a big company buys out a new method when they've got a billion credits sunk in the old? It gets buried and is never heard of again."

"That's right," Quinby sighed. "Robinc would simply strangle it."

"All right. Now look at it straight and say what is going to become of Quinby's Usuform Robots."

"Well," he said simply, "there's only one solution. Change the code."

I groaned. "That's all, huh? Just that. Change the code. And how do you propose to go about that?"

"See the Head of the Council. Explain to him what our idea means to the world—to the system. He's a good man. He'll see us through."

"Dugg," I said, "when you look at things straight I never

know whether you're going to see an amazing truth or the most amazing nonsense that ever was. Sure the Head's a good man. If he could do it without breaking too many political commitments, I think he might help out on an idea as big as this. But how to get to see him when—"

"My brother-in-law tried once," Mike contributed. "He got kind of too persistent. That's how come he's in the hospital now. Hey," he broke off. "Where you going?"

"Come on, Dugg," I said. "Mike, you spend the day looking around the city for a likely factory site. We'll meet you around seventeen at the Sunspot. Quinby and I are going to see the Head of the Council."

We met the first guard about a mile from the office. "Robinc Repair," I said, and waved my card. After all, I assuaged Quinby's conscience, I hadn't actually resigned yet. "Want to check the Head's robot."

The guard nodded. "He's expecting you."

It hadn't been even a long shot. With robots in the state they were in, it was practically a certainty that one of those in direct attendance on the Head would need repair. The gag got us through a mile of guards, some robot, some—more than usual since all the trouble—human, and at last into the presence of the Head himself.

The white teeth gleamed in the black face in that friendly grin so familiar in telecasts. "I've received you in person," he said, "because the repair of this robot is such a confidential matter."

"What are his duties?" I asked.

"He is my private decoder. It is most important that I should have his services again as soon as possible."

"And what's the matter with him?"

"Partly what I gather is, by now, almost the usual thing. Paralysis of the legs. But partly more than that: He keeps talking to himself. Babbling nonsense."

Quinby spoke up. "Just what is he supposed to do?"

The Head frowned. "Assistants bring him every coded or

phered dispatch. His brain was especially constructed for
yptanalysis. He breaks them down, writes out the clear,
nd drops it into a pneumatic chute that goes to a locked
ompartment in my desk."

"He uses books?"

"For some of the codes. The ciphers are entirely brain-
echanics."

Quinby nodded. "Can do. Take us to him."

The robot was saying to himself, "This is the ponderous
me of the decadence of the synaptic reflexes when all
urmudgeons wonkle in the withering wallabies."

Quinby looked after the departing Head. "Some time," he
id, "we're going to see a Venusian as Interplanetary Head."

I snorted.

"Don't laugh. Why, not ten centuries ago people would
ave snorted just like that at the idea of a black as Head
n this planet. Such narrow stupidity seems fantastic to us
ow. Our own prejudices will seem just as comical to our
reat-great-grandchildren."

The robot said, "Over the larking lunar syllogisms lopes
e chariot of funereal ellipses."

Quinby went to work. After a minute—I was beginning to
utch on to this seeing-straight business myself—I saw what
e was doing and helped.

This robot needed nothing but the ability to read, to
anscribe deciphered messages, and to handle papers and
ooks. His legs had atrophied—that was in line with the other
ses. But he was unusual in that he was the rare thing:
robot who had no need at all for communication by speech.
e had the power of speech and was never called upon to
xercise it; result, he had broken down into this fantastic
abbling of nonsense, just to get some exercise of his futile
ower.

When Quinby had finished, the robot consisted only of
is essential cryptanalytic brain, eyes, one arm, and the writer.
his last was now a part of the robot's hookup; so that instead
f using his hands to transcribe the message, he thought it

directly into the writer. He had everything he needed, and nothing more. His last words before we severed the speech connection were, "The runcible rhythm of ravenous raisin rollers through the rookery rambling and raving." His first words when the direct connection with the writer was established were, "This feels good. Thanks boss."

I went to fetch the Head. "I want to warn you," I explained to him, "you may be a little surprised by what you see. But please look at it without preconceptions."

He was startled and silent. He took it well; he didn't blow up hysterically like Thuringer. But he stared at the new thing for a long time without saying a word. Then he took a paper from his pocket and laid it on the decoding table. The eyes looked at it. The arm reached out for a book and opened it. Then a message began to appear on the writer. The Head snatched it up before it went into the tube, read it, and nodded.

"It works," he said slowly. "But it's not a robot any more. It's . . . it's just a decoding machine."

"A robot," I quoted, "is any machine equipped with a Zwergenhaus brain and capable of independent action upon the orders or subject to the guidance of an intelligent being. Planetary Code, paragraph num—"

"But it looks so—"

"It works," I cut in. "And it won't get paralysis of the legs and it won't ever go mad and babble about wonkling curmudgeons. Because, you see, it's a usuform robot." And I hastily sketched out the Quinby project.

The Head listened attentively. Occasionally he flashed his white grin, especially when I explained why we could not turn the notion over to Robinc. When I was through, he paused a moment and then said at last, "It's a fine idea you have there. A great idea. But the difficulties are great, too. I don't need to recount the history of robots to you," he said, proceeding to do so. "How Zwergenhaus' discovery lay dormant for a century and a half because no one dared upset the economic system by developing it. How the Second War of Conquest so nearly depopulated the earth that the use of robot labor became not only possible but necessary. How our society is now so firmly based on it that the lowest laboring rank possible to a being is foreman. The Empire is based on robots; robots are Robinc. We can't fight Robinc."

"Robinc is slowly using up all our resources of metallic and radioactive ore, isn't it?" Quinby asked.

"Perhaps. Scaremongers can produce statistics—"

"And our usuforms will use only a fraction of what Robinc's androids need."

"A good point. An important one. You have convinced me that android robots are a prime example of conspicuous waste, and this epidemic shows that they are, moreover, dangerous. But I cannot attempt to fight Robinc now. My position—I shall be frank, gentlemen—my position is too precarious. I have problems of my own."

"Try Quinby," I said. "I had a problem and tried him, and he saw through it at once."

"Saw through it," the Head observed, "to a far vaster and more difficult problem beyond. Besides, I am not sure if my problem lies in his field. It deals with the question of how to mix a Three Planets cocktail."

The excitement of our enterprise had made me forget my head. Now it began throbbing again at the memory. "A Three Planets?"

The Head hesitated. "Gentlemen," he said at last, "I ask your pledge of the utmost secrecy."

He got it.

"And even with that I cannot give you too many details. But you know that the Empire holds certain mining rights in certain districts of Mars—I dare not be more specific. These rights are essential to maintain our stocks of raw materials. And they are held only on lease, by an agreement that must be renewed quinquennially. It has heretofore been renewed as a matter of course, but the recent rise of the Planetary Party on Mars, which advocates the abolition of all interplanetary contact, makes this coming renewal a highly

doubtful matter. Within the next three days I am to confer
here with a certain high Martian dignitary, traveling in-
cognito. Upon the result of that conference our lease depe____

"And the Three Planets?" I asked. "____
Party want to abolish them as a matt____

"Probably," he smiled. "But t____
party member, and is devoted ____
travel, because only on Mars, he ____
correctly. If I could brighten h____
one perfect Three Planets—"

"Guzub!" I cried. "The barter____
Martian and the drink is his specia____

"I know," the Head agreed sad_____al
in question once said that your G_____g on
this planet who knew how. Everyon_____much or
too little vuzd. But Guzub is an exiled member of the Var-
jinian Loyalists. He hates everything that the present regime
represents. He would never consent to perform his master-
piece for my guest."

"You could order one at the Sunspot and have it sent here
by special—"

"You know that a Three Planets must be drunk within
thirty seconds of mixing for the first sip to have its ideal
flavor."

"Then—"

"All right," Quinby said. "You let us know when your honored guest arrives, and we'll have a Three Planets for him."

The Head looked doubtful. "If you think you can— A bad
one might be more dangerous than none—"

"And if we do," I interposed hastily, "you'll reconsider this
business of the usuform robots?"

"If this mining deal goes through satisfactorily, I should be
strong enough to contemplate facing Robinc."

"Then you'll get your Three Planets," I said calmly, wondering what Quinby had seen straight now.

We met Mike at the Sunspot as arranged. He was drinking a

Three Planets. "This is good," he announced. "This has space-drive and zoomf to it. You get it other places and—"

"I know," I said. "Find a site?"

"A honey. Wait'll I—"

"Hold it. We've got to know have we got anything to go on it. Guzub! One Three Planets."

We watched entranced as he mixed the potion. "Get exactly what he does," Quinby had said. "Then construct a usuform bartender who'll be infallible. It'll satisfy the Martian envoy and at the same time remind the Head of why we're helping him out."

But all we saw was a glittering swirl of tentacles. First a flash as each tentacle picked up its burden—one the shaker, one the lid, one the glass, and three others the bottles of rum, margil, and vuzd. Then a sort of spasm that shook all Guzub's round body as the exact amount of each liquid went in, and finally a gorgeous pinwheel effect of shaking and pouring.

Guzub handed me my drink, and I knew as much as I had before.

By the time I'd finished it, I had courage. "Guzub," I said, "this is wonderful."

"Zure," Guzub glurked. "Always I maig id wondervul."

"Nobody else can make 'em like you, Guz. But tell me. How much vuzd do you put in?"

Guzub made his kind of a shrug. "I dell you, boys, I dunno. Zome dime maybe I wadge myzelv and zee. I juzd go zo! I dunno how mudj."

"Give me another one. Let's see you watch yourself."

"Businezz is good by you, you dring zo many Blanedz? O Gay, ere goes."

But the whirl stopped in the middle. There was Guzub, all his eyes focused sadly on the characteristic green corkscrew-shaped bottle of vuzd. Twice he started to move that tentacle, then drew it back. At last he made a dash with it.

"Exactly two drops," Quinby whispered.

Guzub handed over the drink unhappily. "Dry id," he said.

I did. It was terrible. Too little vuzd, so that you could

taste both the heavy sweetness of the rum and the acrid harsh-
ness of the margil. I said so.

"I know, boys. Wen I zdob do wadge, id bothers me. No
gan do."

I gulped the drink. "Mix up another without watching.
Maybe we can tell."

This one was perfect. And we could see nothing.

The next time he "wadged." He used precisely four and half
drops of vuzd. You tasted nothing but the tart decay of the
vuzd itself.

The next time—

But my memory gets a little vague after that. Like I said,
I'm a whiskey drinker. And four Three Planets in quick succession— I'm told the party went on till closing hour at
twenty-three, after which Guzub accepted Quinby's invitation
to come on and mix for us at my apartment. I wouldn't know.
All I remember is one point where I found a foot in my face.
I bit it, decided it wasn't mine, and stopped worrying about
it. Or about anything.

I'm told that I slept thirty-six hours after that party—a
whole day and more simply vanished out of my existence. I
woke up feeling about twelve and spry for my age, but it took
me a while to reconstruct what had been going on.

I was just beginning to get it straightened out when Quinby
came in. His first words were, "How would you like a Three
Planets?"

I suddenly felt like two hundred and twelve, and on an off
day at that. Not until I'd packed away a superman-size breakfast did he dare repeat the offer. By then I felt brave. "O. K.,"
I said. "But with a whiskey chaser."

I took one sip and said, "Where's Guzub? I didn't know he
was staying here too."

"He isn't."

"But this Three Planets— It's perfect. It's the McCoy. And
Guzub—"

Quinby opened a door. There sat the first original Quinby
Usuform—no remake of a Robinc model, but a brand-new

creation. Quinby said, "Three Planets," and he went into action. He had tentacles, and the motions were exactly like Guzub's except that he was himself the shaker. He poured the liquids into his maw, joggled about, and then poured them out of a hollow hoselike tentacle.

The televisor jangled. Quinby hastily shifted the ike so as to miss the usuform barkeep as I answered. The screen showed the Head himself. He'd been there before on telecasts, but this was the real thing.

He didn't waste time. "Tonight, nineteen thirty," he said. "I don't need to explain?"

"We'll be there," I choked out.

A special diplomatic messenger brought the pass to admit the two of us and "one robot or robotlike machine" to the Council building. I was thankful for that alternative phrase; I didn't want to have to argue with each guard about the technical legal definition of a robot. We were installed in a small room directly off the Head's private reception room. It was soundproofed and there was no window; no chance of our picking up interplanetary secrets of diplomacy. And there was a bar.

A dream of a bar, a rhapsody of a bar. The vuzd, the rum, the margil were all of brands that you hear about and brood about but never think to see in a lifetime. And there was whiskey of the same caliber.

We had hardly set our usuform facing the bar when a servant came in. He was an android. He said, "The Head says now."

Quinby asked me, "Do you want one?"

I shook my head and selected a bottle of whiskey.

"Two Three Planets," Quinby said.

The tentacles flickered, the shaker-body joggled, the hose-tentacle poured. The android took the tray from our usuform. He looked at him with something as close to a mixture of fear, hatred, and envy as his eye cells could express. He went out with the tray.

I turned to Quinby. "We've been busy getting ready for

this party ever since I woke up. I still don't understand how you made him into another Guzub."

There was a click and the room was no longer soundproof. The Head was allowing us to hear the reception of our creation. First his voice came, quiet, reserved and suave. "I think your magnitude would enjoy this insignificant drink. I have been to some slight pains to see that it was worthy of your magnitude's discriminating taste."

There was silence. Then the faintest sound of a sip, a pause, and an exhalation. We could almost hear the Head holding his breath.

"Bervegd!" a deep voice boomed—which, since no Martian has ever yet learned to pronounce a voiceless consonant, means a verdict of "Perfect!"

"I am glad that your magnitude is pleased."

"Bleased is doo mild a word, my dear Ead. And now thad you ave zo delighdvully welgomed me—"

The sound went dead again.

"He liked it, huh?" said Guzub II. "You boys want some, maybe?"

"No thanks," said Quinby. "I wonder if I should have given him a Martian accent—they are the best living bartenders. Perhaps when we get the model into mass production—"

I took a gleefully long swig of whiskey. Its mild warmth felt soothing after memories of last night's Three Planets. "Look," I said. "We have just pulled off the trick that ought to net us a change in the code and a future as the great revolutionists of robot design. I feel like . . . hell, like Ley landing on the Moon. And you sit there with nothing on your mind but a bartender's accent."

"Why not?" Quinby asked. "What is there to do in life but find what you're good for and do it the best you can?"

He had me there. And I began to have some slight inklings of the trouble ahead with a genius who had commercial ideas and the conscience of an otherworldly saint. I said, "All right. I won't ask you to kill this bottle with me, and in return I expect you not to interfere with my assassinating it. But as to what you're good for—how did you duplicate Guzub?"

"Oh, that. That was simple—"

"—when you looked at it straight," I ended.

"Yes." That was another thing about Quinby; he never knew if he was being ribbed. "Yes. I got one of those new electronic cameras—you know, one thousand exposures per second. Hard to find at that time of night, but we made it."

"We?"

"You helped me. You kept the man from overcharging me. Or maybe you don't remember? So we took pictures of Guzub making a Three Planets, and I could construct this one to do it exactly right down to the thousandth of a second. The proper proportion of vuzd, in case you're interested, works out to three-point-six-five-four-seven-eight-two-three drops. It's done with a flip of the third joint of the tentacle on the down beat. It didn't seem right to use Guzub to make a robot that would compete with him and probably drive him out of business; so we've promised him a generous pension from the royalties on usuform barkeeps."

"We?" I said again, more feebly.

"You drew up the agreement."

I didn't argue. It was fair enough. A good businessman would have slipped Guzub a fiver for posing for pictures and then said the hell with him. But I was beginning to see that running Q. U. R. was not going to be just good business.

When the Head finally came in, he didn't need to say a word, though he said plenty. I've never seen that white grin flash quite so cheerfully. That was enough; the empire had its Martian leases, and Q. U. R. was a fact.

When I read back over this story, I can see there's one thing wrong. That's about the giller. I met Dugg Quinby, and you met him through me, in the act of rescuing a Venusian from a giller-baiting mob. By all the rights of storytelling, the green being should have vowed everlasting gratitude to his rescuer, and at some point in our troubles he should have showed up and made everything fine for us.

That's how it should have been. In actual fact, the giller grabbed his inhalator and vanished without so much as a "thank you." If anybody helped us, it was Mike, who had been our most vigorous enemy in the battle.

Which means, I think, that seeing straight can work with things and robots, but not with beings, because no being is really straight, not even to himself.

Except maybe Dugg Quinby.

Robinc

You'd think maybe it meant clear sailing after we'd got the Council's OK. You'd maybe suppose that'd mean the end of our troubles and the end of android robots for the world.

That's what Dugg Quinby thought, anyway. But Quinby may have had a miraculous gift of looking straight at problems and at things and at robots and getting the right answer; but he was always too hopeful about looking straight at people. Because, like I kept saying to him, people aren't straight, not even to themselves. And our future prospects weren't anywhere near as good as he thought.

That's what the Head of the Council was stressing when we saw him that morning just after the Council had passed the bill. His black face was sober—no trace of that flashing white grin that was so familiar on telecasts. "I've put your bill through, boys," he was saying. "God knows I'm grateful—the whole Empire should be grateful to you for helping me put over the renewal of those Martian mining concessions, and the usuform barkeep you made me is my greatest treasure; but I can't help you any more. You're on your own now."

That didn't bother Quinby. He said, "The rest ought to be easy. Once people understand what usuform robots can do for them—"

"I'm afraid, Mr. Quinby, it's you who don't quite understand. Your friend here doubtless does; he has a more realistic slant on things. But you—I wouldn't say you idealize people, but you flatter them. You expect them to see things as clearly as you do. I'm afraid they usually don't."

"But surely when you explained to the Council the advantages of usuforms—"

"Do you think the Council passed the bill only because they saw those advantages? They passed it because I backed it, and because the renewal of the Martian concessions has for the moment put me in a powerful position. Oh, I know, we're supposed to have advanced immeasurably beyond the political corruption of the earlier states; but let progress be what it may, from the cave man on up to the illimitable future, there are three things that people always have made and always will make: love, and music, and politics. And if there's any difference between me and an old-time political leader, it's simply that I'm trying to put my political skill at the service of mankind."

I wasn't listening too carefully to all this. The service of mankind wasn't exactly a hobby of mine. Quinby and the Head were all out for usuforms because they were a service to man and the Empire of Earth; I was in it because it looked like a good thing. Of course, you can't be around such a mixture of a saint, a genius, and a moron as Quinby without catching a little of it; but I tried to keep my mind fixed clear on what was in it for me.

And that was plenty. For the last couple of centuries our civilization had been based on robots—android robots. Quinby's usuform robots—Q. U. R.—robots shaped not as mechanical men, but as independently thinking machines formed directly for their intended function—threatened the whole robot set-up. They were the biggest thing since Zwergenhaus invented the mechanical brain, and I was in on the ground floor.

With the basement shaking under me.

It was an android guard that interrupted the conference here. We hadn't really got started on usuform manufacture yet, and anyway, Quinby was inclined to think that androids might be retained in some places for guards and personal attendants. He said, "Mr. Grew says that you will see him."

The Head frowned. "Robinc has always thought it owned the Empire. Now Mr. Grew thinks he owns me. Well, show him in." As the guard left, he added to us, "This Grew-Quinby meeting has to take place sometime. I'd rather like to see it."

The president-owner of Robinc—Robots Incorporated, but nobody ever said it in full—was a quiet old man with silvery hair and a gentle sad smile. It seemed even sadder than usual today. He greeted the Head and then spoke my name with a sort of tender reproach that near hurt me.

"You," he said. "The best trouble shooter that Robinc ever had, and now I find you in the enemy's camp."

But I knew his technique, and I was armed against being touched by it. "*In* the enemy's camp?" I said. "I *am* the enemy. And it's because I was your best trouble shooter that I learned the real trouble with Robinc's androids: They don't work, and the only solution is to supersede them."

"Supersede is a kind word," he said wistfully. "But the unkind act is destruction. Murder. Murder of Robinc itself, draining the lifeblood of our Empire."

The Head intervened. "Not draining, Mr. Grew, but transfusing. The blood stream, to carry on your own metaphor, is tainted; we want fresh blood, and Mr. Quinby provides it."

"I am not helpless, you know," the old man murmured gently.

"I'm afraid possibly you are, sir, and for the first time in your life. But you know the situation: In the past few months there has been an epidemic of robot breakdowns. Parts unnecessary and unused, but installed because of our absurd insistence on an android shape, have atrophied. Sometimes even the brain has been affected; my own confidential cryptanalyst went totally mad. Quinby's usuforms forestall any such problem."

"The people will not accept them. They are conditioned to androids."

"They must accept them. You know, better than most, the

problems of supply that the Empire faces. The conservation of mineral resources is one of our essential aims. And usuforms will need variously from seventy to only thirty percent of the metal that goes into your androids. This is no mere matter of business rivalry; it is conflict between the old that depletes the Empire and the new that strengthens it."

"And the old must be cast aside and rejected?"

"You," I began, "have, of course, always shown such tender mercy to your business compet—" but Quinby broke in on me.

"I realize, Mr. Grew, that this isn't fair to you. But there are much more important matters than you involved."

"Thank you." The gentle old voice was frigid.

"But I wouldn't feel right if you were simply, as you put it, cast aside and rejected. If you'll come to see us and talk things over, I'm pretty sure we can—"

"Sir!" Sanford Grew rose to his full short height. "I do not ask favors from puppies. I have only one request." He turned to the Head. "The repeal of this ridiculous bill depriving Robinc of its agelong monopoly which has ensured the safety of the Empire."

"I'm sorry, Mr. Grew. That is impossible."

The hair was still silvery and the smile was still sad and gentle. But the words he addressed to us were, "Then you understand that this is war?"

Then he left. I didn't feel too comfortable. Saving the Empire is all very well. Being a big shot in a great new enterprise is swell. But a war with something the size of Robinc is not what the doctor usually orders.

"The poor man," said Quinby.

The Head flashed an echo of the famous grin. "No wonder he's upset. It's not only the threatened loss of power, I heard that yesterday his android cook broke down completely. And you know how devoted he is to unconcentrated food."

Quinby brightened. "Then perhaps we—"

The Head laughed. "Your only hope is that a return to a concentrated diet will poison him. You've no chance of winning over Sanford Grew alive."

We went from there to the Sunspot. "It's funny," Quinby used to say. "I don't much like to drink, but a bar's always good for heavy thinking." And who was I to argue?

Guzub, that greatest of bartenders, spotted us as we came in and had one milk and one straight whiskey poured by the time we reached our usual back table. He served them to us himself, with a happy flourish of his tentacles.

"What are you so beamish about?" I asked gruffly.

Guzub shut his middle eye in the Martian expression of happiness. "Begauze yóu boys are going to 'ave a gread zugzezz with your uxuvorm robods and you invended them righd 'ere in the Zunzbod." He produced another tentacle holding a slug of straight vuzd and downed it. "Good lugg!"

I glowered after him. "We need luck. With Grew as our sworn enemy, we're on the—"

Quinby had paper spread out before him. He looked up now, took a sip of milk, and said, "Do you cook?"

"Not much. Concentrates do me most of the time."

"I can sympathize with Grew. I like old-fashioned food myself, and I'm fairly good at cooking it. I just thought you might have some ideas."

"For what?"

"Why, a usuform cook, of course. Grew's android cook broke down. We'll present him with a usuform, and that will convert him, too—"

"Convert hell!" I snorted. "Nothing can convert that sweetly smiling old— But maybe you have got something there; get at a man through his hobby— Could work."

"Now, usually," Quinby went on, "androids break down because they don't use all their man-shaped body. But an android cook would go nuts because man's body isn't enough. I've cooked; I know. So we'll give the usuform more. For instance, give him Martoid tentacles instead of arms. Maybe instead of legs give him an automatic sliding height adjustment to avoid all the bending and stooping, with a roller base for quick movement. And make the tentacles functionally specialized."

I didn't quite get that last, and I said so.

"Half your time in cooking is wasted reaching around for what you need next. We can build in a lot of that stuff. For instance, one tentacle can be a registering thermometer. Tapering to a fine point—stick it in a roast and— One can end in a broad spoon for stirring—heat-resistant, of course. One might terminate in a sort of hand, of which each of the digits was a different-sized measuring spoon. And best of all—why the nuisance of bringing food to the mouth to taste? Install taste buds in the end of one tentacle."

I nodded. Quinby's pencil was covering the paper with tentative hookups. Suddenly he paused. "I'll bet I know why android cooks were never too successful. Nobody ever included the Verhaeren factor in their brains."

The Verhaeren factor, if you've studied this stuff at all, is what makes robots capable of independent creative action. For instance, it's used in the robots that turn out popular fiction—in very small proportion, of course.

"Yes, that's the trouble. They never realized that a cook is an artist as well as a servant. Well, we'll give him in his brain what he needs for creation, and in his body the tools he needs to carry it out. And when Mr. Grew has had his first meal from a usuform cook—"

It was an idea, I admitted, that might have worked on anybody but Sanford Grew—get at a man and convert him through what's dearest to his heart. But I'd worked for Grew. I knew him. And I knew that no hobby, not even his passion for unconcentrated food, could be stronger than his pride in his power as president of Robinc.

So while Quinby worked on his usuform cook and our foreman, Mike Warren, got our dowser ready for the first big demonstration, I went ahead with the anti-Robinc campaign.

"We've got four striking points," I explained to Quinby. "Android robots atrophy or go nuts; usuforms are safe. Android robots are almost as limited as man in what they can do without tools and accessories; usuforms can be constructed to do anything. Android robots are expensive because you've got to buy an all-purpose one that can do more than you need; usuforms save money because they're specialized. Android robots use up mineral resources; usuforms save them."

"The last reason is the important one," Quinby said.

I smiled to myself. Sure it was, but can you sell the people on anything as abstract as conservation? Hell no. Tell 'em they'll save credits, tell 'em they'll get better service, and you've got 'em signed up already. But tell 'em they're saving their grandchildren from a serious shortage and they'll laugh in your face.

So as usual, I left Quinby to ideas and followed my own judgment on people, and by the time he'd sent the cook to Grew I had all lined up the campaign that could blast Grew and Robinc out of the Empire. The three biggest telecommentators were all sold on usuforms. A major solly producer was set to do a documentary on them. Orders were piling up about twice as fast as Mike Warren could see his way clear to turning them out.

So then came the day of the big test.

We'd wanted to start out with something big and new that no android could possibly compete with, and we'd had the luck to run onto Mike's brother-in-law, who'd induced in robot brains the perception of that nth sense that used to enable dowsers to find water. Our usuform dowser was God's gift to explorers and fresh, exciting copy. So the Head had arranged a big demonstration on a specially prepared field, with grandstands and fireworks and two bands—one human, one android—and all the trimmings.

We sat in our box, Mike and Quinby and I. Mike had a shakerful of Three Planets cocktails mixed by our usuform barkeep; they aren't so good when they stand, but they were still powerful enough to keep him going. I was trying to get along on sheer will power, but little streams of sweat were running down my back and my nails were carving designs in my palms.

Quinby didn't seem bothered. He kept watching the android band and making notes. "You see," he explained, "it's idiotic waste to train a robot to play an instrument, when you could make an instrument that *was* a robot. Your real robot band would be usuforms, and wouldn't be anything but a flock of instruments that could play themselves. You could even work out new instruments, with range and versatility and flexibility beyond the capacity of human or android fingers and lungs. You could—"

"Oh-oh," I said. There was Sanford Grew entering our box.

The smile was still gentle and sad, but it had a kind of warmth about it that puzzled me. I'd never seen that on Grew's face before. He advanced to Quinby and held out his hand. "Sir," he said, "I have just dined."

Quinby rose eagerly, his blond head towering above the little old executive. "You mean my usuform—"

"Your usuform, sir, is indubitably the greatest cook since the Golden Age before the devilish introduction of concentrates. Do you mind if I share your box for this great exhibition?"

Quinby beamed and introduced him to Mike. Grew shook hands warmly with our foreman, then turned to me and spoke even my name with friendly pleasure. Before anybody could say any more, before I could even wipe the numb dazzle off my face, the Head's voice began to come over the speaker.

His words were few—just a succinct promise of the wonders of usuforms and their importance to our civilization—and by the time he'd finished the dowser was in place on the field.

To everybody watching but us, there was never anything that looked less like a robot. There wasn't a trace of an android trait to it. It looked like nothing but a heavy duralite box mounted on caterpillar treads.

But it was a robot by legal definition. It had a Zwergenhaus brain and was capable of independent action under human commands or direction. That box housed the brain, with its nth-sensory perception, and eyes and ears, and the spike-laying apparatus. For when the dowser's perception of water reached a certain level of intensity, it laid a metal spike into the ground. An exploring party could send it out on its own to survey the territory, then follow its tracks at leisure and dig where the spikes were.

After the Head's speech there was silence. Then Quinby leaned over to the mike in our box and said, "Go find water."

The dowser began to move over the field. Only the Head himself knew where water had been cached at various levels and in various quantities. The dowser raced along for a bit, apparently finding nothing. Then it began to hesitate and veer. Once it paused for noticeable seconds. Even Quinby looked tense. I heard sharp breaths from Sanford Grew, and Mike almost drained his shaker.

Then the dowser moved on. There was water, but not enough to bother drilling for. It zoomed about a little more, then stopped suddenly and definitely. It had found a real treasure trove.

I knew its mechanism. In my mind I could see the Zwergenhaus brain registering and communicating its needs to the metal muscles of the sphincter mechanism that would lay the spike. The dowser sat there apparently motionless, but when you knew it you had the impression of a hen straining to lay.

Then came the explosion. When my eyes could see again through the settling fragments, there was nothing in the field but a huge crater.

It was Quinby, of course, who saw right off what had happened. "Somebody," my numb ears barely heard him say, "substituted for the spike an explosive shell with a contact-fuse tip."

Sanford Grew nodded. "Plausible, young man. Plausible. But I rather think that the general impression will be simply that usuforms don't work." He withdrew, smiling gently.

I held Mike back by pouring the rest of the shaker down his throat. Mayhem wouldn't help us any.

"So you converted him?" I said harshly to Quinby. "Brother, the next thing you'd better construct is a good guaranteed working usuform converter."

The next week was the low point in the history of Q. U. R. I know now, when Quinby's usuforms are what makes the world tick, it's hard to imagine Q. U. R. ever hitting a low point. But one reason I'm telling this is to make you realize that no big thing is easy, and that a lot of big things depend for their success on some very little thing, like that chance remark of mine I just quoted.

Not that any of us guessed then how important that remark was. We had other things to worry about. The fiasco of that demonstration had just about cooked our goose. Sure, we explained it must've been sabotage, and the Head backed us up; but the wiseacres shook their heads and muttered "Not bad for an alibi, *but*—"

Two or three telecommentators who had been backing us switched over to Grew. The solly producer abandoned his plans for a documentary. I don't know if this was honest conviction or the power of Robinc; it hit us the same either way. People were scared of usuforms now; they might go *boom!* And the biggest and smartest publicity and advertising campaign of the past century was fizzling out *ffft* before our helpless eyes.

It was the invaluable Guzub who gave us our first upward push. We were drinking at the Sunspot when he said, "Ah, boys— Zo things are going wrong with you, bud you zdill gome 'ere. No madder wad abbens, beoble zdill wand three things: eading and dringing and—"

Quinby looked up with the sharp pleasure of a new idea. "There's nothing we can do with the third," he said. "But eating and drinking— Guzub, you want to see usuforms go over, don't you?"

"And remember," I added practically, "you've got a royalty interest in our robot barkeep."

Guzub rolled all his eyes up once and down once—the Martian trick of nodding assent.

"All right," said Quinby. "Practically all bartenders are Martians, the tentacles are so useful professionally. Lots of them must be good friends of yours?"

"Lodz," Guzub agreed.

"Then listen . . ."

That was how we launched the really appealing campaign.

Words? Sure, people have read and heard millions upon billions of words, and one set of them is a lot like another. But when you get down to Guzub's three essentials—

Within a fortnight there was one of our usuform barkeeps in one bar out of five in the influential metropolitan districts. Guzub's friends took orders for drinks, gave them to the usuforms, served the drinks, and then explained to the satisfied customers how they'd been made—pointing out besides that there had *not* been an explosion. The customers would get curious. They'd order more to watch the usuform work. (It had Martoid tentacles and its own body was its shaker.) The set-up was wonderful for business—and for us.

That got at the men. Meanwhile we had usuform cooks touring the residential districts and offering to prepare old-fashioned meals free. There wasn't a housewife whose husband didn't say regularly once a week, "Why can't we have more old-fashioned food instead of all these concentrates? Why, my mother used to—"

Few of the women knew the art. Those of them who could afford android cooks hadn't found them too satisfactory. And husbands kept muttering about Mother. The chance of a happy home was worth the risk of these dreadful dangerous new things. So our usuform cooks did their stuff and husbands were rapturously pleased and everything began to look swell. (We remembered to check up on a few statistics three quarters later—it seemed we had in a way included Guzub's third appeal after all.)

So things were coming on sweetly until one day at the Sunspot I looked up to see we had a visitor. "I heard that I might find you here," Sanford Grew said, smiling. He beckoned to Guzub and said, "Your oldest brandy."

Guzub knew him by sight. I saw one tentacle flicker hesitantly toward a bottle of mikiphin, that humorously named but none the less effective knockout liquor. I shook my head, and Guzub shrugged resignedly.

"Well?" Quinby asked directly.

"Gentlemen," said Sanford Grew, "I have come here to make a last appeal to you."

"You can take your appeal," I said, "and—"

Quinby shushed me. "Yes, sir?"

"This is not a business appeal, young men. This is an appeal to your consciences, to your duty as citizens of the Empire of Earth."

I saw Quinby looking a little bothered. The smiling old boy was shrewd; he knew that the conscience was where to aim a blow at Quinby. "Our consciences are clear—I think and trust."

"Are they? This law that you finagled through the Council, that destroyed what you call my monopoly—it did more than that. That 'monopoly' rested on our control of the factors that make robots safe and prevent them from ever harming living beings. You have removed that control."

Quinby laughed with relief. "Is that all? I knew you'd been using that line in publicity, but I didn't think you expected us to believe it. There are other safety factors beside yours. We're using them, and the law still insists on the use of some, though not necessarily Robinc's. I'm afraid my conscience is untouched."

"I do not know," said Sanford Grew, "whether I am flattering or insulting you when I say I know that it is no use trying to buy you out at any price. You are immune to reason—"

"Because it's on our side," said Quinby quietly.

"I am left with only one recourse." He rose and smiled a gentle farewell. "Good day, gentlemen."

He'd left the brandy untouched. I finished it, and was glad I'd vetoed Guzub's miki.

"One recourse—" Quinby mused. "That must mean—"

I nodded.

But it started quicker than we'd expected. It started, in fact, as soon as we left the Sunspot. Duralite arms went around my body and a duralite knee dug into the small of my back.

The first time I ever met Dugg Quinby was in a truly major and wondrous street brawl, where the boy was a whirlwind. Quinby was mostly the quiet kind, but when something touched him off—and injustice was the spark that usually did it—he could fight like fourteen Martian mountaineers defending their idols.

But who can fight duralite? Me, I have some sense; I didn't even try. Quinby's temper blinded his clear vision for a moment. The only result was a broken knuckle and some loss of blood and skin.

The next thing was duralite fingers probing for the proper spots at the back of my head. Then a sudden deft pressure, and blackness.

We were in a workshop of some sort. My first guess was one of the secret workshops that honeycomb the Robinc plant, where nobody but Grew's most hand-picked man ever penetrate. We were cuffed to the wall. They'd left only one of the androids to guard us.

It was Quinby who spoke to him, and straight to the point. "What happens to us?"

"When I get my next orders," the android said in his completely emotionless voice, "I kill you."

I tried to hold up my morale by looking as indifferent as he did. I didn't make it.

"The last recourse—" Quinby said.

I nodded. Then, "But look!" I burst out. "This can't be what it looks like. He can't be a Robinc android because he's going—" I gulped a fractional gulp "—to kill us. Robinc's products have the safety factor that prevents them from harming a living being, even on another being's orders."

"No," said Quinby slowly. "Remember that Robinc manufactures androids for the Empire's army? Obviously those can't have the safety factor. And Mr. Grew has apparently held out a few for his own bootleg banditti."

I groaned. "Trust you," I said. "We're chained up with a murderous android, and trust you to stand there calmly and look at things straight. Well, are you going to see straight enough to get us out of this?"

"Of course," he said simply. "We can't let Grew destroy the future of usuforms."

There was at least one other future that worried me more,

but I knew there was no use bringing up anything so personal. I just stood there and watched Quinby thinking—what time I wasn't watching the android's hand hovering around his holster and wondering when he'd get his next orders.

And while I was waiting and watching, half scared sweatless, half trusting blindly in Quinby, half wondering impersonally what death was like—yes, I know that makes three halves of me, but I was in no state for accurate counting—while I waited, I began to realize something very odd.

It wasn't me I was most worried about. It was Dugg Quinby. Me going all unselfish on me! Ever since Quinby had first seen the nonsense in androids—no, back of that, ever since that first magnifiscrumptious street brawl, I'd begun to love that boy like a son—which'd have made me pretty precocious.

There was something about him—that damned mixture of almost stupid innocence, combined with the ability to solve any problem by his—not ingenuity, precisely, just his inborn capacity for looking at things straight.

Here I was feeling selfless. And here he was coming forth with the first at all tricky or indirect thing I'd ever known him to pull. Maybe it was like marriage—the way two people sort of grow together and average up.

Anyway, he said to the android now, "I bet you military robots are pretty good marksmen, aren't you?"

"I'm the best Robinc ever turned out," the android said.

I'd worked for Robinc; I knew that each of them was conditioned with the belief that he was the unique best. It gave them confidence.

Quinby reached out his unfettered hand and picked a plastic disk off the worktable. "While you're waiting for orders, why don't you show us some marksmanship? It'll pass the time."

The robot nodded, and Quinby tossed the disk in the air. The android grabbed at its holster. And the gun stuck.

The metal of the holster had got dented in the struggle of kidnaping us. Quinby must have noticed that; his whole plan developed from that little point.

The robot made comments on the holster; military androids had a soldier's vocabulary built in, so we'll skip that.

Quinby said, "That's too bad. My friend here's a Robinc repairman, or used to be. If you let him loose, he could fix that."

The robot frowned. He wanted the repair, but he was no dope. Finally he settled on chaining my foot before releasing my hand, and keeping his own digits constantly on my wrist so he could clamp down if I got any funny notions about snatching the gun and using it. I began to think Quinby's plan was fizzling, but I went ahead and had the holster repaired in no time with the tools on the worktable.

"Does that happen often?" Quinby asked.

"A little too often." There was a roughness to the android's tones. I recognized what I'd run onto so often in trouble shooting: an android's resentment of the fact that he didn't work perfectly.

"I see," Quinby went on, as casually as though we were here on social terms. "Of course the trouble is that you have to use a gun."

"I'm a soldier. Of course I have to use one."

"You don't understand. I mean the trouble is that you have to *use* one. Now, if you could *be* a gun—"

It took some explaining. But when the android understood what it could mean to be a usuform, to have an arm that didn't need to snatch at a holster because it was itself a firing weapon, his eye cells began to take on a new bright glow.

"You could do that to me?" he demanded of me.

"Sure," I said. "You give me your gun and I'll—"

He drew back mistrustfully. Then he looked around the room, found another gun, unloaded it, and handed it to me. "Go ahead," he said.

It was a lousy job. I was in a state and in a hurry, and the sweat running down my forehead and dripping off my eyebrows didn't help any. The workshop wasn't too well equipped, either, and I hate working from my head. I like a nice diagram to look at.

But I made it somehow, very crudely, replacing one hand with the chamber and barrel and attaching the trigger so that it would be worked by the same nerve currents as actuated the finger movements to fire a separate gun.

The android loaded himself awkwardly. I stood aside, and Quinby tossed up the disk. You never saw a prettier piece of instantaneous trapshooting. The android stretched his face into that very rare thing, a robot grin, and expressed himself in pungently jubilant military language.

"You like it?" Quinby asked.

All that I can quote of the robot's reply is "Yes," but he made it plenty emphatic.

"Then—"

But I stepped in. "Just a minute. I've got an idea to improve it." Quinby was probably trusting to our guard's gratitude; I wanted a surer hold on him. "Let me take this off just a second—" I removed the chamber and barrel; I still had his hand. "Now," I said, "we want out."

He brought up the gun in his other hand, but I said, "Ah, ah! Naughty! You aren't supposed to kill us till you get orders, and if you do they'll find you here with one hand. Fine state for a soldier. You can't repair yourself; you need two hands for it. But if we get out, you can come with us and be made over as much as you want into the first and finest efficient happy usuform soldier."

It took a little argument, but with the memory of that one perfect shot in his mind it didn't take much. As Quinby said afterward, "Robinc built pride into its robots to give them self-confidence. But that pride also gave them vanity and dissatisfaction with anything less than perfection. That was what we could use. It was all perfectly simple—"

"—when you looked at it straight," I chorused with him.

"And besides," he said, "now we know how to lick Robinc forever."

That was some comfort, I suppose, though he wouldn't say another word to explain it. And I needed comfort, because just then things took a nasty turn again. We stuck close to our factory and didn't dare go out. We were taking no chances on more kidnapings before Quinby finished his new inspiration.

Quinby worked on that alone, secret even from us. I figured out some extra touches of perfection on the usuform soldier, who was now our bodyguard—Grew would never dare complain of the theft because he'd had no legal right to possess such an android anyway. Mike and his assistants, both living and usuform, turned out barkeeps and dowsers and cooks— our three most successful usuform designs so far.

We didn't go out, but we heard enough. It was the newest and nastiest step in Grew's campaign. He had men following up our cooks and bartenders and managing to slip concentrated doses of ptomaine alkaloids into their products. No serious poisoning, you understand; just an abnormally high proportion of people taken sick after taking usuform-prepared food or drink. And a rumor going around that the usuforms secreted a poisonous fluid, which was objective nonsense, but enough to scare a lot of people.

"It's no use," Mike said to me one day. "We're licked. Two new orders in a week. We're done for. No use keeping up production."

"The hell we're licked," I said.

"If you want to encourage me, you'd ought to sound like you believed it yourself. No, we're sunk. While *he* sits in there and— I'm going down to the Sunspot and drink Three Planets till this one spins. And if Grew wants to kidnap me, he's welcome to me."

It was just then the message came from the Head. I read it, and knew how the camel feels about that last straw. It said:

> I can't resist popular pressure forever. I know and you know what Grew is up to; but the public is demanding re-enactment of the law giving Robinc exclusive rights. Unless Quinby can see straight through the hat to the rabbit, that re-enactment is going to pass.

"We'll see what he has to say to this," I said to Mike. I started for the door, and even as I did so Quinby came out.

"I've got it!" he said. "It's done." He read the Head's message with one glance, and it didn't bother him. He grabbed me by the shoulders and beamed. I've never heard my name spoken so warmly. "Mike, too. Come on in and see the greatest usuform we've hit on yet. Our troubles are over."

We went in. We looked. And we gawked. For Quinby's greatest usuform, so far as our eyes could tell, was just another android robot.

Mike went resolutely off to the Sunspot to carry out his threat of making this planet spin. I began to think myself that the tension had affected Quinby's clear-seeing mind. I didn't listen especially when he told me I'd given him the idea myself. I watched the usuform-android go off on his mysterious mission and I even let him take my soldier along. And I didn't care. We were done for now, if even Dugg Quinby was slipping.

But I didn't have time to do much worrying that morning. I was kept too busy with androids that came in wanting repairs. Very thoroughgoing repairs, too, that turned them, like my soldier, practically into usuforms. We always had a few such requests—I think I mentioned how they all want to be perfect—but this began to develop into a cloudburst. I stopped the factory lines and put every man and robot on repair.

Along about midafternoon I began to feel puzzled. It took me a little while to get it, and then it hit me. The last three that I'd repaired had been brand-new. Fresh from the Robinc factory, and rushing over here to be remade into . . . into usuforms!

As soon as I finished adjusting drill arms on the robot miner, I hurried over to where Quinby was installing an infrared color sense on a soldier intended for camouflage spotting. He looked up and smiled when he saw me. "You get it now?"

"I get what's happening. But how . . . who—"

"I just followed your advice. Didn't you say what we needed was a guaranteed working usuform converter?"

"I don't need to explain, do I? It's simple enough once you look at it straight."

We were sitting in the Sunspot. Guzub was very happy; it was the first time the Head had ever honored his establishment.

"You'd better," I said, "remember I'm a crooked-viewing dope."

"But it's all from things you've said. You're always saying I'm good at things and robots, but lousy at people because people don't see or act straight. Well, we were stymied with people. They couldn't see the real importance of usuforms through all the smoke screens that Grew threw up. But you admit yourself that robots see straight, so I went direct to them. And you said we needed a usuform converter, so I made one."

The Head smiled. "And what is the utile form of a converter?"

"He had to look like an android, because otherwise they wouldn't accept him. But he was the sturdiest, strongest android ever made, with several ingenious new muscles. If it came to fighting, he was sure to make converts that way. And besides, he had something that's never been put in a robot brain before—the ability to argue and convince. With that, he had the usuform soldier as a combination bodyguard and example. So he went out among the androids, even to the guards at Robinc and from then on inside; and since he was a usuform converter, well—he converted."

The Head let the famous grin play across his black face. "Fine work, Quinby. And if Grew hadn't had the sense to see at last that he was licked, you could have gone on with your usuform converters until there wasn't an android left on Earth. Robinc would have toppled like a wooden building with termites."

"And Grew?" I asked. "What's become of him?"

"I think, in a way, he's resigned to his loss. He told me that since his greatest passion was gone, he was going to make the most of his second greatest. He's gone off to his place in the mountains with the usuform cook you gave him, and he swears he's going to eat himself to death."

"Me," said Mike, with appropriate business, "I'd like a damper death."

"And from now on, my statisticians assure me, we're in no danger of ever using up our metal stockpile. The savings on usuforms will save us. Do you realize, Quimby, that you're just about the most important man in the Empire today?"

That was when I first heard the band approaching. It got louder while Quinby got red and gulped. It was going good when he finally said, "You know, if I'd ever thought of that, I . . . I don't think I could have done it."

He meant it, too. You've never seen an unhappier face than his when the crowd burst into the Sunspot yelling "Quinby!" and "Q. U. R.!"

But you've never seen a prouder face than mine as I saw it then in the bar mirror. Proud of myself, sure, but only because it was me that discovered Dugg Quinby.

Snulbug

"*T*hat's a hell of a spell you're using," said the demon, "if I'm the best you can call up."

He wasn't much, Bill Hitchens had to admit. He looked lost in the center of that pentacle. His basic design was impressive enough—snakes for hair, curling tusks, a sharp-tipped tail, all the works—but he was something under an inch tall.

Bill had chanted the words and lit the powder with the highest hopes. Even after the feeble flickering flash and the damp fizzling *zzzt* which had replaced the expected thunder and lightning, he had still had hopes. He had stared up at the space above the pentacle waiting to be awe-struck until he had heard that plaintive little voice from the floor wailing, "Here I am."

"Nobody's wasted time and power on a misfit like me for years," the demon went on. "Where'd you get the spell?"

"Just a little something I whipped up," said Bill modestly.

The demon grunted and muttered something about people that thought they were magicians.

"But I'm not a magician," Bill explained. "I'm a biochemist."

The demon shuddered. "I land the damnedest cases," he mourned. "Working for that psychiatrist wasn't bad enough, I should draw a biochemist. Whatever that is."

Bill couldn't check his curiosity. "And what did you do for a psychiatrist?"

"He showed me to people who were followed by little men and told them I'd chase the little men away." The demon pantomimed shooting motions.

"And did they go away?"

"Sure. Only then the people decided they'd sooner have little men than me. It didn't work so good. Nothing ever does," he added woefully. "Yours won't either."

Bill sat down and filled his pipe. Calling up demons wasn't so terrifying after all. Something quiet and homey about it. "Oh, yes it will," he said. "This is foolproof."

"That's what they all think. People—" The demon wistfully eyed the match as Bill lit his pipe. "But we might as well get it over with. What do you want?"

"I want a laboratory for my embolism experiments. If this method works, it's going to mean that a doctor can spot an embolus in the blood stream long before it's dangerous and remove it safely. My ex-boss, that screwball old occultist Reuben Choatsby, said it wasn't practical—meaning there wasn't a fortune in it for him—and fired me. Everybody else thinks I'm wacky too, and I can't get any backing. So I need ten thousand dollars."

"There!" the demon sighed with satisfaction. "I told you it wouldn't work. That's out for me. They can't start fetching money on demand till three grades higher than me. I told you."

"But you don't," Bill insisted, "appreciate all my fiendish subtlety. Look—Say, what is your name?"

The demon hesitated. "You haven't got another of those things?"

"What things?"

"Matches."

"Sure."

"Light me one, please?"

Bill tossed the burning match into the center of the pentacle. The demon scrambled eagerly out of the now cold ashes of the powder and dived into the flame, rubbing himself with the brisk vigor of a man under a needle shower, "There!" he gasped joyously. "That's more like it."

"And now what's your name?"

The demon's face fell again. "My name? You really want to know?"

"I've got to call you something."

"Oh, no you don't. I'm going home. No money games for me."

"But I haven't explained yet what you are to do. What's your name?"

"Snulbug." The demon's voice dropped almost too low to be heard.

"Snulbug?" Bill laughed.

"Uh-huh. I've got a cavity in one tusk, my snakes are falling out, I haven't got troubles enough, I should be named Snulbug."

"All right. Now listen, Snulbug, can you travel into the future?"

"A little. I don't like it much, though. It makes you itch in the memory."

"Look, my fine snake-haired friend. It isn't a question of what you like. How would you like to be left there in that pentacle with nobody to throw matches at you?" Snulbug shuddered. "I thought so. Now, you can travel into the future?"

"I said a little."

"And," Bill leaned forward and puffed hard at his corncob as he asked the vital question, "can you bring back material objects?" If the answer was no, all the fine febrile fertility of his spell-making was useless. And if that was useless, heaven alone knew how the Hitchens Embolus Diagnosis would ever succeed in ringing down the halls of history, and incidentally saving a few thousand lives annually.

Snulbug seemed more interested in the warm clouds of pipe smoke than in the question. "Sure," he said. "Within reason I can—" He broke off and stared up piteously. "You don't mean— You can't be going to pull that old gag again?"

"Look, baby. You do what I tell you and leave the worrying to me. You can bring back material objects?"

"Sure. But I warn you—"

Bill cut him off short. "Then as soon as I release you from that pentacle, you're to bring me tomorrow's newspaper."

Snulbug sat down on the burned match and tapped his forehead sorrowfully with his tail tip. "I knew it," he wailed. "I knew it. Three times already this happens to me. I've got limited powers, I'm a runt, I've got a funny name, so I should run foolish errands."

"Foolish errands?" Bill rose and began to pace about the bare attic. "Sir, if I may call you that, I resent such an imputa- tion. I've spent weeks on this idea. Think of the limitless power in knowing the future. Think of what could be done with it: swaying the course of empire, dominating mankind. All I want is to take this stream of unlimited power, turn it into the simple channel of humanitarian research, and get me $10,000; and you call that a foolish errand!"

"That Spaniard," Snulbug moaned. "He was a nice guy, even if his spell was lousy. Had a solid, comfortable brazier where an imp could keep warm. Fine fellow. And he had to ask to see tomorrow's newspaper. I'm warning you—"

"I know," said Billy hastily. "I've been over in my mind all the things that can go wrong. And that's why I'm laying three conditions on you before you get out of that pentacle. I'm not falling for the easy snares."

"All right." Snulbug sounded almost resigned. "Let's hear 'em. Not that they'll do any good."

"First: This newspaper must not contain a notice of my own death or of any other disaster that would frustrate what I can do with it."

"But shucks," Snulbug protested. "I can't guarantee that. I you're slated to die between now and tomorrow, what can I do about it? Not that I guess you're important enough to crash the paper."

"Courtesy, Snulbug. Courtesy to your master. But I tell you what: When you go into the future, you'll know then if I'm going to die? Right. Well, if I am, come back and tell me and we'll work out other plans. This errand will be off."

"People," Snulbug observed, "make such an effort to make trouble for themselves. Go on."

"Second: The newspaper must be of this city and in English. I can just imagine you and your little friends presenting some dope with the Omsk and Tomsk *Daily Vuskutsukt*."

"We should take so much trouble," said Snulbug.

"And third: The newspaper must belong to this space-time continuum, to this spiral of the serial universe, to this Wheel of If. However you want to put it. It must be a newspaper of the tomorrow that I myself shall experience, not of some other, to me hypothetical, tomorrow."

"Throw me another match," said Snulbug.

"Those three conditions should cover it, I think. There's not a loophole there, and the Hitchens Laboratory is guaranteed."

Snulbug grunted. "You'll find out."

Bill took a sharp blade and duly cut a line of the pentacle with cold steel. But Snulbug simply dived in and out of the flame of his second match, twitching his tail happily, and seemed not to give a rap that the way to freedom was now open.

"Come on!" Bill snapped impatiently. "Or I'll take the match away."

Snulbug got as far as the opening and hesitated. "Twenty-four hours is a long way."

"You can make it."

"I don't know. Look." He shook his head, and a microscopic dead snake fell to the floor. "I'm not at my best. I'm shot to pieces lately, I am. Tap my tail."

"Do what?"

"Go on. Tap it with your fingernail right there where it joins on."

Bill grinned and obeyed. "Nothing happens."

"Sure nothing happens. My reflexes are all haywire. I don't know as I can make twenty-four hours." He brooded, and his snakes curled up into a concentrated clump. "Look. All you want is tomorrow's newspaper, huh? Just tomorrow's, not the edition that'll be out exactly twenty-four hours from now?"

"It's noon now," Bill reflected. "Sure, I guess tomorrow morning's paper'll do."

"OK. What's the date today?"

"August 21."

"Fine. I'll bring you a paper for August 22. Only I'm warning you: It won't do any good. But here goes nothing. Good-bye now. Hello again. Here you are." There was a string in Snulbug's horny hand, and on the end of the string was a newspaper.

"But hey!" Bill protested. "You haven't been gone."

"People," said Snulbug feelingly, "are dopes. Why should it take any time out of the present to go into the future? I leave this point, I come back to this point. I spent two hours hunting for this damned paper, but that doesn't mean two hours of your time here. People—" he snorted.

Bill scratched his head. "I guess it's all right. Let's see the paper. And I know: You're warning me." He turned quickly to the obituaries to check. No Hitchens. "And I wasn't dead in the time you were in?"

"No," Snulbug admitted. "Not *dead*," he added, with the most pessimistic implications possible.

"What was I, then? Was I—"

"I had salamander blood," Snulbug complained. "They thought I was an undine like my mother and they put me in the cold-water incubator when any dope knows salamandry is a dominant. So I'm a runt and good for nothing but to run errands, and now I should make prophecies! You read your paper and see how much good it does you."

Bill laid down his pipe and folded the paper back from the obituaries to the front page. He had not expected to find anything useful there—what advantage could he gain from knowing who won the next naval engagement or which cities were bombed?—but he was scientifically methodical. And this time method was rewarded. There it was, streaming across the front page in vast black blocks:

MAYOR ASSASSINATED
FIFTH COLUMN KILLS CRUSADER

Bill snapped his fingers. This was it. This was his chance. He jammed his pipe in his mouth, hastily pulled a coat on his shoulders, crammed the priceless paper into a pocket, and started out of the attic. Then he paused and looked around. He'd forgotten Snulbug. Shouldn't there be some sort of formal discharge?

The dismal demon was nowhere in sight. Not in the pentacle or out of it. Not a sign or a trace of him. Bill frowned. This was definitely not methodical. He struck a match and held it over the bowl of his pipe.

A warm sigh of pleasure came from inside the corncob.

Bill took the pipe from his mouth and stared at it. "So that's where you are!" he said musingly.

"I told you salamandry was a dominant," said Snulbug, peering out of the bowl. "I want to go along. I want to see just what kind of a fool you make of yourself." He withdrew his head into the glowing tobacco, muttering about newspapers, spells, and, with a wealth of unhappy scorn, people.

The crusading mayor of Granton was a national figure of splendid proportions. Without hysteria, red baiting, or strike-breaking, he had launched a quietly purposeful and well-directed program against subversive elements which had rapidly converted Granton into the safest and most American city in the country. He was also a persistent advocate of national, state, and municipal subsidy of the arts and sciences —the ideal man to wangle an endowment for the Hitchens Laboratory, if he were not so surrounded by overly skeptical assistants that Bill had never been able to lay the program before him.

This would do it. Rescue him from assassination in the very nick of time—in itself an act worth calling up demons to perform—and then when he asks, "And how, Mr. Hitchens, can I possibly repay you?" come forth with the whole great plan of research. It couldn't miss.

No sound came from the pipe bowl, but Bill clearly heard the words, "Couldn't it just?" ringing in his mind.

He braked his car to a fast stop in the red zone before the city hall, jumped out without even slamming the door, and dashed up the marble steps so rapidly, so purposefully, that pure momentum carried him up three flights and through four suites of offices before anybody had the courage to stop him and say, "What goes?"

The man with the courage was a huge bull-necked plain-clothes man, whose bulk made Bill feel relatively about the size of Snulbug. "All right, there," this hulk rumbled. "All right. Where's the fire?"

"In an assassin's gun," said Bill. "And it had better stay there."

Bullneck had not expected a literal answer. He hesitated long enough for Bill to push him to the door marked MAYOR —PRIVATE. But though the husky's brain might move slowly, his muscles made up for the lag. Just as Bill started to shove the door open, a five-pronged mound of flesh lit on his neck and jerked.

Bill crawled from under a desk, ducked Bullneck's left, reached the door, executed a second backward flip, climbed down from the table, ducked a right, reached the door, sailed back in reverse, and lowered himself nimbly from the chandelier.

Bullneck took up a stand in front of the door, spread his legs in ready balance, and drew a service automatic from its holster. "You ain't going in there," he said, to make the situation perfectly clear.

Bill spat out a tooth, wiped the blood from his eyes, picked up the shattered remains of his pipe, and said, "Look. It's now 12:30. At 12:32 a redheaded hunchback is going to come out on that balcony across the street and aim through the open window into the mayor's office. At 12:33 His Honor is going to be slumped over his desk, dead. Unless you help me get him out of range."

"Yeah?" said Bullneck. "And who says so?"

"It says so here. Look. In the paper."

Bullneck guffawed. "How can a paper say what ain't even happened yet? You're nuts, brother, if you ain't something worse. Now go on. Scram. Go peddle your paper."

Bill's glance darted out the window. There was the balcony facing the mayor's office. And there coming out on it—

"Look!" he cried. "If you won't believe me, look out the window. See on that balcony? The redheaded hunchback? Just like I told you. Quick!"

Bullneck stared despite himself. He saw the hunchback peer across into the office. He saw the sudden glint of metal in the hunchback's hand. "Brother," he said to Bill, "I'll tend to you later."

The hunchback had his rifle halfway to his shoulder when Bullneck's automatic spat and Bill braked his car in the red zone, jumped out, and dashed through four suites of offices before anybody had the courage to stop him.

The man with the courage was a huge bull-necked plain-clothes man, who rumbled, "Where's the fire?"

"In an assassin's gun," said Bill, and took advantage of Bullneck's confusion to reach the door marked MAYOR— PRIVATE. But just as he started to push it open, a vast hand lit on his neck and jerked.

As Bill descended from the chandelier after his third try, Bullneck took up a stand in front of the door, with straddled legs and drawn gun. "You ain't going in," he said clarifyingly.

Bill spat out a tooth and outlined the situation. "—at 12:33," he ended, "His Honor is going to be slumped over the desk dead. Unless you help me get him out of range. See? It says so here. In the paper."

"How can it? Gwan. Go peddle your paper."

Bill's glance darted to the balcony. "Look, if you won't believe me. See the redheaded hunchback? Just like I told you. Quick! We've got to—"

Bullneck stared. He saw the sudden glint of metal in the hunchback's hand. "Brother," he said, "I'll tend to you later."

The hunchback had his rifle halfway to his shoulder when Bullneck's automatic spat and Bill braked his car in the red zone, jumped out, and dashed through four suites before anybody stopped him.

The man who did was a bull-necked plain-clothes man, who rumbled—

"Don't you think," said Snulbug, "you've had about enough of this?"

Bill agreed mentally, and there he was sitting in his roadster
in front of the city hall. His clothes were unrumpled, his eyes
were bloodless, his teeth were all there, and his corncob was
still intact. "And just what," he demanded of his pipe bowl,
"has been going on?"

Snulbug popped his snaky head out. "Light this again, will
you? It's getting cold. Thanks."

"What happened?" Bill insisted.

"People!" Snulbug moaned. "No sense. Don't you see? So
long as the newspaper was in the future, it was only a possibility. If you'd had, say, a hunch that the mayor was in danger
maybe you could have saved him. But when I brought it into
now, it became a fact. You can't possibly make it untrue."

"But how about man's free will? Can't I do whatever
want to do?"

"Sure. It was your precious free will that brought the paper
into now. You can't undo your own will. And, anyway, your
will's still free. You're free to go getting thrown around
chandeliers as often as you want. You probably like it. You
can do anything up to the point where it would change what's
in that paper. Then you have to start in again and again and
again until you make up your mind to be sensible."

"But that—" Bill fumbled for words, "that's just as bad as
. . . as fate or predestination. If my soul wills to—"

"Newspapers aren't enough. Time theory isn't enough. So
I should tell him about his soul! People—" and Snulbug withdrew into the bowl.

Bill looked up at the city hall regretfully and shrugged his
resignation. Then he folded his paper to the sports page and
studied it carefully.

Snulbug thrust his head out again as they stopped in the
many-acred parking lot. "Where is it this time?" he wanted
to know. "Not that it matters."

"The racetrack."

"Oh—" Snulbug groaned, "I might have known it. You're
all alike. No sense in the whole caboodle. I suppose you found
a long shot?"

"Darned tooting I did. Alhazred at twenty to one in the fourth. I've got $500, the only money I've got left on earth. Plunk on Alhazred's nose it goes, and there's our $10,000."

Snulbug grunted. "I hear his lousy spell, I watch him get caught on a merry-go-round, it isn't enough, I should see him lay a bet on a long shot."

"But there isn't a loophole in this. I'm not interfering with the future; I'm just taking advantage of it. Alhazred'll win this race whether I bet on him or not. Five pretty hundred-dollar parimutuel tickets, and behold: The Hitchens Laboratory!" Bill jumped spryly out of his car and strutted along joyously. Suddenly he paused and addressed his pipe: "Hey! Why do I feel so good?"

Snulbug sighed dismally. "Why should anybody?"

"No, but I mean: I took a hell of a shellacking from that plug-ugly in the office. And I haven't got a pain or an ache."

"Of course not. It never happened."

"But I felt it then."

"Sure. In a future that never was. You changed your mind, didn't you? You decided not to go up there?"

"O.K., but that was after I'd already been beaten up."

"Uh-uh," said Snulbug firmly. "It was before you hadn't been." And he withdrew again into the pipe.

There was a band somewhere in the distance and the raucous burble of an announcer's voice. Crowds clustered around the $2 windows, and the $5 weren't doing bad business. But the $100 window, where the five beautiful pasteboards lived that were to create an embolism laboratory, was almost deserted.

Bill buttonholed a stranger with a purple nose. "What's the next race?"

"Second, Mac."

Swell, Bill thought. Lots of time. And from now on—He hastened to the $100 window and shoved across the five bills that he had drawn from the bank that morning. "Alhazred, on the nose," he said.

The clerk frowned with surprise, but took the money and turned to get the tickets.

Bill buttonholed a stranger with a purple nose. "What's the next race?"

"Second, Mac."

Swell, Bill thought. And then he yelled, "Hey!"

A stranger with a purple nose paused and said, " 'Smatter, Mac?"

"Nothing," Bill groaned. "Just everything."

The stranger hesitated. "Ain't I seen you someplace before?"

"No," said Bill hurriedly. "You were going to, but you haven't. I changed my mind."

The stranger walked away shaking his head and muttering how the ponies could get a guy.

Not till Bill was back in his roadster did he take the corncob from his mouth and glare at it. "All right!" he barked. "What was wrong this time? Why did I get on a merry-go-round again? I didn't try to change the future!"

Snulbug popped his head out and yawned a tuskful yawn. "I warn him, I explain it, I warn him again, now he wants I should explain it all over."

"But what did I do?"

"What did he do? You changed the odds, you dope. That much folding money on a long shot at a parimutuel track, and the odds change. It wouldn't have paid off at twenty to one, the way it said in the paper."

"Nuts," Bill muttered. "And I suppose that applies to anything? If I study the stock market in this paper and try to invest my $500 according to tomorrow's market—"

"Same thing. The quotations wouldn't be quite the same if you started in playing. I warned you. You're stuck," said Snulbug. "You're stymied. It's no use." He sounded almost cheerful.

"Isn't it?" Bill mused. "Now look, Snulbug. Me, I'm a great believer in Man. This universe doesn't hold a problem that Man can't eventually solve. And I'm no dumber than the average."

"That's saying a lot, that is," Snulbug sneered. "People—"

"I've got a responsibility now. It's more than just my $10,000. I've got to redeem the honor of Man. You say this is the insoluble problem. I say there *is* no insoluble problem."

"I say you talk a lot."

Bill's mind was racing furiously. How can a man take advantage of the future without in any smallest way altering that future? There must be an answer somewhere, and a man who devised the Hitchens Embolus Diagnosis could certainly crack a little nut like this. Man cannot refuse a challenge.

Unthinking, he reached for his tobacco pouch and tapped out his pipe on the sole of his foot. There was a microscopic thud as Snulbug crashed onto the floor of the car.

Bill looked down half-smiling. The tiny demon's tail was lashing madly, and every separate snake stood on end. "This is too much!" Snulbug screamed. "Dumb gags aren't enough, insults aren't enough, I should get thrown around like a damned soul. This is the last straw. Give me my dismissal!"

Bill snapped his fingers gleefully. "Dismissal!" he cried. "I've got it, Snully. We're all set."

Snulbug looked up puzzled and slowly let his snakes droop more amicably. "It won't work," he said, with an omnisciently sad shake of his serpentine head.

It was the dashing act again that carried Bill through the Choatsby Laboratories, where he had been employed so recently, and on up to the very anteroom of old R. C.'s office.

But where you can do battle with a bull-necked guard, there is not a thing you can oppose against the brisk competence of a young lady who says, "I shall find out if Mr. Choatsby will see you." There was nothing to do but wait.

"And what's the brilliant idea this time?" Snulbug obviously feared the worst.

"R. C.'s nuts," said Bill. "He's an astrologer and a pyramidologist and a British Israelite—American Branch Reformed—and Heaven knows what else. He . . . why, he'll even believe in you."

"That's more than I do," said Snulbug. "It's a waste of energy."

"He'll buy this paper. He'll pay anything for it. There's nothing he loves more than futzing around with the occult.

He'll never be able to resist a good solid slice of the future, with illusions of a fortune thrown in."

"You better hurry, then."

"Why such a rush? It's only 2:30 now. Lots of time. And while that girl's gone there's nothing for us to do but cool our heels."

"You might at least," said Snulbug, "warm the heel of your pipe."

The girl returned at last. "Mr. Choatsby will see you."

Reuben Choatsby overflowed the outsize chair behind his desk. His little face, like a baby's head balanced on a giant suet pudding, beamed as Bill entered. "Changed your mind, eh?" His words came in sudden soft blobs, like the abrupt glugs of pouring syrup. "Good. Need you in K-39. Lab's not the same since you left."

Bill groped for the exactly right words. "That's not it, R. C. I'm on my own now and I'm doing all right."

The baby face soured. "Damned cheek. Competitor of mine, eh? What you want now? Waste my time?"

"Not at all." With a pretty shaky assumption of confidence, Bill perched on the edge of the desk. "R. C.," he said, slowly and impressively, "what would you give for a glimpse into the future?"

Mr. Choatsby glugged vigorously. "Ribbing me? Get out of here! Have you thrown out—Hold on! You're the one— Used to read queer books. Had a grimoire here once." The baby face grew earnest. "What d'you mean?"

"Just what I said, R. C. What would you give for a glimpse into the future?"

Mr. Choatsby hesitated. "How? Time travel? Pyramid? You figured out the King's Chamber?"

"Much simpler than that. I have here"—he took it out of his pocket and folded it so that only the name and the date line were visible—"tomorrow's newspaper."

Mr. Choatsby grabbed. "Let me see."

"Uh-uh. Naughty. You'll see after we discuss terms. But there it is."

"Trick. Had some printer fake it. Don't believe it."

"All right. I never expected you, R. C., to descend to such unenlightened skepticism. But if that's all the faith you have —" Bill stuffed the paper back in his pocket and started for the door.

"Wait!" Mr. Choatsby lowered his voice. "How'd you do it? Sell your soul?"

"That wasn't necessary."

"How? Spells? Cantrips? Incantations? Prove it to me. Show me it's real. Then we'll talk terms."

Bill walked casually to the desk and emptied his pipe into the ash tray.

"I'm underdeveloped. I run errands. I'm named Snulbug. It isn't enough—now I should be a testimonial!"

Mr. Choatsby stared rapt at the furious little demon raging in his ash tray. He watched reverently as Bill held out the pipe for its inmate, filled it with tobacco, and lit it. He listened awe-struck as Snulbug moaned with delight at the flame.

"No more questions," he said. "What terms?"

"Fifteen thousand dollars." Bill was ready for bargaining.

"Don't put it too high," Snulbug warned. "You better hurry."

But Mr. Choatsby had pulled out his checkbook and was scribbling hastily. He blotted the check and handed it over. "It's a deal." He grabbed up the paper. "You're a fool, young man. Fifteen thousand! *Hmf!*" He had it open already at the financial page. "With what I make on the market tomorrow, never notice $15,000. Pennies."

"Hurry up," Snulbug urged.

"Goodbye, sir," Bill began politely, "and thank you for—" But Reuben Choatsby wasn't even listening.

"What's all this hurry?" Bill demanded as he reached the elevator.

"People!" Snulbug sighed. "Never you mind what's the hurry. You get to your bank and deposit that check."

So Bill, with Snulbug's incessant prodding, made a dash to

the bank worthy of his descents on the city hall and on the Choatsby Laboratories. He just made it, by stop-watch fractions of a second. The door was already closing as he shoved his way through at three o'clock sharp.

He made his deposit, watched the teller's eyes bug out at the size of the check, and delayed long enough to enjoy the incomparable thrill of changing the account from William Hitchens to The Hitchens Research Laboratory.

Then he climbed once more into his car, where he could talk with his pipe in peace. "Now," he asked as he drove home, "what was the rush?"

"He'd stop payment."

"You mean when he found out about the merry-go-round? But I didn't promise anything. I just sold him tomorrow's paper. I didn't guarantee he'd make a fortune off it."

"That's all right. But—"

"Sure, you warned me. But where's the hitch? R. C.'s a bandit, but he's honest. He wouldn't stop payment."

"Wouldn't he?"

The car was waiting for a stop signal. The newsboy in the intersection was yelling "Uxtruh!" Bill glanced casually at the headline, did a double take, and instantly thrust out a nickel and seized a paper.

He turned into a side street, stopped the car, and went through this paper. Front page: MAYOR ASSASSINATED. Sports page: Alhazred at twenty to one. Obituaries: The same list he'd read at noon. He turned back to the date line. August 22. Tomorrow.

"I warned you," Snulbug was explaining. "I told you I wasn't strong enough to go far into the future. I'm not a well demon, I'm not. And an itch in the memory is something fierce. I just went far enough ahead to get a paper with tomorrow's date on it. And any dope knows that a Tuesday paper comes out Monday afternoon."

For a moment Bill was dazed. His magic paper, his fifteen-thousand-dollar paper, was being hawked by newsies on every corner. Small wonder R. C. might have stopped payment! And then he saw the other side. He started to laugh. He couldn't stop.

"Look out!" Snulbug shrilled. "You'll drop my pipe. And what's so funny?"

Bill wiped tears from his eyes. "I was right. Don't you see, Snulbug? Man can't be licked. My magic was lousy. All it could call up was you. You brought me what was practically a fake, and I got caught on the merry-go-round of time trying to use it. You were right enough there; no good could come of that magic.

"But without the magic, just using human psychology, knowing a man's weaknesses, playing on them, I made a syrup-voiced old bandit endow the very research he'd tabooed, and do more good for humanity than he's done in all the rest of his life. I was right, Snulbug. You can't lick Man."

Snulbug's snakes writhed into knots of scorn. "People!" he snorted. "You'll find out." And he shook his head with dismal satisfaction.

Mr. Lupescu

*T*he teacups rattled, and flames flickered over the logs.

"Alan, I *do* wish you could do something about Bobby."

"Isn't that rather Robert's place?"

"Oh you know *Robert*. He's so busy doing good in nice abstract ways with committees in them."

"And headlines."

"He can't be bothered with things like Mr. Lupescu. After all, Bobby's only his *son*."

"And yours, Marjorie."

"And mine. But things like this take a *man*, Alan."

The room was warm and peaceful; Alan stretched his long legs by the fire and felt domestic. Marjorie was soothing even when she fretted. The firelight did things to her hair and the curve of her blouse.

A small whirlwind entered at high velocity and stopped only when Marjorie said, "Bob-*by*! Say hello nicely to Uncle Alan."

Bobby said hello and stood tentatively on one foot.

"Alan . . ." Marjorie prompted.

Alan sat up straight and tried to look paternal. "Well, Bobby," he said. "And where are you off to in such a hurry?"

"See Mr. Lupescu 'f course. He usually comes afternoons."

"Your mother's been telling me about Mr. Lupescu. He must be quite a person."

"Oh gee I'll say he is, Uncle Alan. He's got a great big red nose and red gloves and red eyes—not like when you've been crying but really red like yours're brown—and little red wings that twitch only he can't fly with them cause they're ruddermentary he says. And he talks like—oh gee I can't do it, but he's swell, he is."

"Lupescu's a funny name for a fairy godfather, isn't it, Bobby?"

"Why? Mr. Lupescu always says why do all the fairies have to be Irish because it takes all kinds, doesn't it?"

"*Alan!*" Marjorie said. "I don't see that you're doing a *bit* of good. You talk to him seriously like that and you simply make him think it *is* serious. And you *do* know better, don't you, Bobby? You're just joking with us."

"Joking? About *Mr. Lupescu?*"

"Marjorie, you don't— Listen, Bobby. Your mother didn't mean to insult you or Mr. Lupescu. She just doesn't believe in what she's never seen, and you can't blame her. Now, supposing you took her and me out in the garden and we could all see Mr. Lupescu. Wouldn't that be fun?"

"Uh-uh." Bobby shook his head gravely. "Not for Mr. Lupescu. He doesn't like people. Only little boys. And he says if I ever bring people to see him, then he'll let Gorgo get me. G'bye now." And the whirlwind departed.

Marjorie sighed. "At least thank heavens for Gorgo. I never can get a very clear picture out of Bobby, but he says Mr. Lupescu tells the most *terrible* things about him. And if there's any trouble about vegetables or brushing teeth, all I have to say is *Gorgo* and hey presto!"

Alan rose. "I don't think you need worry, Marjorie. Mr. Lupescu seems to do more good than harm, and an active imagination is no curse to a child."

"You haven't *lived* with Mr. Lupescu."

"To live in a house like this, I'd chance it," Alan laughed. "But please forgive me now—back to the cottage and the typewriter . . . Seriously, why don't you ask Robert to talk with him?"

Marjorie spread her hands helplessly.

"I know. I'm always the one to assume responsibilities. And yet you married Robert."

Marjorie laughed. "I don't know. Somehow there's something *about* Robert . . ." Her vague gesture happened to include the original Degas over the fireplace, the sterling tea service, and even the liveried footman who came in at that moment to clear away.

Mr. Lupescu was pretty wonderful that afternoon, all right. He had a little kind of an itch like in his wings and they kept twitching all the time. Stardust, he said. It tickles. Got it up in the Milky Way. Friend of mine has a wagon route up there.

Mr. Lupescu had lots of friends, and they all did something you wouldn't ever think of, not in a squillion years. That's why he didn't like people, because people don't do things you can tell stories about. They just work or keep house or are mothers or something.

But one of Mr. Lupescu's friends, now, was captain of a ship, only it went in time, and Mr. Lupescu took trips with him and came back and told you all about what was happening this very minute five hundred years ago. And another of the friends was a radio engineer, only he could tune in on all the kingdoms of faery and Mr. Lupescu would squidgle up his red nose and twist it like a dial and make noises like all the kingdoms of faery coming in on the set. And then there was Gorgo, only he wasn't a friend—not exactly; not even to Mr. Lupescu.

They'd been playing for a couple of weeks—only it must've been really hours, cause Mamselle hadn't yelled about supper yet, but Mr. Lupescu says Time is funny—when Mr. Lupescu screwed up his red eyes and said, "Bobby, let's go in the house."

"But there's people in the house, and you don't—"

"I know I don't like people. That's why we're going in the house. Come on, Bobby, or I'll—"

So what could you do when you didn't even want to hear him say Gorgo's name?

He went into Father's study through the French window, and it was a strict rule that nobody *ever* went into Father's study, but rules weren't for Mr. Lupescu.

Father was on the telephone telling somebody he'd try to be at a luncheon but there was a committee meeting that same morning but he'd see. While he was talking, Mr. Lupescu went over to a table and opened a drawer and took something out.

When Father hung up, he saw Bobby first and started to be very mad. He said, "Young man, you've been trouble enough to your Mother and me with all your stories about your red-winged Mr. Lupescu, and now if you're to start bursting in—"

You have to be polite and introduce people. "Father, this is Mr. Lupescu. And see, he does too have red wings."

Mr. Lupescu held out the gun he'd taken from the drawer and shot Father once right through the forehead. It made a little clean hole in front and a big messy hole in back. Father fell down and was dead.

"Now, Bobby," Mr. Lupescu said, "a lot of people are going to come here and ask you a lot of questions. And if you don't tell the truth about exactly what happened, I'll send Gorgo to fetch you."

Then Mr. Lupescu was gone through the French window.

"It's a curious case, Lieutenant," the medical examiner said. "It's fortunate I've dabbled a bit in psychiatry; I can at least give you a lead until you get the experts in. The child's statement that his fairy godfather shot his father is obviously a simple flight mechanism, susceptible of two interpretations. A, the father shot himself; the child was so horrified by the sight that he refused to accept it and invented this explanation. B, the child shot the father, let us say by accident, and shifted the blame to his imaginary scapegoat. B has, of course, its more sinister implications: if the child had resented his father and created an ideal substitute, he might make the substitute destroy the reality. . . . But there's the solution to your eyewitness testimony; which alternative is true, Lieutenant, I leave up to your researches into motive and the evidence of ballistics and fingerprints. The angle of the wound jibes with either."

The man with the red nose and eyes and gloves and wings walked down the back lane to the cottage. As soon as he got inside, he took off his coat and removed the wings and the mechanism of strings and rubber that made them twitch. He laid them on top of the ready pile of kindling and lit the fire. When it was well started, he added the gloves. Then he took off the nose, kneaded the putty until the red of its outside vanished into the neutral brown of the mass, jammed it into a crack in the wall, and smoothed it over. Then he took the red-irised contact lenses out of his brown eyes and went into the kitchen, found a hammer, pounded them to powder, and washed the powder down the sink.

Alan started to pour himself a drink and found, to his pleased surprise, that he didn't especially need one. But he did feel tired. He could lie down and recapitulate it all, from the invention of Mr. Lupescu (and Gorgo and the man with the Milky Way route) to today's success and on into the future when Marjorie—pliant, trusting Marjorie—would be more desirable than ever as Robert's widow and heir. And Bobby would need a *man* to look after him.

Alan went into the bedroom. Several years passed by in the few seconds it took him to recognize what was waiting on the bed, but then, Time is funny.

Alan said nothing.

"Mr. Lupescu, I presume?" said Gorgo.

They Bite

*T*here was no path, only the almost vertical
ascent. Crumbled rock for a few yards, with the roots of sage
finding their scanty life in the dry soil. Then jagged outcrop-
pings of crude crags, sometimes with accidental footholds,
sometimes with overhanging and untrustworthy branches of
greasewood, sometimes with no aid to climbing but the lever-
age of your muscles and the ingenuity of your balance.

The sage was as drably green as the rock was drably brown.
The only color was the occasional rosy spikes of a barrel cactus.

Hugh Tallant swung himself up onto the last pinnacle. It
had a deliberate, shaped look about it—a petrified fortress of
Lilliputians, a Gibraltar of pygmies. Tallant perched on its
battlements and unslung his field glasses.

The desert valley spread below him. The tiny cluster of
buildings that was Oasis, the exiguous cluster of palms that
gave name to the town and shelter to his own tent and to the
shack he was building, the dead-ended highway leading
straightforwardly to nothing, the oiled roads diagraming the
vacant blocks of an optimistic subdivision.

Tallant saw none of these. His glasses were fixed beyond the
oasis and the town of Oasis on the dry lake. The gliders were
clear and vivid to him, and the uniformed men busy with
them were as sharply and minutely visible as a nest of ants
under glass. The training school was more than usually active.

One glider in particular, strange to Tallant, seemed the focus of attention. Men would come and examine it and glance back at the older models in comparison.

Only the corner of Tallant's left eye was not preoccupied with the new glider. In that corner something moved, something little and thin and brown as the earth. Too large for a rabbit, much too small for a man. It darted across that corner of vision, and Tallant found gliders oddly hard to concentrate on.

He set down the bifocals and deliberately looked about him. His pinnacle surveyed the narrow, flat area of the crest. Nothing stirred. Nothing stood out against the sage and rock but one barrel of rosy spikes. He took up the glasses again and resumed his observations. When he was done, he methodically entered the results in the little black notebook.

His hand was still white. The desert is cold and often sunless in winter. But it was a firm hand, and as well trained as his eyes, fully capable of recording faithfully the designs and dimensions which they had registered so accurately.

Once his hand slipped, and he had to erase and redraw, leaving a smudge that displeased him. The lean, brown thing had slipped across the edge of his vision again. Going toward the east edge, he would swear, where that set of rocks jutted like the spines on the back of a stegosaur.

Only when his notes were completed did he yield to curiosity, and even then with cynical self-reproach. He was physically tired, for him an unusual state, from this daily climbing and from clearing the ground for his shack-to-be. The eye muscles play odd nervous tricks. There could be nothing behind the stegosaur's armor.

There was nothing. Nothing alive and moving. Only the torn and half-plucked carcass of a bird, which looked as though it had been gnawed by some small animal.

It was halfway down the hill—hill in Western terminology, though anywhere east of the Rockies it would have been considered a sizable mountain—that Tallant again had a glimpse of a moving figure.

But this was no trick of a nervous eye. It was not little nor thin nor brown. It was tall and broad and wore a loud red-and-black lumberjacket. It bellowed, "Tallant!" in a cheerful and lusty voice.

Tallant drew near the man and said, "Hello." He paused and added, "Your advantage, I think."

The man grinned broadly. "Don't know me? Well, I daresay ten years is a long time, and the California desert ain't exactly the Chinese rice fields. How's stuff? Still loaded down with Secrets for Sale?"

Tallant tried desperately not to react to that shot, but he stiffened a little. "Sorry. The prospector getup had me fooled. Good to see you again, Morgan."

The man's eyes had narrowed. "Just having my little joke," he smiled. "Of course you wouldn't have no serious reason for mountain climbing around a glider school, now, would you? And you'd kind of need field glasses to keep an eye on the pretty birdies."

"I'm out here for my health." Tallant's voice sounded unnatural even to himself.

"Sure, sure. You were always in it for your health. And come to think of it, my own health ain't been none too good lately. I've got me a little cabin way to hell-and-gone around here, and I do me a little prospecting now and then. And somehow it just strikes me, Tallant, like maybe I hit a pretty good lode today."

"Nonsense, old man. You can see—"

"I'd sure hate to tell any of them Army men out at the field some of the stories I know about China and the kind of men I used to know out there. Wouldn't cotton to them stories a bit, the Army wouldn't. But if I was to have a drink too many and get talkative-like—"

"Tell you what," Tallant suggested brusquely. "It's getting near sunset now, and my tent's chilly for evening visits. But drop around in the morning and we'll talk over old times. Is rum still your tipple?"

"Sure is. Kind of expensive now, you understand—"

"I'll lay some in. You can find the place easily—over by the oasis. And we . . . we might be able to talk about your prospecting, too."

Tallant's thin lips were set firm as he walked away.

The bartender opened a bottle of beer and plunked it on the damp-circled counter. "That'll be twenty cents," he said, then added as an afterthought, "Want a glass? Sometimes tourists do."

Tallant looked at the others sitting at the counter—the red-eyed and unshaven old man, the flight sergeant unhappily drinking a Coke—it was after Army hours for beer—the young man with the long, dirty trench coat and the pipe and the new-looking brown beard—and saw no glasses. "I guess I won't be a tourist," he decided.

This was the first time Tallant had had a chance to visit the Desert Sport Spot. It was as well to be seen around in a community. Otherwise people begin to wonder and say, "Who is that man out by the oasis? Why don't you ever see him anyplace?"

The Sport Spot was quiet that night. The four of them at the counter, two Army boys shooting pool, and a half-dozen of the local men gathered about a round poker table, soberly and wordlessly cleaning a construction worker whose mind seemed more on his beer than on his cards.

"You just passing through?" the bartender asked sociably.

Tallant shook his head. "I'm moving in. When the Army turned me down for my lungs, I decided I better do something about it. Heard so much about your climate here I thought I might as well try it."

"Sure thing," the bartender nodded. "You take up until they started this glider school, just about every other guy you meet in the desert is here for his health. Me, I had sinus, and look at me now. It's the air."

Tallant breathed the atmosphere of smoke and beer suds, but did not smile. "I'm looking forward to miracles."

"You'll get 'em. Whereabouts you staying?"

"Over that way a bit. The agent called it 'the old Carker place.' "

Tallant felt the curious listening silence and frowned. The bartender had started to speak and then thought better of it. The young man with the beard looked at him oddly. The old man fixed him with red and watery eyes that had a faded glint of pity in them. For a moment, Tallant felt a chill that had nothing to do with the night air of the desert.

The old man drank his beer in quick gulps and frowned as though trying to formulate a sentence. At last he wiped beer from his bristly lips and said, "You wasn't aiming to stay in the adobe, was you?"

"No. It's pretty much gone to pieces. Easier to rig me up a little shack than try to make the adobe livable. Meanwhile, I've got a tent."

"That's all right, then, mebbe. But mind you don't go poking around that there adobe."

"I don't think I'm apt to. But why not? Want another beer?"

The old man shook his head reluctantly and slid from his stool to the ground. "No thanks. I don't rightly know as I—"

"Yes?"

"Nothing. Thanks all the same." He turned and shuffled to the door.

Tallant smiled. "But why should I stay clear of the adobe?" he called after him.

The old man mumbled.

"What?"

"They bite," said the old man, and went out shivering into the night.

The bartender was back at his post. "I'm glad he didn't take that beer you offered him," he said. "Along about this time in the evening I have to stop serving him. For once he had the sense to quit."

Tallant pushed his own empty bottle forward. "I hope I didn't frighten him away."

"Frighten? Well, mister, I think maybe that's just what you did do. He didn't want beer that sort of came, like you might say, from the old Carker place. Some of the old-timers here, they're funny that way."

Tallant grinned. "Is it haunted?"

"Not what you'd call haunted, no. No ghosts there that I ever heard of." He wiped the counter with a cloth and seemed to wipe the subject away with it.

The flight sergeant pushed his Coke bottle away, hunted in his pocket for nickels, and went over to the pinball machine. The young man with the beard slid onto his vacant stool. "Hope old Jake didn't worry you," he said.

Tallant laughed. "I suppose every town has its deserted homestead with a grisly tradition. But this sounds a little different. No ghosts, and they bite. Do you know anything about it?"

"A little," the young man said seriously. "A little. Just enough to—"

Tallant was curious. "Have one on me and tell me about it."

The flight sergeant swore bitterly at the machine.

Beer gurgled through the beard. "You see," the young man began, "the desert's so big you can't be alone in it. Ever notice that? It's all empty and there's nothing in sight, but there's always something moving over there where you can't quite see it. It's something very dry and thin and brown, only when you look around it isn't there. Ever see it?"

"Optical fatigue—" Tallant began.

"Sure. I know. Every man to his own legend. There isn't a tribe of Indians hasn't got some way of accounting for it. You've heard of the Watchers? And the twentieth-century white man comes along, and it's optical fatigue. Only in the nineteenth century things weren't quite the same, and there were the Carkers."

"You've got a special localized legend?"

"Call it that. You glimpse things out of the corner of your mind, same like you glimpse lean, dry things out of the corner of your eye. You encase 'em in solid circumstance and they're not so bad. That is known as the Growth of Legend. The Folk Mind in Action. You take the Carkers and the things you don't quite see and you put 'em together. And they bite."

Tallant wondered how long that beard had been absorbing

beer. "And what were the Carkers?" he prompted politely.

"Ever hear of Sawney Bean? Scotland—reign of James First, or maybe the Sixth, though I think Roughead's wrong on that for once. Or let's be more modern—ever hear of the Benders? Kansas in the 1870s? No? Ever hear of Procrustes? Or Polyphemus? Or Fee-fi-fo-fum?

"There are ogres, you know. They're no legend. They're fact, they are. The inn where nine guests left for every ten that arrived, the mountain cabin that sheltered travelers from the snow, sheltered them all winter till the melting spring uncovered their bones, the lonely stretches of road that so many passengers traveled halfway—you'll find 'em everywhere. All over Europe and pretty much in this country too before communications became what they are. Profitable business. And it wasn't just the profit. The Benders made money, sure; but that wasn't why they killed all their victims as carefully as a kosher butcher. Sawney Bean got so he didn't give a damn about the profit; he just needed to lay in more meat for the winter.

"And think of the chances you'd have at an oasis."

"So these Carkers of yours were, as you call them, ogres?"

"Carkers, ogres—maybe they were Benders. The Benders were never seen alive, you know, after the townspeople found those curiously butchered bodies. There's a rumor they got this far west. And the time checks pretty well. There wasn't any town here in the eighties. Just a couple of Indian families, last of a dying tribe living on at the oasis. They vanished after the Carkers moved in. That's not so surprising. The white race is a sort of super-ogre, anyway. Nobody worried about them. But they used to worry about why so many travelers never got across this stretch of desert. The travelers used to stop over at the Carkers', you see, and somehow they often never got any farther. Their wagons'd be found maybe fifteen miles beyond in the desert. Sometimes they found the bones, too, parched and white. Gnawed-looking, they said sometimes."

"And nobody ever did anything about these Carkers?"

"Oh, sure. We didn't have King James Sixth—only I still

think it was First—to ride up on a great white horse for a gesture, but twice Army detachments came here and wiped them all out."

"Twice? One wiping-out would do for most families." Tallant smiled.

"Uh-uh. That was no slip. They wiped out the Carkers twice because, you see, once didn't do any good. They wiped 'em out and still travelers vanished and still there were gnawed bones. So they wiped 'em out again. After that they gave up, and people detoured the oasis. It made a longer, harder trip, but after all—"

Tallant laughed. "You mean to say these Carkers were immortal?"

"I don't know about immortal. They somehow just didn't die very easy. Maybe, if they were the Benders—and I sort of like to think they were—they learned a little more about what they were doing out here on the desert. Maybe they put together what the Indians knew and what they knew, and it worked. Maybe Whatever they made their sacrifices to understood them better out here than in Kansas."

"And what's become of them—aside from seeing them out of the corner of the eye?"

"There's forty years between the last of the Carker history and this new settlement at the oasis. And people won't talk much about what they learned here in the first year or so. Only that they stay away from that old Carker adobe. They tell some stories— The priest says he was sitting in the confessional one hot Saturday afternoon and thought he heard a penitent come in. He waited a long time and finally lifted the gauze to see was anybody there. Something was there, and it bit. He's got three fingers on his right hand now, which looks funny as hell when he gives a benediction."

Tallant pushed their two bottles toward the bartender. "That yarn, my young friend, has earned another beer. How about it, bartender? Is he always cheerful like this, or is this just something he's improvised for my benefit?"

The bartender set out the fresh bottles with great solemnity. "Me, I wouldn't've told you all that myself, but then, he's a stranger too and maybe don't feel the same way we do here. For him it's just a story."

"It's more comfortable that way," said the young man with the beard, and he took a firm hold on his beer bottle.

"But as long as you've heard that much," said the bartender, "you might as well— It was last winter, when we had that cold spell. You heard funny stories that winter. Wolves coming into prospectors' cabins just to warm up. Well, business wasn't so good. We don't have a license for hard liquor, and the boys don't drink much beer when it's that cold. But they used to come in anyway because we've got that big oil burner.

"So one night there's a bunch of 'em in here—old Jake was here, that you was talking to, and his dog Jigger—and I think I hear somebody else come in. The door creaks a little. But I don't see nobody, and the poker game's going, and we're talking just like we're talking now, and all of a sudden I hear a kind of a noise like *crack!* over there in that corner behind the juke box near the burner.

"I go over to see what goes and it gets away before I can see it very good. But it was little and thin and it didn't have no clothes on. It must've been damned cold that winter."

"And what was the cracking noise?" Tallant asked dutifully.

"That? That was a bone. It must've strangled Jigger without any noise. He was a little dog. It ate most of the flesh, and if it hadn't cracked the bone for the marrow it could've finished. You can still see the spots over there. The blood never did come out."

There had been silence all through the story. Now suddenly all hell broke loose. The flight sergeant let out a splendid yell and began pointing excitedly at the pinball machine and yelling for his payoff. The construction worker dramatically deserted the poker game, knocking his chair over in the process, and announced lugubriously that these guys here had their own rules, see?

Any atmosphere of Carker-inspired horror was dissipated. Tallant whistled as he walked over to put a nickel in the juke-box. He glanced casually at the floor. Yes, there was a stain, for what that was worth.

He smiled cheerfully and felt rather grateful to the Carkers. They were going to solve his blackmail problem very neatly.

Tallant dreamed of power that night. It was a common dream with him. He was a ruler of the new American Corporate State that would follow the war; and he said to this man, "Come!" and he came, and to that man, "Go!" and he went, and to his servants, "Do this!" and they did it.

Then the young man with the beard was standing before him, and the dirty trench coat was like the robes of an ancient prophet. And the young man said, "You see yourself riding high, don't you? Riding the crest of the wave—the Wave of the Future, you call it. But there's a deep, dark undertow that you don't see, and that's a part of the Past. And the Present and even your Future. There is evil in mankind that is blacker even than your evil, and infinitely more ancient."

And there was something in the shadows behind the young man, something little and lean and brown.

Tallant's dream did not disturb him the following morning. Nor did the thought of the approaching interview with Morgan. He fried his bacon and eggs and devoured them cheerfully. The wind had died down for a change, and the sun was warm enough so that he could strip to the waist while he cleared land for his shack. His machete glinted brilliantly as it swung through the air and struck at the roots of the brush.

When Morgan arrived his full face was red and sweating.

"It's cool over there in the shade of the adobe," Tallant suggested. "We'll be more comfortable." And in the comfortable shade of the adobe he swung the machete once and clove Morgan's full, red, sweating face in two.

It was so simple. It took less effort than uprooting a clump of sage. And it was so safe. Morgan lived in a cabin way to hell-and-gone and was often away on prospecting trips. No one would notice his absence for months, if then. No one had any reason to connect him with Tallant. And no one in Oasis would hunt for him in the Carker-haunted adobe.

The body was heavy, and the blood dripped warm on Tallant's bare skin. With relief he dumped what had been Morgan on the floor of the adobe. There were no boards, no flooring. Just the earth. Hard, but not too hard to dig a grave in. And no one was likely to come poking around in this taboo territory to notice the grave. Let a year or so go by, and the grave and the bones it contained would be attributed to the Carkers.

The corner of Tallant's eye bothered him again. Deliberately he looked about the interior of the adobe.

The little furniture was crude and heavy, with no attempt to smooth down the strokes of the ax. It was held together with wooden pegs or half-rotted thongs. There were age-old cinders in the fireplace, and the dusty shards of a cooking jar among them.

And there was a deeply hollowed stone, covered with stains that might have been rust, if stone rusted. Behind it was a tiny figure, clumsily fashioned of clay and sticks. It was something like a man and something like a lizard, and something like the things that flit across the corner of the eye.

Curious now, Tallant peered about further. He penetrated to the corner that the one unglassed window lighted but dimly. And there he let out a little choking gasp. For a moment he was rigid with horror. Then he smiled and all but laughed aloud.

This explained everything. Some curious individual had seen this, and from his accounts had burgeoned the whole legend. The Carkers had indeed learned something from the Indians, but that secret was the art of embalming.

It was a perfect mummy. Either the Indian art had shrunk bodies, or this was that of a ten-year-old boy. There was no flesh. Only skin and bone and taut, dry stretches of tendon between. The eyelids were closed; the sockets looked hollow under them. The nose was sunken and almost lost. The scant lips were tightly curled back from the long and very white teeth, which stood forth all the more brilliantly against the deep-brown skin.

It was a curious little trove, this mummy. Tallant was

already calculating the chances for raising a decent sum of money from an interested anthropologist—murder can produce such delightfully profitable chance by-products—when he noticed the infinitesimal rise and fall of the chest.

The Carker was not dead. It was sleeping.

Tallant did not dare stop to think beyond the instant. This was no time to pause to consider if such things were possible in a well-ordered world. It was no time to reflect on the disposal of the body of Morgan. It was a time to snatch up your machete and get out of there.

But in the doorway he halted. There, coming across the desert, heading for the adobe, clearly seen this time, was another—a female.

He made an involuntary gesture of indecision. The blade of the machete clanged ringingly against the adobe wall. He heard the dry shuffling of a roused sleeper behind him.

He turned fully now, the machete raised. Dispose of this nearer one first, then face the female. There was no room even for terror in his thoughts, only for action.

The lean brown shape darted at him avidly. He moved lightly away and stood poised for its second charge. It shot forward again. He took one step back, machete arm raised, and fell headlong over the corpse of Morgan. Before he could rise, the thin thing was upon him. Its sharp teeth had met through the palm of his left hand.

The machete moved swiftly. The thin dry body fell headless to the floor. There was no blood.

The grip of the teeth did not relax. Pain coursed up Tallant's left arm—a sharper, more bitter pain than you would expect from the bite. Almost as though venom—

He dropped the machete, and his strong white hand plucked and twisted at the dry brown lips. The teeth stayed clenched, unrelaxing. He sat bracing his back against the wall and gripped the head between his knees. He pulled. His flesh ripped, and blood formed dusty clots on the dirt floor. But the bite was firm.

His world had become reduced now to that hand and that

head. Nothing outside mattered. He must free himself. He raised his aching arm to his face, and with his own teeth he tore at that unrelenting grip. The dry flesh crumbled away in desert dust, but the teeth were locked fast. He tore his lip against their white keenness, and tasted in his mouth the sweetness of blood and something else.

He staggered to his feet again. He knew what he must do. Later he could use cautery, a tourniquet, see a doctor with a story about a Gila monster—their heads grip too, don't they? —but he knew what he must do now.

He raised the machete and struck again.

His white hand lay on the brown floor, gripped by the white teeth in the brown face. He propped himself against the adobe wall, momentarily unable to move. His open wrist hung over the deeply hollowed stone. His blood and his strength and his life poured out before the little figure of sticks and clay.

The female stood in the doorway now, the sun bright on her thin brownness. She did not move. He knew that she was waiting for the hollow stone to fill.

Expedition

*T*he following is a transcript of the recorded two-way messages between Mars and the field expedition to the satellite of the third planet.

First Interplanetary Exploratory Expedition to Central Receiving Station:

What has the Great One achieved?

Murvin, Central Receiving Station, to First Interplanetary Exploratory Expedition:

All right, boys. I'll play games. What *has* the Great One achieved? And when are we going to get a report on it?

Falzik, First Interplanetary Exploratory Expedition, to Murvin, Central Receiving Station:

Haven't you any sense of historical moments? That was the first interplanetary message ever sent. It had to be worthy of the occasion. Trubz spent a long time working on the psychology of it while I prepared the report. Those words are going to live down through the ages of our planet.

Murvin to Falzik:

All right. Swell. You'll be just as extinct while they live on. Now, how's about that report?

Report of First Interplanetary Exploratory Expedition, presented by Falzik, specialist in reporting:

The First Interplanetary Exploratory Expedition has landed successfully upon the satellite of the third planet. The personnel of this expedition consists of Karnim, specialist in astrogation; Halov, specialist in life sciences; Trubz, specialist in psychology; Lilil, specialist in the art; and Falzik, specialist in reporting.

The trip itself proved unimportant for general reporting. Special aspects of difficulties encountered and overcome will appear in the detailed individual report of Karnim after the return of the expedition. The others, in particular Trubz and Lilil were largely unaware of these difficulties. To anyone save the specialist in astrogation, the trip seemed nowise different, except in length, from a vacation excursion to one of our own satellites.

The majority theory is apparently vindicated here on this satellite of the third planet. It does not sustain life. According to Halov, specialist in life sciences, it is not a question of cannot, since life of some strange sort might conceivably exist under any conditions save those of a perfect vacuum. But so far as can be ascertained there is no life of any remotely recognizable form upon this satellite.

This globe is dead. It is so dead that one may say the word without fear. The euphemism *extinct* would be too mild for the absolute and utter deadness here. It is so dead that the thought of death is not terrifying.

Trubz is now working on the psychology of that.

Observation checks the previous calculations that one face of this satellite is always turned toward its world and one always away from it, the period of rotation coinciding exactly with the orbital period. There seems to be no difference in nature between the two sides; but obviously the far side is the proper site for the erection of our temporary dome. If the hypothetical inhabitants of the third planet have progressed to the use of astronomical instruments, we do not wish to give them warning of our approach by establishing ourselves in the full sight of those instruments.

The absence of life on this satellite naturally proved a serious disappointment to Halov, but even more so to Lilil, who felt inspired to improvise a particularly ingenious specimen of his art. Fortunately, the stores of the ship had provided for such an emergency, and the resultant improvisation was one of the greatest triumphs of Lilil's great career. We are now about to take our first rest after the trip, and our minds are aglow with the charm and beauty of his exquisite work.

Murvin to Falzik:

All right. Report received and very welcome. But can't you give us more color? Physical description of the satellite— minerals present—exploitation possibilities—anything like that? Some of us are more interested in those than in Trubz's psychology or even Lilil's practice of the art.

Falzik to Murvin:

What are you asking for? You know as well as I do the purpose of this expedition: to discover other intelligent forms of life. And you know the double purpose behind that purpose: to verify by comparison the psychological explanation of our race-dominant fear of death (if this were a formal dispatch I'd censor that to "extinction"), and to open up new avenues of creation in the art.

That's why the personnel of this expedition, save for the astrogator, was chosen for its usefulness *if* we discover life. Until we do, our talents as specialists are wasted. We don't know about minerals and topography. Wait for the next expedition's report on them.

If you want color, our next report should have it. It will come from the third planet itself. We've established our temporary base here easily and are blasting off very soon for what our scientists have always maintained is the most probable source of life in this system.

Murvin to Falzik:

All right. And if you find life, I owe you a sarbel dinner at Noku's.

Falzik to Murvin:

Sarbel for two, please! Though what we've found, the Great One only—but go on to the report.

Report of First Interplanetary Exploratory Expedition, presented by Falzik, specialist in reporting:

The site of the Expedition's landing on the third planet was chosen more or less at random. It is situated on the third in size of the five continents, not far from the shore of the largest ocean. It is approximately indicated by the coordinates —— and —— * in Kubril's chart of the planet.

In the relatively slow final period of our approach, we were able to observe that the oceans of the third planet are indeed true liquids and not merely beds of molten metal, as has been conjectured by some of our scientists. We were more elated to observe definite signs of intelligent life. We glimpsed many structures which only the most unimaginative materialist could attribute to natural accident, and the fact that these structures tend to cluster together in great numbers indicates an organized and communal civilization.

That at least was our first uplifting emotional reaction, as yet not completely verified. The place of our landing is free of such structures, and of almost everything else. It is as purely arid a desert as the region about Krinavizhd, which in some respects it strongly resembles.

At first we saw no signs of life whatsoever, which is as we would have wished it. An exploratory expedition does not want a welcoming committee, complete with spoken speeches and even-string sridars. There was a sparse amount of vegetation, apparently in an untended state of nature, but nothing to indicate the presence of animal life until we saw the road.

It was an exceedingly primitive and clumsy road, consisting of little more than a ribbon of space from which the vegetation had been cleared; but it was a sign, and we followed it, to be rewarded shortly by our first glimpse of moving life. This was some form of apodal being, approximately one-fifth

---

* The mathematical signs indicating these coordinates are, unfortunately, topographically impossible to reproduce in this publication.—EDITOR

of the length of one of us, which glided across the road and disappeared before we could make any attempt at communication.

We continued along the road for some time, suffering severely from the unaccustomed gravity and the heavy atmosphere, but spurred on by the joyous hope of fulfilling the aim of the expedition. Lilil in particular evinced an inspired elation at the hope of finding new subjects for his great compositions.

The sun, markedly closer and hotter here on the third planet, was setting when at last we made our first contact with third-planet life. This being was small, about the length of the first joint of one's foreleg, covered with fur of pure white, save for the brown dust of the desert, and quadrupedal. It was frisking in a patch of shade, seeming to rejoice in the setting of the sun and the lowering of the temperature. With its forelegs it performed some elaborate and to us incomprehensible ritual with a red ball.

Halov approached it and attracted its attention by a creaking of his wing rudiments. It evinced no fear, but instantly rolled the red ball in his direction. Halov deftly avoided this possible weapon. (We later examined it and found it to be harmless, at least to any form of life known to us; its purpose remains a mystery. Trubz is working on the psychology of it.) He then—optimistically, but to my mind foolishly—began the fifth approach, the one developed for beings of a civilization roughly parallel to our own.

It was a complete failure. The white thing understood nothing of what Halov scratched in the ground, but persisted in trying to wrench from his digits the stick with which he scratched. Halov reluctantly retreated through the approaches down to approach one (designed for beings of the approximate mental level of the Narbian aborigines), but the creature paid no heed to them and insisted upon performing with the moving stick some ritual similar to that which it had practiced with the ball.

By this time we were all weary of these fruitless efforts, s that it came as a marked relief when Lilil announced that he had been inspired to improvise. The exquisite perfection of his art refreshed us and we continued our search with renewed vitality, though not before Halov had examined the corpse of the white creature and determined that it was indubitably similar to the mammals, though many times larger than any form of mammalian life has ever become on our planet.

Some of us thought whimsically of that favorite fantasy of the science-fiction composers, the outsize mammals who will attack and destroy our race. But we had not yet seen anything.

Murvin to Falzik:

That's a fine way to end a dispatch. You've got me all agog. Has the Monster Mammal King got you in his clutches?

Falzik to Murvin:

Sorry. I didn't intend to be sensational. It is simply that we've been learning so much here through—well, you can call him the Monster Mammal King, though the fictionists would be disappointed in him—that it's hard to find time enough for reports. But here is more.

Report of First Interplanetary Exploratory Expedition, presented by Falzik, specialist in reporting:

The sun was almost down when we saw the first intelligent being ever beheld by one of our race outside of our planet. He (for we learned afterward that he was male, and it would be unjust to refer to an intelligent being as *it*) was lying on the ground in the shade of a structure—a far smaller structure than those we had glimpsed in passing, and apparently in a sad state of dilapidation.

In this posture the fact was not markedly noticeable, but he is a biped. Used as we are on our own planet to many forms of life—octopods (though the Great One be thanked that those terrors are nearly wiped out), ourselves hexapods, and the pesky little mammalian tetrapods—a biped still seems to us something strange and mythical. A logical possibility, but not a likelihood. The length of body of this one is approximately that of a small member of our own race.

He held a container apparently of glass in one foreleg (there must be some other term to use of bipeds, since the front limbs are not used as legs) and was drinking from it when he spied us. He choked on his drink, looked away, then returned his gaze to us and stared for a long time. At last he blinked his eyes, groaned aloud, and hurled the glass container far away.

Halov now advanced toward him. He backed away, reached one forelimb inside the structure, and brought it out clasping a long metal rod, with a handle of some vegetable material. This he pointed at Halov, and a loud noise ensued. At the time some of us thought this was the being's speech, but now we know it came from the rod, which apparently propelled some form of metal missile against Halov.

The missile, of course, bounced harmlessly off Halov's armor (he prides himself on keeping in condition), and our specialist in life sciences continued to advance toward the biped, who dropped the rod and leaned back against the structure. For the first time we heard his voice, which is extraordinarily low in pitch. We have not yet fully deciphered his language, but I have, as instructed, been keeping full phonetic transcriptions of his every remark. Trubz has calculated psychologically that the meaning of this remark must be:

"Ministers of the Great One, be gracious to me!"

The phonetic transcription is as follows:*

AND THEY TALK ABOUT PINK ELEPHANTS!

He watched awestruck as Halov, undaunted by his former experience, again went directly into the fifth approach. The stick in Halov's digit traced a circle in the dirt with rays coming out of it, then pointed up at the setting sun.

The biped moved his head forward and back and spoke again. Trubz's conjecture here is:

* For the convenience of the reader, these transcriptions have been retranscribed into the conventional biped spelling.—EDITOR

"The great sun, the giver of life."

Phonetic transcription:

BUGS THAT DRAW PRETTY PICTURES YET!

Then Halov drew a series of concentric ellipses of dotted lines about the figure of the sun. He drew tiny circles on these orbits to indicate the first and second planets, then larger ones to indicate the third and our own. The biped was by now following the drawing with intense absorption.

Halov now pointed to the drawing of the third planet, then to the biped, and back again. The biped once more moved his head forward, apparently as a gesture of agreement. Finally Halov in like manner pointed to the fourth planet, to himself, and back again, and likewise in turn for each of us.

The biped's face was blank for a moment. Then he himself took a stick and pointed from the fourth planet to Halov, saying, according to Trubz:

"This is really true?"

Transcription:

YOU MEAN YOU'RE MARTIANS?

Halov imitated the head movement of agreement. The biped dropped his stick and gasped out sounds which Trubz is sure were the invocation of the name of a potent deity. Transcription:

ORSON WELLES!

We had all meanwhile been groping with the biped's thought patterns, though no success had attended our efforts. In the first place, his projection was almost nil; his race is apparently quite unaccustomed to telepathic communication. In the second place, of course, it is next to impossible to read alien thought patterns without some fixed point of reference.

Just as we could never have deciphered the ancient writings of the Khrugs without the discovery of the Burdarno Stone which gave the same inscription in their language and in an antique form of our own, so we could not attempt to decode this biped's thought patterns until we knew what they were like on a given known subject.

We now began to perceive some of his patterns of the Solar System and for our respective worlds. Halov went on to the second stage of the fifth approach. He took a group of small rocks, isolated one, held up one digit, and drew the figure one in the dirt. The biped seemed puzzled. Then Halov added another rock to the first, held up two digits, and drew the figure two, and so on for three and four. Now the biped seemed enlightened and made his agreement gesture. He also held up one digit and drew a figure beside Halov's.

His *one* is the same as ours—a not too surprising fact. Trubz has been working on the psychology of it and has decided that the figure one is probably a simple straight line in almost any numerical system. His other figures differed markedly from ours, but his intention was clear and we could to some extent follow his patterns.

Using both forelegs, Halov went on to five, six, and seven with the biped writing down his number likewise. Then Halov held up all his digits and wrote a one followed by the dot which represents zero and is the essence of any mathematical intelligence. This was the crucial moment—did these bipeds know how to calculate or was their numerical system purely primitive?

The biped held up eight digits and wrote a new figure, a conjoined pair of circles. Halov, looking worried, added another rock to his group and wrote down two ones. The biped wrote a circle with a tail to it. Halov added another rock and wrote a one followed by a two. The biped wrote a one followed by a circle.

Then Halov understood. We have always used an octonary system, but our mathematicians have long realized the possibility of others: a system of two, for instance, in which 11 would mean three, a system of four (the folk speech even contains survivals of such a system) in which 11 would mean five. For 11 means simply the first power of the number which is your base, plus one. This system of the bipeds obviously employs a decimal base.

(Trubz has been working on the psychology of this. He explains it by the fact that the bipeds have five digits on each forelimb, or a total of ten, whereas we have four each, a total of eight.)

Halov now beckoned to Karnim, who as astrogator is the best mathematician among us, and asked him to take over. He studied for a moment the biped's numbers, adjusted his mind rapidly to the (for the layman) hopeless confusion of a decimal system, and went ahead with simple mathematical operations. The biped followed him not unskillfully, while the rest of us concentrated on his thought patterns and began to gather their shape and nature.

The growing darkness bothered the biped before it incommoded Karnim. He rose from his squatting position over the numerals and went into the structure, the interior of which was soon alight. He came back to the doorway and beckoned us to enter. As we did so, he spoke words which Trubz conjectures to mean:

"Enter my abode and stay in peace, O emissaries from the fourth planet."

Phonetic transcription:

YOU'LL BE GONE IN THE MORNING, AND WILL I HAVE A HEAD!

Murvin to Falzik:

What a yarn! A planet of intelligent beings! What a future for the art! Maybe I never was sold on this expedition, but I am now. Keep the reports coming. And include as much phonetic transcription as you can—the specialists are working on what you've sent and are inclined to doubt some of Trubz's interpretations. Also tell Trubz to get to work as soon as possible on the psychological problem of extinction. If this being's a mammal, he should help.

[Several reports are omitted here, dealing chiefly with the gradually acquired skill of the expedition in reading a portion of the biped's thought patterns and in speaking a few words of his language.]

Report of First Interplanetary Exploratory Expedition, presented by Falzik, specialist in reporting:

Halov and Trubz agree that we should stay with this *man* (for such we have by now learned is the name of his race) until we have learned as much from him as we can. He has accepted us now and is almost at ease with us, though the morning after our arrival, for some peculiar reason, he seemed even more surprised to see us than when we first appeared.

We can learn much more from him, now that he is used to us, than we could from the dwellers in the large massed structures, and after we are well versed in his civilization we stand much more chance of being accepted peaceably.

We have been here now for three of the days of this planet, absorbed in our new learning. (All save Lilil, who is fretful because he has not practiced his art for so long. I have occasionally seen him eyeing the *man* speculatively.) By using a mixture of telepathy, sign language, and speech, we can by now discuss many things, though speech comes with difficulty to one who has used it only on formal and fixed occasions.

For instance, we have learned why this *man* lives alone, far from his fellows. His specialty is the making of pictures with what he calls a *camera*, a contrivance which records the effect of differing intensities of light upon a salt of silver—a far more complex method than our means of making pictures with photosensitized elduron, but one producing much the same results. He has taken pictures of us, though he seems doubtful that any other *man* will ever believe the record of his *camera*.

At present he is engaged in a series of pictures of aspects of the desert, an undertaking that he seems to regard not as a useful function but as an art of some strange sort. Trubz is working on the psychology of it and says that a reproductive and imitative art is conceivable, but Lilil is scornful of the notion.

Today he showed us many pictures of other *mans* and of their cities and structures. *Man* is a thin-skinned and almost hairless animal. This *man* of ours goes almost naked, but that is apparently because of the desert heat. Normally a *man* makes up for his absence of hair by wearing a sort of artificial fur of varying shapes known as *clothes*. To judge from the pictures shown us by the *man*, this is true only of the male

f the species. The female never covers her bare skin in any
way.

Examination of these pictures of females shown us by our
man fully confirms our theory that the animal *man* is a
mammal.

The display of pictures ended with an episode still not quite
clear to us. Ever since our arrival, the *man* has been worrying and talking about something apparently lost—something
called a *kitten*. The thought pattern was not familiar enough
to permit us to gather its nature, until he showed us a picture
of the small white beast which we had first met, and we recognized in his mind this *kitten*-pattern. He seemed proud of
the picture, which showed the beast in its ritual with the ball,
but still worried, and asked us, according to Trubz, if we
knew anything of its whereabouts. Transcription:

YOU WOULDN'T ANY OF YOU BIG BUGS KNOW
WHAT THE DEVIL'S BECOME OF THAT KITTEN,
WOULD YOU?

Thereupon Lilil arose in his full creative pride and led the
man to the place where we had met the *kitten*. The corpse
was by now withered in the desert sun, and I admit that it
was difficult to gather from such a spectacle the greatness of
Lilil's art, but we were not prepared for the *man*'s reaction.

His face grew exceedingly red, and a fluid formed in his
eyes. He clenched his digits and made curious gestures with
them. His words were uttered brokenly and exceedingly difficult to transcribe. Trubz has not yet conjectured their meaning but the transcription reads:

YOU DID THAT? TO A POOR, HARMLESS LITTLE
KITTEN? WHY, YOU——*

His attitude has not been the same toward us since. Trubz
is working on the psychology of it.

Murvin to Falzik:

Tell Trubz to work on the major psychological problem.
Our backers are getting impatient.

* The remainder of this transcription has been suppressed for this
audience.—EDITOR

Falzik to Murvin:

I think that last report was an aspect of it. But I'm still puzzled. See what you can make of this one.

Report of First Interplanetary Exploratory Expedition, presented by Falzik, specialist in reporting:

Tonight Halov and Trubz attempted to present the great psychological problem to the *man.* To present such a problem in our confusion of thoughts, language, and gesture is not easy, but I think that to some extent they succeeded.

They stated it in its simplest form: Our race is obsessed by a terrible fear of extinction. We will each of us do anything to avoid his personal extinction. No such obsession has ever been observed among the minute mammalian pests of our planet.

Now, is our terror a part of our intelligence? Does intelligence necessarily imply and bring with it a frantic clinging to the life that supports us? Or does this terror stem from our being what we are, rather than mammals? A mammal brings forth its young directly; the young are a direct continuation of the life of the old. But with us a half dozen specialized individuals bring forth all the young. The rest of us have no part in it; our lives are dead ends, and we dread the approach of that blank wall.

Our psychologists have battled over this question for generations. Would another—say, a mammalian—form of intelligent life have such an obsession? Here we had an intelligent mammal. Could he answer us?

I give the transcription of his answer, as yet not fully deciphered:

I THINK I GET WHAT YOU MEAN. AND I THINK THE ANSWER IS A LITTLE OF BOTH. OK, SO WE'RE INTELLIGENT MAMMALS. WE HAVE MORE FEAR OF DEATH THAN THE UNINTELLIGENT, LIKE THE POOR LITTLE KITTEN YOU BUTCHERED; BUT CERTAINLY NOT SUCH A DOMINANT OBSESSION AS I GATHER YOUR RACE HAS.

Trubz thinks that this was an ambiguous answer, which will not satisfy either party among our specialists in psychology.

We then proposed, as a sub-question, the matter of the art. Is it this same psychological manifestation that has led us to develop such an art? That magnificent and highest of arts which consists in the extinction with the greatest aesthetic subtlety of all other forms of life?

Here the *man's* reactions were as confusing as they had been beside the corpse of the *kitten*. He said.

SO THAT'S WHAT HAPPENED TO SNOWPUSS? ART . . . ! ART, YOU CALL IT, YET! AND YOU'VE COME HERE TO PRACTICE THAT ART ON THIS WORLD? I'LL SEE YOU FRIED CRISP ON BOTH SIDES ON HADES' HOTTEST GRIDDLE FIRST!

Trubz believes that the extremely violent emotion expressed was shock at realization of the vast new reaches of aesthetic experience which lay before him.

Later, when he thought he was alone, I overheard him talking to himself. There was something so emphatically inimical in his thought patterns that I transcribed his words, though I have not yet had a chance to secure Trubz's opinion on them. He beat the clenched digits of one forelimb against the other and said:

SO THAT'S WHAT YOU'RE UP TO! WE'LL SEE ABOUT THAT. BUT HOW? HOW . . . ? GOT IT! THOSE PICTURES I TOOK FOR THE PUBLIC HEALTH CAMPAIGN . . .

I am worried. If this attitude indicated by his thought patterns persists, we may have to bring about his extinction and proceed at once by ourselves. At least it will give Lilil a chance to compose one of his masterpieces.

Final report of the First Interplanetary Exploratory Expedition, presented by Falzik, specialist in reporting:

How I could so completely have misinterpreted the *man's* thought patterns I do not understand. Trubz is working on the psychology of it. Far from any hatred or enmity, the *man* was even then resolving to save our lives. The First Interplanetary Exploratory Expedition owes him a debt that it can never repay.

It was after sunup the next day that he approached us with his noble change of heart. As I describe this scene I cannot unfortunately give his direct words; I was too carried away by my own emotions to remember to transcribe. Such phrases as I attribute to him here are reconstructed from the complex of our intercourse and were largely a matter of signs and pictures.

What he did first was to show us one of his pictures. We stared at it and drew back horrified. For it represented a being closely allied to us, almost to be taken for one of us, meeting extinction beneath a titanic weapon wielded by what was obviously the characteristic five-digited forelimb of a *man*. And that forelimb was many, many times the size of the being resembling us.

"I've been keeping this from you," he informed us. "I'll admit I've been trying to trap you. But the truth is: I'm a dwarf *man*. The real ones are as much bigger than me as you are bigger than the *kitten*. More, even. And their favorite pastime—only they call it a sport, not art—is killing bugs like you."

We realized now what should have struck us before—the minute size of his structure compared with those which we had seen before. Obviously he spoke the truth—he was a dwarf specimen of his race.

Then he produced more pictures—horrible, terrifying, monstrous pictures, all showing something perturbingly like us meeting cruel extinction at the whim of a *man*.

"I've just been keeping you here," he said, "until some real members of my race could come and play with you. They'd like it. But I haven't got the heart to do it. I like you, and what you told me about your art convinces me that you don't deserve extinction like that. So I'm giving you your chance: Clear out of here and stay away from this planet. It's the most unsafe place in the universe for your kind. If you dread extinction, stay away from the third planet!"

His resolve to spare our lives had made him happy. His face kept twisting into that grimace which we had learned to recognize as a sign of *man*'s pleasure. But we hardly watched him or even listened to him. Our eyes kept returning with awful fascination to those morbidly terrifying pictures. Then our thoughts fused into one, and with hardly a word of farewell to our savior we sped back to the ship.

This is our last report. We are now on the temporary base established on the satellite and will return as soon as we have recovered from the shock of our narrow escape. Lilil has achieved a new composition with a captive pergut from the ship which has somewhat solaced us.

Murvin to First Interplanetary Exploratory Expedition:

You dopes! You low mammalian idiots! It's what comes of sending nothing but specialists on an expedition. I tried to convince them you needed a good general worker like me, but no. And look at you!

It's obvious what happened. On our planet, mammals are minute pests and the large intelligent beings are arthropodal hexapods. All right. On the third planet things have worked out the other way round. *Bugs,* as the *man* calls our kin, are tiny, insignificant things. You saw those pictures and thought the *mans* were enormous; actually they meant only that the *bugs* were minute!

That *man* tricked you unpardonably, and I like him for it. Specialists . . . ! You deserve extinction for this, and you know it. But Vardanek has another idea. Stay where you are. Develop the temporary base in any way you can. We'll send others to help you. We'll build up a major encampment on that side of the satellite, and in our own sweet time we can invade the third planet with enough sensible ones to counteract the boners of individual specialists.

We can do it, too. We've got all the time we need to build up our base, even if that *man* has warned his kind—who probably wouldn't believe him anyway. Because remember this always, and feel secure: *No being on the third planet ever knows what is happening on the other side of its satellite.*

We Print the Truth

"**A**ll right, then, tell me this: If God can do anything—" Jake Willis cleared his throat and paused, preparatory to delivering the real clincher.

The old man with the scraggly beard snorted and took another shot of applejack. "—can He make a weight so heavy He can't lift it? We know that one, Jake, and it's nonsense. It's like who wakes the bugler, or who shaves the barber, or how many angels can dance how many sarabands on the point of a pin. It's just playing games. It takes a village atheist to beat a scholastic disputant at pure verbal hogwash. Have a drink."

Jake Willis glared. "I'd sooner be the village atheist," he said flatly, "than the town drunkard. You know I don't drink." He cast a further sidewise glare at the little glass in Father Byrne's hand, as though the priest were only a step from the post of town drunkard himself.

"You're an ascetic without mysticism, Jake, and there's no excuse for it. Better be like me: a mystic without ary a trace of asceticism. More fun."

"Stop heckling him, Luke," Father Byrne put in quietly. "Let's hear what if God can do anything."

Lucretius Sellers grunted and became silent. MacVeagh said, "Go ahead, Jake," and Chief Hanby nodded.

They don't have a cracker barrel in Grover, but they still

have a hot-stove league. It meets pretty regularly in the back room of the *Sentinel*. Oh, once in a while someplace else. On a dull night in the police station they may begin to flock around Chief Hanby, or maybe even sometimes they get together with Father Byrne at the parish house. But mostly it's at the *Sentinel*.

There's lots of spare time around a weekly paper, even with the increase in job printing that's come from all the forms and stuff they use out at the Hitchcock plant. And Editor John MacVeagh likes to talk, so it's natural for him to gather around him all the others that like to talk too. It started when Luke Sellers was a printer, before he resigned to take up drinking as a career.

The talk's apt to be about anything. Father Byrne talks music mostly; it's safer than his own job. With John MacVeagh and Chief Hanby it's shop talk: news and crime—not that there's much of either in Grover, or wasn't up to this evening you're reading about.

But sometime in the evening it's sure to get around to Is there a God? And if so why doesn't He— Especially when Jake Willis is there. Jake's the undertaker and the coroner. He says, or used to say then, that when he's through with them, he knows they're going to stay dead, and that's enough for him.

So here Jake had built up to his usual poser again. Only this time it wasn't the weight that Omnipotence couldn't lift. Everybody was pretty tired of that. It was, "If God can do anything, why doesn't he stop the war?"

"For once, Jake, you've got something," said John MacVeagh. "I know the problem of Evil is the great old insoluble problem; but Evil on a scale like this begins to get you. From an Old Testament God, maybe yes; but it's hard to believe in the Christian God of love and kindness permitting all this mass slaughter and devastation and cruelty."

"We just don't know," Chief Hanby said slowly. "We don't understand. 'For my thoughts are not your thoughts, neither are your ways my ways, saith the Lord. For as the Heavens are higher than the earth, so are my ways higher than your ways and my thoughts than your thoughts.' Isaiah, fifty-five, eight and nine. We just don't understand."

"Uh-uh, Chief." MacVeagh shook his head. "That won't wash. That's the easy way out. The one thing we've got to know and understand about God is that He loves good and despises evil, which I'll bet there's a text for, only I wouldn't know."

"He loves truth," said Chief Hanby. "We don't know if His truth is our 'good.' "

Lucretius Sellers refilled his glass. "If the Romans thought there was truth in wine, they should've known about apple jack. But what do you say, Father?"

Father Byrne sipped and smiled. "It's presumptuous to try to unravel the divine motives. Isaiah and the Chief are right: His thoughts are not our thoughts. But still I think we can understand the answer to Jake's question. If you were God—'

They never heard the end to this daring assumption; not that night, anyway. For just then was when Philip Roger burst in. He was always a little on the pale side—thin, too, only the word the girls used for it was "slim," and they liked the pallor, too. Thought it made him look "interesting," with those clean, sharp features and those long dark eyelashes. Ever Laura Hitchcock liked the features and the lashes and the pallor. Ever since she read about Byron in high school.

But the girls never saw him looking as pale as this, and they wouldn't have liked it. Laura, now, might have screamed at the sight of him. It isn't right, it isn't natural for the human skin to get that pale—as though a patriotic vampire had lifted your whole stock of blood for the plasma drive.

He fumbled around with noises for almost a minute before he found words. The men were silent. Abstract problems of evil didn't seem so important when you had concrete evidence of some kind of evil right here before you. Only evil could drain blood like that.

Finally one of his choking glurks sounded like a word. The word was "Chief!"

Chief Hanby got up. "Yes, Phil? What's the matter?"

Wordlessly, Luke Sellers handed over the bottle of applejack. It was a pretty noble gesture. There was only about two drinks left, and Phil Rogers took them both in one swallow.

"I thought you'd be over here, Chief," he managed to say. "You've got to come. Quick. Out to Aunt Agnes'."

"What's the matter out there? Burglary?" Chief Hanby asked with an optimism he didn't feel.

"Maybe. I don't know. I didn't look. I couldn't. All that blood— Look. Even on my trousers where I bent down— I don't know why. Any fool could see she was dead—"

"Your aunt?" Chief Hanby gasped. Then the men were silent. They kept their eyes away from the young man with blood on his trousers and none in his face. Father Byrne said something softly to himself and to his God. It was a good thirty seconds before the professional aspects of this news began to strike them.

"You mean murder?" Chief Hanby demanded. Nothing like this had ever happened in Grover before. Murder of H. A. Hitchcock's own sister! "Come on, boy. We won't waste any time."

John MacVeagh's eyes were alight. "No objections to the press on your heels, chief? I'll be with you as soon as I see Whalen."

Hanby nodded. "Meet you there, Johnny."

Father Byrne said, "I know your aunt never quite approved of me or my church, Philip. But perhaps she won't mind too much if I say a mass for her in the morning."

Jake Willis said nothing, but his eyes gleamed with interest. It was hard to tell whether the coroner or the undertaker in him was more stirred by the prospect.

Lucretius Sellers headed for the door. "As the only man here without a professional interest in death, I bid you boys good night." He laid his hand on the pale young man's arm and squeezed gently. "Sorry, Phil."

Father Byrne was the last to leave, and Molly bumped into him in the doorway. She returned his greeting hastily and turned to John MacVeagh, every inch of her plump body trembling with excitement. "What's happening, boss? What goes? It must be something terrific to break up the bull session this early."

MacVeagh was puffing his pipe faster and hotter than was good for it. "I'll say something's happened, Molly. Agnes Rogers has been killed. Murdered."

"Whee!" Molly yelled. "Stop the presses! Is that a story! Is that a— Only you can't stop the presses when we don't come out till Friday, can you?"

"I've got to talk to Whalen a minute—and about that very thing—and then I'll be off hotfooting it after the chief. It's the first local news in three years that's rated an extra, and it's going to get one."

"Wonderful!" Her voice changed sharply. "The poor crazy old woman— We're vultures, that's what we are—"

"Don't be melodramatically moral, Molly. It's our job. There have to be . . . well, vultures; and that's us. Now let me talk to Whalen, and I'll—"

"Boss?"

"Uh-huh?"

"Boss, I've been a good girl Friday, haven't I? I keep all the job orders straight and I never make a mistake about who's just been to the city and who's got relatives staying with them and whose strawberry jam won the prize at the Fair—"

"Sure, sure. But look, Molly—"

"And when you had that hangover last Thursday and I fed you tomato juice all morning and beer all afternoon and we got the paper out OK, you said you'd do anything for me, didn't you?"

"Sure. But—"

"All right. Then you stay here and let me cover this murder."

"That's absurd. It's my job to—"

"If you knew how much I want to turn out some copy that isn't about visiting and strawberry jam— And besides, this'll be all tied up with the Hitchcocks. Maybe even Laura'll be there. And when you're . . . well, involved a little with peo-ple, how can you be a good reporter? Me, I don't give a damn about Hitchcocks. But with you, maybe you'd be in a spot where you'd have to be either a lousy reporter or a lousy friend."

MacVeagh grinned. "As usual, Friday, you make sense. Go on. Get out there and bring me back the best story the *Sentinel* ever printed. Go ahead. Git."

"Gee, boss—" Molly groped for words, but all she found was another and even more heartfelt "*Gee*—." Then she was gone.

MacVeagh smiled to himself. Swell person, Molly. He'd be lost without her. Grand wife for some man, if he liked them a little on the plump side. If, for instance, he had never seen the superb slim body of Laura Hitchcock—

But thoughts of Laura now would only get in the way. He'd have to see her tomorrow. Offer his condolences on the death of her aunt. Perhaps in comforting her distress—

Though it would be difficult, and even unconvincing, to display too much grief at Agnes Rogers' death. She had been Grover's great eccentric, a figure of fun, liked well enough, in a disrespectful way, but hardly loved. A wealthy widow—she held an interest in the Hitchcock plant second only to H. A.'s own—she had let her fortune take care of itself—and of her—while she indulged in a frantic crackpot quest for the Ultimate Religious Truth. At least once a year she would proclaim that she had found it, and her house would be filled with the long-robed disciples of the Church of the Eleven Apostles—which claimed that the election by lot of Matthias had been fraudulent and invalidated the apostolic succession of all other churches; or the sharp-eyed, businesslike emissaries of Christoid Thought—which seemed to preach the Gospel according to St. Dale.

It was hard to take Agnes Rogers' death too seriously. But that ultimate seriousness transfigures, at least for the moment, the most ludicrous of individuals.

Whalen was reading when John MacVeagh entered his cubbyhole off the printing room. One of those books that no one, not even Father Byrne, had ever recognized the letters of. It made MacVeagh realize again how little he knew of this last survival of the race of tramp printers, who came out of nowhere to do good work and vanish back into nowhere.

Brownies, he thought. With whiskey in their saucers instead of milk.

Not that Whalen looked like any brownie. He was taller than MacVeagh himself, and thinner than Phil Rogers. The funniest thing about him was that when you called up a memory image of him, you saw him with a beard. He didn't have any, but there was something about the thin long nose, the bright deepset eyes— Anyway, you saw a beard.

You could almost see it now, in the half-light outside the circle that shone on the unknown alphabet. He looked up as MacVeagh came in and said, "John. Good. I wanted to see you."

MacVeagh had never had a printer before who called him by his formal first name. A few had ventured on "Johnny," Luke Sellers among them, but never "John." And still, whatever came from Whalen sounded right.

"We've got work to do, Whalen. We're going to bring out an extra tomorrow. This town's gone and busted loose with the best story in years, and it's up to us to—"

"I'm sorry, John," Whalen said gravely. His voice was the deepest MacVeagh had ever heard in ordinary speech. "I'm leaving tonight."

"Leaving—" MacVeagh was almost speechless. Granted that tramp printers were unpredictable; still after an announcement such as he'd just made—

"I must, John. No man is master of his own movements. I must go, and tonight. That is why I wished to see you. I want to know your wish."

"My wish? But look, Whalen: We've got work to do. We've got to—"

"I must go." It was said so simply and sincerely that it stood as absolute fact, as irrevocable as it was incomprehensible. "You've been a good employer, John. Good employers have a wish when I go. I'll give you time to think about it; never make wishes hastily."

"But I— Look, Whalen. I've never seen you drink, but I've never known a printer that didn't. You're babbling. Sleep it off, and in the morning we'll talk about leaving."

"You never did get my name straight, John," Whalen went on. "It was understandable in all that confusion the day you hired me after Luke Sellers had retired. But Whalen is only my first name. I'm really Whalen Smith. And it isn't quite Whalen—"

"What difference does that make?"

"You still don't understand? You don't see how some of us had to take up other trades with the times? When horses went and you still wanted to work with metal, as an individual worker and not an ant on an assembly line— So you don't believe I can grant your wish, John?"

"Of course not. Wishes—"

"Look at the book, John."

MacVeagh looked. He read:

> At this point in the debate His Majesty waxed exceeding wroth and smote the great oaken table with a mighty oath. "Nay," he swore, "all of our powers they shall not take from us. We will sign the compact, but we will not relinquish all. For unto us and our loyal servitors must remain—"

"So what?" he said. "Fairy tales?"

Whalen Smith smiled. "Exactly. The annals of the court of His Majesty King Oberon."

"Which proves what?"

"You read it, didn't you? I gave you the eyes to read—"

John MacVeagh looked back at the book. He had no great oaken table to smite, but he swore a mighty oath. For the characters were again strange and illegible.

"I can grant your wish, John," said Whalen Smith with quiet assurance.

The front doorbell jangled.

"I'll think about it," said MacVeagh confusedly. "I'll let you know—"

"Before midnight, John. I must be gone then," said the printer.

Even an outsider to Grover would have guessed that the man waiting in the office was H. A. Hitchcock. He was obviously a man of national importance, from the polished tips of his shoes to the equally polished top of his head. He was well preserved and as proud of his figure as he was of his daughter's or his accountant's; but he somehow bulked as large as though he weighed two hundred.

The top of his head was gleaming with unusual luster at the moment, and his cheeks were red. "Sit down, MacVeagh," he said, as authoritatively as though this was his own office.

John MacVeagh sat down, said, "Yes, Mr. Hitchcock?" and waited.

"Terrible thing," Mr. Hitchcock sputtered. "Terrible. Poor Agnes— Some passing tramp, no doubt."

"Probably," John agreed. Inhabitants of Grover were hard to picture as murderers. "Anything taken?"

"Jewelry from the dressing table. Loose cash. Didn't find the wall safe, fortunately. Chief Hanby's quite satisfied. Must have been a tramp. Sent out a warning to state highway police."

"That was wise." He wondered why H. A. Hitchcock had bothered to come here just for this. Molly would bring it to him shortly. He felt a minor twinge of regret—passing tramps aren't good copy, even when their victim is a magnate's sister.

"Hanby's satisfied," Mr. Hitchcock went on. "You understand that?"

"Of course."

"So I don't want you or your girl reporter questioning him and stirring up a lot of confusion. No point to it."

"If the chief's satisfied, we aren't apt to shake him."

"And I don't want any huggermugger. I know you newspapermen. Anything for a story. Look at the way the press associations treated that strike. What happened? Nothing.

Just a little necessary discipline. And you'd think it was a massacre. So I want a soft pedal on poor Agnes' death. You understand? Just a few paragraphs—mysterious marauder— you know."

"It looks," said MacVeagh ruefully, "as though that was all it was going to be worth."

"No use mentioning that Philip and Laura were in the house. Matter of fact, so was I. We didn't see anything. She'd gone upstairs. No point to our evidence. Leave us out of it."

MacVeagh looked up with fresh interest. "All of you there? All of you downstairs and a passing tramp invades the upstairs and gets away with—"

"Damn clever, some of these criminals. Know the ropes. If I'd laid my hands on the— Well, that won't bring Agnes back to life. Neither will a scare story. Had enough unfavorable publicity lately. So keep it quiet. Don't trust that reporter of yours; don't know what wild yarns she might bring back to you. Thought I'd get it all straight for you."

"Uh-huh." MacVeagh nodded abstractedly. "You were all together downstairs, you and Laura and Philip?"

"Yes," said Mr. Hitchcock. He didn't hesitate, but Mac-Veagh sensed a lie.

"Hm-m-m," was all he said.

"Don't you believe me? Ask Laura. Ask Philip."

"I intend to," said John MacVeagh quietly.

Mr. Hitchcock opened his mouth and stared. "There's no need for that, young man. No need at all. Any necessary facts you can get from me. I'd sooner you didn't bother my daughter or my nephew or the chief. They have enough trouble."

MacVeagh rose from behind his desk. "There's been a murder," he said slowly. "The people of Grover want to know the truth. Wherever there's an attempt to cover up, you can be pretty sure that there's something to cover. Whatever it is, the *Sentinel's* going to print it. Good night, Mr. Hitchcock."

With the full realization of what MacVeagh meant, Mr. Hitchcock stopped spluttering. There was nothing of the turkey cock about him now. He was quiet and deadly as he said, "I'll talk to Mr. Manson tomorrow."

"Sorry to disappoint you. My debt to Manson's bank was paid off last month. We haven't been doing badly since the influx of your workers doubled our circulation."

"And I think that our plant's printing will be more efficiently and economically handled in the city."

"As you wish. We can make out without it." He hoped he sounded more convincing than he felt.

"And you understand that my daughter will hardly be interested in seeing you after this?"

"I understand. You understand, too, that her refusal to see the press might easily be misconstrued under the circumstances?"

Mr. Hitchcock said nothing. He did not even glare. He turned and walked out of the room, closing the door gently. His quiet exit was more effectively threatening than any blustering and slamming could have been.

MacVeagh stood by the desk a moment and thought about Rubicons and stuff. His eyes were hard and his lips firmly set when he looked up as Whalen entered.

"It's almost midnight," the old printer said.

MacVeagh grabbed the phone. "Two three two," he said. "You're still bound to walk out on me, Whalen?"

"Needs must, John."

"OK. I can make out without you. I can make out without H. A. Hitchcock and his— Hello. Mrs. Belden? . . . MacVeagh speaking. Look, I'm sorry to wake you up at this hour, but could you go up and get Luke Sellers out of bed and tell him I want him over here right away? It's important. . . . Thanks." He hung up. "Between us, Molly and I can whip Luke back into some sort of shape as a printer. We'll make out."

"Good, John. I should be sorry to inconvenience you. And have you thought of your wish?"

MacVeagh grinned. "I've had more important things on my mind, Whalen. Go run along now. I'm sorry to lose you; you know that. And I wish you luck, whatever it is you're up to. Goodbye."

"Please John." The old man's deep voice was earnest. "I do

not wish you to lose what is rightfully yours. What is your wish? If you need money, if you need love—"

MacVeagh thumped his desk. "I've got a wish, all right. And it's not love nor money. I've got a paper and I've got a debt to that paper and its readers. What happened tonight'll happen again. It's bound to. And sometime I may not have the strength to fight it, God help me. So I've got a wish."

"Yes, John?"

"Did you ever look at our masthead? Sometimes you can see things so often that you never really see them. But look at that masthead. It's got a slogan on it, under where it says '*Grover Sentinel.*' Old Jonathan Minter put that slogan there, and that slogan was the first words he ever spoke to me when he took me on here. He was a great old man, and I've got a debt to him too, and to his slogan.

"Do you know what a slogan really means? It doesn't mean a come-on, a bait. It doesn't mean Eat Wootsy-Tootsie and Watch Your Hair Curl. It means a rallying call, a battle cry."

"I know, John."

"And that's what this slogan is, the *Sentinel's* battle cry: '*We print the truth.*' So this is my wish, and if anybody had a stack of Bibles handy I'd swear to it on them: May the *Sentinel* never depart from that slogan. May that slogan itself be true, in the fullest meaning of truth. May there never be lies or suppression or evasions in the *Sentinel,* because always and forever *we print the truth.*"

It was impossible to see what Whalen Smith did with his hands. They moved too nimbly. For a moment it seemed as though their intricate pattern remained glowing in the air. Then it was gone, and Whalen said, "I have never granted a nobler wish. Nor," he added, "a more dangerous one."

He was gone before MacVeagh could ask what he meant.

II.

Wednesday's extra of the Grover *Sentinel* carried the full, uncensored story of the murder of Agnes Rogers, and a fine job Molly had done of it. It carried some filling matter too, of course—much of it mats from the syndicate—eked out with local items from the spindles, like the announcement of Old Man Herkimer's funeral and the secretary's report of the meeting of the Ladies' Aid at Mrs. Warren's.

There was no way of telling that one of those local items was infinitely more important to the future of John MacVeagh and of Grover itself than the front-page story.

MacVeagh woke up around two on Wednesday afternoon. They'd worked all night on the extra, he and Molly and Luke. He'd never thought at the time to wonder where the coffee came from that kept them going; he realized now it must have been Molly who supplied it.

But they'd got out the extra; that was the main thing. Sensationalism? Vultures, as Molly had said? Maybe he might have thought so before H. A. Hitchcock's visit. Maybe another approach, along those lines, might have gained Hitchcock's end. But he knew, as well as any man can ever know his own motives, that the driving force that carried them through last night's frantic activity was no lust for sensationalism, no greed for sales, but a clean, intense desire to print the truth for Grover.

The fight wasn't over. The extra was only the start. Tomorrow he would be preparing Friday's regular issue, and in that—

The first stop, he decided, was the station. It might be possible to get something out of Chief Hanby. Though he doubted if the chief was clear enough of debt to Manson's bank, to say nothing of political obligations, to take a very firm stand against H. A. Hitchcock.

MacVeagh met her in the anteroom of the station. She was coming out of the chief's private office, and Phil Rogers was with her. He had just his normal pallor now, and looked almost human. Still not human enough, though, to justify the smile she was giving him and the way her hand rested on his arm.

That smile lit up the dark, dusty little office. It hardly

mattered that she wasn't smiling at MacVeagh. Her smile was beauty itself, in the absolute, no matter who it was aimed at. Her every movement was beauty, and her clothes were a part of her, so that they and her lithe flesh made one smooth loveliness.

And this was H. A. Hitchcock's daughter Laura, and Mac-Veagh was more tongue-tied than he usually was in her presence. He never could approach her without feeling like a high school junior trying to get up nerve to date the belle of the class.

"Laura—" he said.

She had a copy of the extra in one hand. Her fingers twitched it as she said, "I don't think there is anything we could possibly say to each other, Mr. MacVeagh."

Philip Rogers was obviously repressing a snicker. MacVeagh turned to him. "I'm glad to see you looking better, Phil. I was worried about you last night. Tell me: how did you happen to find the body?"

Laura jerked at Philip's arm. "Come on, Phil. Don't be afraid of the big, bad editor."

Philip smiled, in the style that best suited his pallid profile. "Quite a journalistic achievement, this extra, Johnny. More credit to your spirit than to your judgment, but quite an achievement. Of course, you were far too carried away by it all to do any proofreading?"

"Come *on*, Phil."

"Hold it, Laura. I can't resist showing our fearless young journalist his triumph of accuracy. Look, Johnny. He took the paper from her and pointed to an inside page. "Your account of Old Man Herkimer's funeral: 'Today under the old oaks of Mountain View Cemetery, the last rites of Josephus R. Herkimer, 17, of this city—'" He laughed. "The old boy ought to enjoy that posthumous youth."

"Seventeen, seventy-seven!" MacVeagh snorted. "If that's all that's gone wrong in that edition, I'm a miracle man. But, Laura—"

"You're quite right, Mr. MacVeagh. There are far worse

things wrong with that edition than the misprint that amuses Philip."

"Will you be home tonight?" he said with harsh abruptness.

"For you, Mr. MacVeagh, I shall never be home. Good day."

Philip followed her. He looked over his shoulder once and grinned, never knowing how close his pallid profile came to being smashed forever.

Chief Hanby was frowning miserably as MacVeagh came into the office. The delicate smoke of his cigar indicated one far above his usual standard—it was easy to guess its source —but he wasn't enjoying it.

"'Render therefore unto Caesar,'" he said, "'the things which are Caesar's; and unto God the things that are God's.' Matthew, twenty-two, twenty-one. Only who knows which is which?"

"Troubles, Chief?" MacVeagh asked.

Chief Hanby had a copy of the extra on his desk. His hand touched it almost reverently as he spoke. "He went to see you, John?"

"Yeah."

"And still you printed this? You're a brave man, John, a brave man."

"You're no coward yourself, Chief. Remember when Nose O'Leary escaped from the state pen and decided Grover'd make a nice hide-out?"

The chief's eyes glowed with the memory of that past exploit. "But that was different, John. A man can maybe risk his life when he can't risk— I'll tell you this much: I'm not talking to you, not right now. Nothing's settled, nothing's ripe, I don't know a thing. But I'm still groping. And I'm not going to stop groping. And if I grope out an answer to anything—whatever the answer is, you'll get it."

MacVeagh thrust out his hand. "I couldn't ask fairer than that, Chief. We both want the truth, and between us we'll get it."

Chief Hanby looked relieved. "I wouldn't blame H. A. too much John. Remember, he's under a strain. These labor troubles are getting him, and with the election coming up at the plant—"

"And whose fault are the troubles? Father Byrne's committee suggested a compromise and a labor-management plan. The men were willing enough—"

"Even they aren't any more. Not since Bricker took over. We've all got our troubles. Take Jake Willis, now— Why, speak of the devil!"

The coroner looked as though he could easily take a prize for worried expressions away from even MacVeagh and the chief. The greeting didn't help it. He said, "There's too much loose talk about devils. It's as barbarous as swearing by God." But his heart wasn't in his conventional protest.

"What *is* the matter, Jake?" the chief asked. "You aren't worried just on account of you've got an inquest coming up, are you?"

"No, it ain't that—" His eyes rested distrustfully on MacVeagh.

"Off the record," said the editor. "You've my word."

"All right, only— No. It ain't no use. You wouldn't believe me if I told you. . . . Either of you going back past my establishment?"

The chief was tied to his office. But John MacVeagh went along, his curiosity stimulated. His questions received no answers. Jake Willis simply plodded along South Street like a man ridden by the devils in which he refused to believe.

And what, MacVeagh asked himself, would Jake think of a tramp printer who claimed to grant wishes? For the matter of that, what do I think— But there was too much else going on for him to spare much thought for Whalen Smith.

Jake Willis led the way past his assistant without a nod, on back into the chapel. There was a casket in place there, duly embanked with floral tributes. The folding chairs were set up; there was a Bible on the lectern and music on the organ. The stage was completely set for a funeral, and MacVeagh remembered about Old Man Herkimer.

"They're due here at three thirty," Jake whined. "And

how'll I dare show it to 'em? I don't know how it happened. Jimmy, he swears he don't know a thing neither. God knows!" he concluded in a despairing rejection of his skepticism.

"It is Old Man Herkimer?"

"It ought to be. That's what I put in there yesterday, Old Man Herkimer's body. And I go to look at it today and—"

The face plate of the coffin was closed. "I'm going to have to leave it that way," he said. "I can't let 'em see— I'll have to tell 'em confidential-like that he looked too— I don't know. I'll have to think of something."

He opened up the plate. MacVeagh looked in. It was a Herkimer, all right. There was no mistaking the wide-set eyes and thin lips of that clan. But Old Man Herkimer, as the original copy for the item in the extra had read, was seventy-seven when he died. The boy in the coffin—

"Don't look a day over seventeen, does he?" said Jake Willis.

"Father Byrne," said John MacVeagh, "I'm asking you this, not as a priest, but as the best-read scholar in Grover: Do miracles happen?"

Father Byrne smiled. "It's hard not to reply as a priest; but I'll try. Do miracles happen? By dictionary definition, I'll say yes; certainly." He crossed the study to the stand that held the large unabridged volume. "Here's what Webster calls a miracle: 'An event or effect in the physical world beyond or out of the ordinary course of things, deviating from the known laws of nature, or,' and this should be put in italics, '*or transcending our knowledge of those laws.*'"

MacVeagh nodded. "I see. We obviously don't know all the laws. We're still learning them. And what doesn't fit in with the little we know—"

"'An event,'" the priest read on, "'which cannot be accounted for by any of the known forces of nature and which is, therefore, attributed to a supernatural force.' So you see, miraculousness is more in the attitude of the beholder than in the nature of the fact."

"And the logical reaction of a reasonable man confronted with an apparent miracle would be to test it by scientific method, to try to find the as yet unknown natural law behind it?"

"I should think so. Again being careful not to speak as a priest."

"Thanks, Father."

"But what brings all this up, John? Don't tell me you have been hearing voices or such? I'd have more hope of converting an atheist like Jake to the supernatural than a good hard-headed agnostic like you."

"Nothing, Father. I just got to thinking— Let you know if anything comes of it."

Philip Rogers was waiting for MacVeagh at the *Sentinel* office. There was a puzzling splash of bright red on his white cheek. Molly was there, too, typing with furious concentration.

"I want to talk to you alone, Johnny," Rogers said.

Molly started to rise, but MacVeagh said, "Stick around. Handy things sometimes, witnesses. Well, Phil?"

Philip Rogers glared at the girl. "I just wanted to give you a friendly warning, Johnny. You know as personnel manager out at the plant I get a pretty good notion of how the men are feeling."

"Too bad you've never put it over to H. A., then."

Philip shrugged. "I don't mean the reds and the malcontents. Let Bricker speak for them—while he's still able. I mean the good, solid American workers, that understand the plant and the management."

"H. A.'s company stooges, in short. OK., Phil, so what are they thinking?"

"They don't like the way you're playing up this murder. They think you ought to show a little sympathy for the boss in his bereavement. They think he's got troubles enough with Bricker and the Congressional committee."

MacVeagh smiled. "Now I get it."

"Get what?"

"I'd forgotten about the committee. So that's what's back of all the hush-hush. A breath of scandal, a suspicion that there might be a murderer in the Hitchcock clan—it could so easily sway a congressman who was trying to evaluate the motives behind H. A.'s deals. He's got to be Caesar's wife. Above suspicion."

"At least," Philip said scornfully, "you have too much journalistic sense to print wild guesses like that. That's something. But remember what I said about the men."

"So?"

"So they might decide to clean out the *Sentinel* some night."

MacVeagh's hand clenched into a tight fist. Then slowly he forced it to relax. "Phil," he said, "I ought to batter that pallor of yours to a nice, healthy pulp. But you're not worth it. Tell the company police I'm saving my fists for their vigilante raid. Now get out of here, while I've still got sense enough to hold myself back."

Philip was smiling confidently as he left, but his face was a trifle paler even than usual.

MacVeagh expressed himself with calculated liberty on Philip Rogers' ancestry, nature, and hobbies for almost a minute before he was aware of Molly. "Sorry," he broke off to say, "but I meant it."

"Say it again for me, boss. And in spades."

"I should have socked him. He—" MacVeagh frowned. "When I came in, it looked as though someone might already have had that pious notion." He looked at Molly queerly. "Did you—"

"He made a pass at me," Molly said unemotionally. "He thought maybe he could enlist me on their side that way, keep me from writing my stuff up. I didn't mind the pass. Why I slapped him was, he seemed to think I ought to be flattered."

MacVeagh laughed. "Good girl." He sat down at the other typewriter and rolled in a sheet of copy paper. "We'll hold the fort." He began to type.

Molly looked up from her own copy. "Get any new leads, boss?"

"No," he said reflectively. "This is just an experiment." He wrote:

A sudden freakish windstorm hit Grover last night. For ten minutes windows rattled furiously, and old citizens began to recall the Great Wind of '97.

The storm died down as suddenly as it came, however. No damage was done except to the statue of General Wigginsby in Courthouse Square, which was blown from its pedestal, breaking off the head and one arm.

C. B. Tooly, chairman of the Grover Scrap Drive, expressed great pleasure at the accident. Members of the Civic Planning Commission were reportedly even more pleased at the removal of Grover's outstanding eyesore.

He tore the sheet out of the typewriter. Then a perversely puckish thought struck him and he inserted another page. He headed it:

WHAT PEOPLE ARE SAYING

Coroner Jake Willis has apparently abandoned his thirty-year standing of strict atheism. "In times like these," he said last night, "we need faith in something outside of ourselves. I've been a stubborn fool for too long."

Molly spoke as he stopped typing. "What kind of experiment, boss?"

"Let you know Friday," he said. "Hold on tight, Molly. If his experiment works—"

For a moment he leaned back in his chair, his eyes aglow with visions of fabulous possibilities. Then he laughed out loud and got on with his work.

III.

No paper was ever gotten out by a more distracted editor than that Friday's issue of the Grover *Sentinel*.

Two things preoccupied John MacVeagh. One, of course,

was his purely rational experiment in scientific methods as applied to miracles. Not that he believed for an instant that whatever gestures Whalen Smith had woven in the air could impart to the *Sentinel* the absolute and literal faculty of printing the truth—and making it the truth by printing it. But the episode of the seventeen-year-old corpse had been a curious one. It deserved checking—rationally and scientifically, you understand.

And the other distraction was the effect upon Grover of the murder.

Almost, John MacVeagh was becoming persuaded that his crusading truthfulness had been a mistake. Perhaps there was some justice in the attitude of the bluenoses who decry sensational publishing. Certainly the town's reaction to the sensational news was not healthy.

On the one hand, inevitably, there was the group—vocally headed by Banker Manson—who claimed that what they called the "smear campaign" was a vile conspiracy between MacVeagh and labor leader Tim Bricker.

That was to be expected. With Manson and his crowd, you pushed certain buttons and you got certain automatic responses. But MacVeagh had not foreseen the reverse of the coin he had minted: the bitterness and resentment among the little people.

"Whatddaya expect?" he overheard in Clem's barber shop. "You take a guy like Hitchcock, you don't think they can do anything to him, do you? Why, them guys can get away with—" The speaker stopped, as though that were a little more than he had meant to say.

But there were other voices to take up his accusation.

"Go ahead, Joe, say it. Get away with murder."

"Sure, who's gonna try to pin a rap on the guy that owns the town?"

"What good's a police chief when he's all sewed up pretty in Hitchcock's pocket?"

"And the *Sentinel* don't dare print half it knows. You all know the editor's got a yen for Hitchcock's daughter. Well—"

"Somebody ought to do something."

That last was the crystallized essence of their feeling. Somebody ought to do something. And those simple words can be meaningful and ugly. They were on many tongues in Germany in the twenties.

John MacVeagh thought about the sorcerer's apprentice, who summoned the powers beyond his control. But, no, that was a pointed but still light and amusing story. This was becoming grim. If he and Molly could only crack this murder, cut through to the solution and dispel once and for all these dissatisfied grumblings—

But how was that to be done? They had so few facts, and nothing to disprove the fantastic notion of a wandering tramp invading the upper story of a fully occupied house without disturbing a soul save his victim. If some trick of psychological pressure could force a confession—

MacVeagh mused on these problems as he walked back to the office after dinner on Thursday, and came regretfully to the conclusion that there was nothing to do but go on as per schedule: print Friday's regular edition with what follow-up was possible on the murder story, and dig and delve as best they could to reach toward the truth.

He frowned as he entered the office. Sidewalk loafers weren't so common on Spruce Street. They hung out more on South, or down near the station on Jackson. But this evening there was quite a flock of them within a few doors of the *Sentinel*.

Lucretius Sellers was chuckling over the copy he was setting up. "That sure is a good one you've got here on Jake, Johnny. Lord, I never did think I'd see the day— Maybe pretty soon we'll see that ascetic atheist taking a drink, too. Which reminds me—"

He caught MacVeagh's eye and paused. "Nope. Don't know what I was going to say, Johnny." He had been sober now since Whalen Smith's departure had caused his sudden drafting back into his old profession. And he knew, and MacVeagh knew, that the only way for him to stay sober was to climb completely on the wagon.

"Making out all right, Luke?" MacVeagh asked.

"Swell, Johnny. You know, you think you forget things, but you don't. Not things you learn with your hands, you don't. You ask me last week could I still set type and I'd say no. But there in my fingers—they still remembered. But look, Johnny—"

"Yes?"

"This item about the Wigginsby statue. It's a swell idea, but it just hasn't happened. I was past there not an hour ago, and the old boy's as big and ugly as ever. And besides, this says 'last night.' That means tonight—how can I set up what hasn't happened yet?"

"Luke, you've been grand to me. You've helped me out of a spot by taking over. But if I can impose on you just a leetle bit more—please don't ask any questions about the general's statue. Just set it up and forget about it. Maybe I'll have something to tell you about that item tomorrow, maybe not. But in any case—"

His voice broke off sharply. He heard loud thumping feet in the front office. He heard Molly's voice shrilling. "What do you want? You can't all of you come crowding in here like this!"

Another voice said, "We're in, ain't we, sister?" It was a calm, cold voice.

"We've got work to do," Molly persisted. "We've got a paper to get out."

"That," said the voice, "is what *you* think." There was a jangling crash that could be made only by a typewriter hurled to the floor.

MacVeagh shucked his coat as he stepped into the front office. No time for rolling up sleeves. He snapped the lock on the door as he came through; that'd keep them from the press for a matter of minutes, anyway. He felt Luke at his heels, but he didn't look. He walked straight to the towering redhead who stood beside Molly's desk, the wrecked typewriter at his feet, and delivered the punch that he had neglected to give Phil Rogers.

The redhead was a second too late to duck, but he rolled

with it. His left came up to answer it with a short jab, but suddenly he staggered back. His face was a dripping black mess, and he let out an angry roar. He charged in wide-open fury, and this time MacVeagh connected.

He'd recognized the redhead. Chief of Hitchcock's company police. He'd heard about him—how he had a tough skull and a tougher belly, but a glass chin. For once, MacVeagh reflected, rumor was right.

It was the silent quickness of the whole episode that impressed the other Hitchcock men and halted them for a moment. MacVeagh blessed Molly for her beautifully timed toss with the ink bottle. He glanced at her and saw that she now held her desk scissors ready in a stabbing grip. Luke Sellers held a wrench.

But they were three, and there were a dozen men in the room besides the fallen redhead. One of them stepped forward now, a swarthy little man whose face was stubbled in blue-black save for the white streak of an old knife scar.

"You shouldn't ought to of done that," he said. "Red didn't mean you no harm, not personal. No roughhouse, see? And if you listen to reason, why, OK."

"And if I don't?" MacVeagh asked tersely.

"If you don't? Well, then it looks like we're going to have to smash up that pretty press of yours, mister. But there don't nobody need to get hurt. You ain't got a chance against the bunch of us. You might as well admit it if you don't want us to have to smash up that pretty puss of yours too."

"What can we do?" Molly whispered. "He's right; we can't stand them all off. But to smash the press—"

Luke Sellers waved his wrench and issued wholesale invitations to slaughter.

Scarface grinned. "Call off the old man, mister. He's apt to get hurt. Well, how's about it? Do you let us in nice and peaceable or do we smash down the door?"

MacVeagh opened a drawer of the desk and put his hand in. "You can try smashing," he said, "if you don't mind bullets."

"We don't mind bluffs," said Scarface dryly. "OK, boys!"

MacVeagh took his empty hand from the drawer. There was only one thing to do, and that was to fight as long as he could. It was foolish, pointless, hopeless. But it was the only thing that a man could do.

The men came. Scarface had somehow managed wisely to drop to the rear of the charge. As they came, MacVeagh stooped. He rose with the wreck of the typewriter and hurled it. It took the first man out and brought the second thudding down with him. MacVeagh followed it with his fists.

Luke Sellers, as a long-standing authority on barroom brawls, claimed that the ensuing fight lasted less than a minute. It seemed closer to an hour to MacVeagh, closer yet to an eternity. Time vanished and there was nothing, no thinking, no reasoning, no problems, no values, nothing but the ache in his body as blows landed on it and the joy in his heart as his own blows connected and the salt warmth of blood in his mouth.

From some place a thousand light-years away he heard a voice bellowing, "Quit it! Lay off!" The words meant nothing. He paid no more attention to them than did the man who at the moment held his head in an elbow lock and pummeled it with a heavy ring-bearing fist. The voice sounded again as MacVeagh miraculously wriggled loose, his neck aching with the strain, and delivered an unorthodox knee blow to the ring wearer. Still the voice meant nothing.

But the shot did.

It thudded into the ceiling, and its echoes rang through the room. The voice bellowed again, "Now do you believe I mean it? Lay off. All of you!"

The sound and smell of powder wield a weighty influence in civilian reactions. The room was suddenly very still. MacVeagh wiped sweat and blood from his face, forced his eyes open, and discovered that he could see a little.

He could see a tall gaunt man with crudely Lincolnian features striding toward him. He recognized the labor leader. "Sergeant Bricker, I presume?" he said groggily.

Bricker looked his surprise. "Sergeant? MacVeagh, you're punchy."

"Uh-huh." MacVeagh cast dim eyes on the two armed body-guards at the door and at the restlessly obedient men of the company's police. "Don't you know? You're the U.S. Marines."

Then somebody pulled a blackdotted veil over the light, which presently went out altogether.

At first John MacVeagh thought it was a hangover. To be sure, he had never had a hangover like this. To be equally sure, he resolved that he never would again. A convention of gnomes was holding high revels in his skull and demonstrating the latest rock-drilling gadgets.

He groaned and tried to roll over. His outflung arm felt emptiness, and his body started to slip. A firm hand shoved him back into place.

He opened his eyes. They ached even more resolutely when open, and he quickly dropped his lids. But he had seen that he was on the narrow couch in the back office, that Molly's hand had rescued him from rolling off, and that it was day-light.

"Are you OK, boss?" Molly's voice was softer than usual.

"I'll be all right as soon as they shovel the dirt in on me."

"Can you listen while I tell you things?"

"I can try. Tell me the worst. What did I do? Climb chandeliers and sing bawdy ballads to the Ladies' Aid?"

He heard Molly laugh. "You weren't plastered, boss. You were in a fight. Remember?"

The shudder that ran through him testified to his memory. "I remember now. Hitchcock's little playmates. And Bricker showed up and staged the grand rescue and I passed out. Fine, upstanding hero I am. Can't take it—"

"You took plenty. Doc Quillan was worried about a con-cussion at first. That's why he had us keep you here—didn't want to risk moving you home. But he looked at you again this morning and he thinks you'll be OK."

"And I never even felt it. Exalted, that's what I must've been. Wonderful thing, lust of battle. This morning! Sun-light!" He forced his eyes open and tried to sit up. "Then it's Friday! The paper should be—"

Molly pushed him back. "Don't worry, boss. The *Sentinel* came out this morning. Everything's hunky-dory. Bricker lent us a couple of men to help, and it's all swell."

"Bricker— Where'd we be without him? A god out of the machinists' union. And the paper's out. . . ." Suddenly he tried to sit up again, then decided against it. "Molly!"

"Yes, boss?"

"Have you been in Courthouse Square this morning?"

"No, boss. Doc Quillan said I ought to— I mean, there's been so much to do here in the office—"

"Have you seen Jake?"

"Uh-huh. That was funny. He dropped in this morning. I think he heard about the ruckus and wanted to see was there anything in his line of business. And has he changed!"

"Changed?" What voice MacVeagh had was breathless.

"He practically delivered a sermon. All about what a fool he's been and man cannot live by bread alone and in times like these and stuff. Grover isn't going to seem the same without Jake's atheism."

"Scientific method," said MacVeagh.

"What do you mean, boss?"

"Molly, there's something I've got to tell you about the *Sentinel*. You'll think I'm crazy maybe, but there's too much to disregard. You've got to believe it."

"Boss, you know I believe every word you say." She laughed, but the laugh didn't succeed in discounting her obvious sincerity.

"Molly—"

"Hi, MacVeagh! Feeling fit again? Ready to take on a dozen more finks?"

MacVeagh focused his eyes on the gangling figure. "Bricker! I'm glad to see you. Almost as glad as I was last night. I don't feel too bright and loquacious yet, but when I do, consider yourself scheduled for the best speech of gratitude ever made in Grover."

Bricker waved one hand. "That's OK. Nothing to it. United front. We've got to gang up—victims of oppression. Collective security."

"Anything I can do for you—"

"You're doing plenty." Bricker pulled up a chair and sat down, his long legs sprawling in front of him. "You know, MacVeagh, I had you figured wrong."

"How so?"

"I thought you were just another editor. You know, a guy who joins liberal committees and prints what the advertisers want. But I had the wrong picture. You've got ideas and the guts to back 'em."

MacVeagh basked. Praise felt good after what he'd been through. But Bricker's next words woke him up.

"How much did *you* try to shake Hitchcock down for?"

"How much— I— Why— Look, Bricker, I don't get you."

Bricker eased himself more comfortably into the chair and said, "He don't shake easy. Don't I know! But a tree with them apples is worth shaking."

"You mean you're . . . you've been blackmailing Hitchcock?"

"I can talk to you, MacVeagh. Nobody else in this town has got the guts or the sense to see my angle. But you've got angles of your own; you can understand. Sure I've been shaking him down. Before I moved in on that local, it sounded like a Socialist Party pink tea. 'Better working conditions. A living wage. Rights of labor.'" He expressed his editorial comment in a ripe raspberry. "I saw the possibilities and I took over. Old Hasenberg and the rest of those boys—they don't know from nothing about politics. A few plants, a little pressure, and I was in—but for good. Then I put it up to H. A.: 'How much is it worth to you to get along without strikes?'"

MacVeagh opened his mouth, but the words stuck there.

"So you see?" Bricker went on calmly. "We can work together. The more pressure you put on Hitchcock with this murder scandal, the more he can't afford to risk labor trouble. And vice, as the fellow says, versa. So you can count on me any time you need help. And when this blows over— There's lots more can happen, MacVeagh, lots more. Between us, we can wind up owning this town.

"Keep the murder story running as long as you can. That's

my advice. If it begins to look like a solution that'll clear Hitchcock and his family, keep it quiet. Keep the pressure on him, and he'll kick through in the end. I know his type. . . . What is it you're really after, MacVeagh? Just cash, or the daughter?"

MacVeagh was still speechless. He was glad that Luke Sellers came in just then. It kept him from sputtering.

Luke was fair-to-middling speechless himself. He nodded at Bricker and Molly, and finally he managed to say, "Johnny, if I hadn't been on the wagon for two days I swear I'd go on and stay there!"

Bricker looked interested. "What's happened?"

"You were in Courthouse Square," said John MacVeagh.

"That's it, all right. I was in Courthouse Square. And General Wigginsby has enlisted in the scrap drive. Funny freak wind last night, the boys at Clem's say. Didn't do any other damage. But, Johnny, how you knew—"

"What is all this?" Bricker broke in. "What's the angle on the statue, MacVeagh?"

The editor smiled wearily. "No angle, Bricker. Not the way you mean. Nothing you'd understand. But maybe something that's going to make a big difference to you and your angles."

Bricker glanced at Molly and touched his head. "Still don't feel so good, huh? Well, I've got to be getting along. I'll drop in again off and on, MacVeagh. We've got plans to make. Glad I helped you last night, and remember: keep up the good work."

Luke Sellers looked after the lean figure. "What's he mean by that?"

"Not what he thinks he means," said John MacVeagh, "I hope. Out of the frying pan—"

Molly shuddered. "He's as bad as H. A. Hitchcock."

"Just about. And if I hush up the murder, I'm playing H. A.'s game, and if I give it a big play, I'm stooging for Bricker's racket. I guess," he said thoughtfully, "there's only one thing to do. Molly, Luke! We're getting out another extra."

"Life," said Luke Sellers, "used to be a sight simpler before

I went and got sober. Now nothing makes any sense. An extra? What for?"

"We're going to get out another extra," MacVeagh repeated. "Tomorrow. And the banner head is going to be: MURDERER CONFESSES."

"But, boss, how do we know—"

Luke Sellers was thinking of General Wigginsby. "Hush, Molly," he said. "Let's see what happens."

IV.

MURDERER CONFESSES

At a late hour last night, the murderer of Mrs. Agnes Rogers walked into the Grover police station and gave himself up. Police Chief J. B. Hanby is holding him incommunicado until his confession has been checked.

The murderer's identity, together with a full text of his confession, will be released in time for a further special edition of the *Sentinel* later today, Chief Hanby promises.

This story was set up and printed in the Grover *Sentinel* late Friday night and was on sale early Saturday morning. At eleven fifty-five P.M. Friday, Neville Markham, butler to Mrs. Agnes Rogers, walked into the police station and confessed to the murder.

"'The butler did it,'" said Molly between scornful quotation marks.

"After all," said John MacVeagh, "I suppose sometime the butler must do it. Just by the law of averages."

It was Saturday night, and the two of them were sitting in the office talking after the frantic strain of getting out the second extra of the day. Luke Sellers had gone home and gone to bed with a fifth.

"A man can stay a reformed character just so long," he said, "and you won't be needing me much for a couple of days.

Unless," he added, "you get any more brilliant inspirations before the fact. Tell me, Johnny, how did you . . ." But he let the query trail off unfinished and went home, clutching his fifth as though it were the one sure thing in a wambling world.

The second extra had carried the butler's whole story: how he, a good servant of the Lord, had endured as long as he could his mistress' searching for strange gods until finally a Voice had said to him, "Smite thou this evil woman," and he smote. Afterward he panicked and tried to make it look like robbery. He thought he had succeeded until Friday night, when the same Voice said to him, "Go thou and proclaim thy deed," and he went and proclaimed.

MacVeagh wished he'd been there. He'd bet the butler and Chief Hanby had fun swapping texts.

"'The butler did it,'" Molly repeated. "And I never so much as mentioned the butler in my stories. You don't even *think* of butlers—not since the twenties."

"Well, anyway, the murder is solved. That's the main thing. No more pressure from either Hitchcock or Bricker. No more mumbling dissension in Grover."

"But don't you feel . . . oh, I don't know . . . cheated? It's no fun when a murder gets solved that way. If you and I could've figured it out and broken the story, or even if Chief Hanby had cracked it with dogged routine . . . But this way it's so flat!"

"Weary, flat, and stale, Molly, I agree. But not unprofitable. We learned the truth, and the truth has solved a lot of our problems."

"Only,—"

"Yes, Molly?"

"Only, boss— How? I've got to know how. How could you know that the butler was going to hear another Voice and confess? And that isn't all. Luke told me about General Wigginsby."

Molly had never seen John MacVeagh look so serious. "All right," he said. "I've got to tell somebody, anyway. It eats at me. . . . OK. You remember how Whalen left so abruptly? Well,—"

Molly sat wide-eyed and agape when he finished the story. "Ordinarily," she said at last, "I'd say you were crazy, boss. But Old Man Herkimer and General Wigginsby and the butler . . . What *was* Whalen—"

MacVeagh had wondered about that too. Sometimes he could still almost feel around the office the lingering presence of that gaunt old man with the books you couldn't read and the beard that wasn't there. What had he been?

"And what're you going to do, boss? It looks like you can do practically anything. If anything we print in the paper turns out to be the truth— What *are* you going to do?"

"Come in!" MacVeagh yelled, as someone knocked on the door.

It was Father Byrne, followed by a little man whose blue eyes were brightly alive in his old, seamed face. "Good evening, John, Molly. This is Mr. Hasenberg—you've probably met him. Used to head the union out at the Hitchcock plant before Tim Bricker moved in."

"Evening, folks," said Mr. Hasenberg. He tipped his cap with a hand that was as sensitive and alive as his eyes—the hardened, ready hand of a skilled workman.

MacVeagh furnished his guests with chairs. Then he said, "To what am I indebted and such?"

"Mr. Hasenberg has a problem, John, and it's mine too. And it's yours and everybody's. Go on, sir."

Mr. Hasenberg spoke in a dry, precise tone. "Bricker's called a strike. We don't want to strike. We don't like or trust Hitchcock, but we do trust the arbitration committee that Father Byrne's on. We've accepted their decision, and we still hope we can get the management to. But Bricker put over the strike vote with some sharp finagling, and that'll probably mean the Army taking over the plant."

"And I know Bricker . . ." said MacVeagh. "But where do I come in?"

"Advice and publicity," said Father Byrne. "First, have you

any ideas? Second, will you print the statement Mr. Hasenberg's preparing on the real stand of the men, without
Bricker's trimmings?"

"Second, of course. First—" he hesitated. "Tell me, Mr.
Hasenberg, if you were free of Bricker, do you think you could
get the management to come to terms?"

"Maybe. They ain't all like Hitchcock and Phil Rogers.
There's some of them want to get the stuff out and the war
won as bad as we do. Now, ever since Mathers went to Washington, the post of general manager's been vacant. Suppose,
now, Johansen should get that appointment—he'd string along
with the committee's decision, I'm pretty sure."

MacVeagh pulled a scratch pad toward him. "Johansen—
First name?"

"Boss! You aren't going to—"

"*Sh*, Molly. And now, Father, if you could give me an out-
line of the committee's terms . . ."

So Ingve Johansen became general manager of the Hitchcock plant, and Mr. Hasenberg resumed control of the union,
after evidence had been uncovered which totally discredited
Tim Bricker, and the arbitrated terms of the committee were
accepted by labor and management, and the joint labor-management council got off to a fine start—all of which the
burghers of Grover read with great pleasure in the *Sentinel*.

There was another important paragraph in that Friday's
issue: an announcement that starting in another week the
Sentinel was to become a daily.

"We've got to, Molly," MacVeagh had insisted. "There's so
much we can do for Grover. If we can settle the troubles at
Hitchcock, that's just a start. We can make this over into the
finest community in the country. And we haven't space in one
small weekly edition. With a daily we can do things gradually,
step by step . . ."

"And what, boss, do we use for money? That'll mean more
presses, more men, more paper. Where's the money coming
from?"

"That," said John MacVeagh, "I don't know."

And he never did. There was simply a small statement in the paper:

ANONYMOUS
BENEFACTOR
ENDOWS *SENTINEL*

Mr. Manson was never able to find a teller who remembered receiving that astonishingly large deposit made to the credit of the *Sentinel's* account; but there it was, all duly entered.

And so the Grover *Sentinel* became a daily, printing the truth.

V.

If it's all right with you, we'll skip pretty fast over the next part of the story. The days of triumph never make interesting reading. The rise and fall—that's your dramatic formula. The build-up can be stirring and the letdown can be tragic, but there's no interest in the flat plateau at the top.

So there's no need to tell in detail all that happened in Grover after the *Sentinel* went daily. You can imagine the sort of thing: How the Hitchcock plant stepped up its production and turned out a steady flow of war matériel that was the pride of the county, the state, and even the country. How Doc Quillan tracked down, identified, and averted the epidemic that threatened the workers' housing project. How Chief Hanby finally got the goods on the gamblers who were moving in on the South Side and cleaned up the district. How the Grover Red Cross drive went a hundred percent over its quota. How the expected meat shortage never materialized . . . You get the picture.

All this is just the plateau, the level stretch between the rise and the fall. Not that John MacVeagh expected the fall. Nothing like that seemed possible, even though Molly worried.

"You know, boss," she said one day, "I was reading ove
some of the books I used to love when I was a kid. This wish
—it's magic, isn't it?"

MacVeagh snapped the speaking box on his desk and gav
a succinct order to the assistant editor. He was the chief exec
utive of a staff now. Then he turned back and said, "Why, yes
Molly, I guess you might call it that. Magic, miracle—wha
do we care so long as it enables us to accomplish all we'r
doing?"

"I don't know. But sometimes I get scared. Those books
especially the ones by E. Nesbit—"

MacVeagh grinned. "Scared of kids' books?"

"I know it sounds silly, boss, but kids' books are the onl
place you can find out about magic. And there seems to b
only one sure thing about it: You can know there's a catch t
it. There's always a catch."

MacVeagh didn't think any further about that. What stuc
in his mind was phrases like those he heard down at Clem'
barber shop:

"Hanged if I know what's come over this burg. Seems lik
for a couple of months there just can't nothing go wron;
Ever since that trouble out at the plant when they got rid c
Bricker, this burg is just about perfect, seems like."

Those were fine words. They fed the soul. They made yo
forget that little, nagging, undefined discontent that was ra
kling underneath and threatening to spoil all this wonderf
miracle—or magic, if you prefer. They even made you b
polite to H. A. Hitchcock when he came to pay his respects t
you after the opening of the new *Sentinel* Building.

He praised MacVeagh as an outstanding example of fre
enterprise. (A year or so ago he would have said rugged ind
vidualism, but the phrase had been replaced in his vocabular
by its more noble-sounding synonym.) He probed with ma
to-man frankness trying to learn where the financial backin
had come from. He all but apologized for the foolish misu
derstanding over the butler's crime. And he ended up with
dinner invitation in token of reconciliation.

MacVeagh accepted. But his feelings were mixed, and they were even more mixed when he dropped into the office on the night of the dinner, resplendent in white tie and tails, to check up some last-minute details on the reports of the election for councilman. He had just learned that Grizzle had had some nasty semi-Fascist tie-ups a year earlier, and must not be allowed to be elected.

"I don't know what's the matter," he confided to Molly after he'd attended to business. "I ought to be sitting on top of the world, and somehow I'm not. Maybe I almost see what the trouble is: No heavy."

"What does that mean, boss?"

"No opposition. Nothing to fight against. Just wield my white magic benevolently and that's that. I need a black magician to combat me on my own level. You've got to have a heavy."

"Are you so sure," Molly asked, "that yours is white magic?"

"Why—"

"Skip it, boss. But I think I know one thing that's the matter. And I think, God help me, that you'll realize it tonight?"

Molly's words couldn't have been truer if she had printed them in the *Sentinel*.

The party itself was painful. Not the dinner; that was as admirable as only H. A. Hitchcock's chef could contrive. But the company had been carefully chosen to give MacVeagh the idea that, now that he was making such a phenomenal success of himself, he was to be welcomed among the Best People of Grover.

There were the Mansons, of course, and Phil Rogers, and Major General Front, U.S.A., retired, and a half dozen others who formed a neat tight little society of mutual admiration and congratulation. The only halfway human person present seemed to be the new general manager of the plant, Johansen; but he sat at the other end of the table from MacVeagh, in the dominating shadow of Mrs. Manson's bosom.

MacVeagh himself was loomed over by Mrs. Front, who gave her own interpretation of the general's interpretation of the plans of the High Command. He nodded dutifully and gave every impression of listening, while he saw and heard and felt nothing but Laura Hitchcock across the table.

Every man dreams of Helen, but to few is it ever given to behold the face that can launch a thousand ships. This is well. Life is complicated enough, if often pleasantly so, when we love a pretty girl, a charming girl, a sweet girl. But when we see beauty, pure and radiant and absolute, we are lost.

MacVeagh had been lost since he first arrived in Grover and old Jonathan Minter sent him to cover Laura's coming-out party. After that she had gone east to college and he had told himself that it was all the champagne. He couldn't have seen what his heart remembered.

Then she came back, and since then no moment of his life had ever seemed quite complete. He never knew how he stood with her; he never even knew what she was like. He would begin to get acquainted with her, and then she would be off to visit her aunt in Florida or her cousins, before the war, in France. Since the war she had stayed in Grover, busy with the various volunteer activities entailed by her position as H. A. Hitchcock's daughter. He was beginning to know her, he thought; he was beginning to reach a point where—

And then came the murder and the quarrel with Hitchcock. And this was the first time that he had seen her since then.

She smiled and seemed friendly. Evidently, like her father, she looked upon MacVeagh with a new regard since he had begun his mysteriously spectacular climb to success.

She even exchanged an intimate and shuddering glance with him after dinner, when Mrs. Manson began to sing American folk ballads in the drawing room. MacVeagh took courage and pointed to the open French window behind her.

His throat choked when she accepted the hint. He joined her on the lawn, and they strolled quietly over to the pond where the croaking monotone of the frogs drowned out the distant shrilling of Mrs. Manson.

"What gets me," MacVeagh grunted, "is the people that call all that wonderful stuff 'ballads.' They're just plain songs, and good ones. And where they belong is a couple of guys that love them trying them out with one foot on the rail and the barkeep joining in the harmony. When the fancy folk begin singing them in drawing rooms with artistically contrived accompaniments—"

"I guess I'll just have to do without them then," said Laura. "I can't see myself in your barroom."

"Can't you?" There must have been something in the moon that stirred MacVeagh's daring. "Why not? There's a good, plain, honest bar not a mile from here that I like. Why don't we ditch the party and go—"

"Oh, John. Don't be silly. We couldn't. We're not bright young people, and it isn't smart to be like that any more. Everybody's serious now; this is war. And besides, you know, you have to think more of the company you're seen in now."

"Me?"

"Of course, John. Father's been telling me how wonderfully you're coming on. You're getting to be somebody. You have to look out for appearances."

"I'm afraid"—MacVeagh grinned—"I have congenitally low tastes. Can't I be a big-shot editor and still love the riff and the raff?"

"Of course not." She was perfectly serious, and MacVeagh felt a twinge of regret that such perfection of beauty was apparently not compatible with the least trace of humor. "You have to be thinking about settling down now."

"Settling down—" he repeated. This was so pat a cue, if he could get that lump out of his throat and go on with it. "You're right, Laura. At my age—" His voice was as harsh a croak as the frogs'.

"What's the matter, John?"

He harrumphed. "Something in my throat. But it's true. A man needs a wife. A man—"

"Marriage is a wonderful thing, isn't it? I've only just lately been realizing how wonderful."

He leaned toward her. "Laura—"

"John, I feel like telling you something, if you'll promise not to go printing it."

"Yes—"

"It's a secret yet, but—I'm going to be married."

There was a distant patter of applause for Mrs. Manson, and the frogs croaked louder than ever. These were the only noises that accompanied the end of the world.

For a moment there was a blankness inside John MacVeagh. He felt as though he had received a harder blow than any taken in the fight with Hitchcock's stooges. And then came the same reaction as he had known to those blows: the lust for battle. The lump in his throat was gone and words were pouring out. He heard the words only half-consciously, hardly aware that his own brain must be formulating them. He heard them, and was aghast that any man could lay bare his desires so plainly, his very soul.

They were pitiful words, and yet powerful—plaintive, and yet demandingly vigorous. And they were finally stopped by Laura's voice cutting across them with a harsh, "John!"

"John," she said again more softly. "I— Believe me, I never knew you felt like this. I never would have— You're nice. You're sweet, and I like you. But I couldn't ever love you. I couldn't ever possibly marry you. Let's go back inside, John. Mrs. Manson must be through by now. What's the matter? Aren't you coming? John. Please."

But John MacVeagh stood motionless by the pool while Laura went on back to the big house. He listened to the frogs for a while and then he went to the good, plain, honest bar not a mile away and listened to some "ballads."

After the third whiskey the numbness began to lift. He began to see what he had to do. It must be Phil Rogers she was marrying. But he was her cousin, wasn't he? Oh, no—he was her aunt's husband's nephew. That made it all right.

But there was a way out. There was the one sure way. All right, so it was selfish. So it was abusing a great and mysterious power for private ends. But the custodian of that power had some privileges, didn't he? And if he had one and only one prayer on earth—

After the seventh whiskey he went back to the office. It took him three tries to turn out legible copy. He hadn't written a word for the Social Notes since Molly had joined the staff, and besides, the machine seemed to resent the drunken pawing of his fingers.

But he made it at last, and it appeared in the next day's *Sentinel,* and H. A. Hitchcock said to his daughter, "Wish you'd told me, first, Laura. But I must say I think it's a fine idea. He's a comer, that boy. And maybe if you can use a little influence with him— Useful thing, having a newspaper editor in the family. You can keep him in hand."

What came next is more plateau that we don't need to examine in detail. At least, apparently plateau; a discerning eye might see the start of the fall already. Because lives don't make nice, clear graphs. The rise and the fall can be going on at once, and neither of them noticeable.

So we can accept as read all the inevitable preparations for such an event as the wedding of H. A. Hitchcock's daughter to the most promising young man in Grover. We can pass over the account of the white splendor of the wedding day and the curiously anticlimactic night that followed.

That was the night, too, when Molly, who never drank anything but beer, brought two fifths of whiskey to Luke Sellers' boardinghouse and sat up all night discussing them and other aspects of life. But the scene would be difficult to record. Most of what she said wouldn't make any sense to a reader. It didn't make much sense to Luke, nor to Molly herself the next morning.

We can skip by the details of how Grover solved the manpower shortage in the adjacent farming territory, and of how liberalism triumphed in the council election. We can go on to a Saturday night three months after Whalen Smith departed, leaving a wish behind him.

John MacVeagh had been seeing quite a bit of Ingve Johansen since the Hitchcock dinner party. He was a man you kept running into at the luncheons you had to attend, and as your father-in-law's general manager he was a man you had to have to dinner occasionally.

And MacVeagh's first impression was confirmed: he was a good guy, this Johansen. A guy you'd be happy to have in a cracker-barrel session, only those sessions never seemed to come off any more. Running a daily was a very different job from being editor of the old weekly *Sentinel*. And when so much responsibility rested on your slightest word—you didn't have time for a good bull session any more.

But Johansen would have belonged, just as Mr. Hasenberg would. Sometime he must get the two of them together away from the plant. For an executive like Johansen no more deserved to be judged by H. A. than Mr. Hasenberg did to be rated like Bricker.

Besides all the lines of race or religion or country or class, MacVeagh was beginning to feel, there was another basic dividing line among men: There are the good guys, the Men of Good Will, if you want to be fancy about it, and there are —others.

Ingve Johansen was of the first; and that's why it hurt MacVeagh, when he dropped in that Saturday at his good, plain, honest bar for a quick one, to find Johansen reduced to telling the bartender the story of his life.

MacVeagh stayed in the bar longer than he'd intended. He steered the manager over to the corner table and tried gently to find out what was eating him. For this was no ordinary drinking, but some compelling obsession.

"Look," MacVeagh said finally, "I know it's none of my business, and if you want to tell me to go jump in a lake I'll try and find one. But you've got something gnawing inside you, and if there's anything I can do to help you—" You can't tell men that you have the power to ease their troubles; but if you can once learn the troubles . . .

Johansen laughed. His heavy shock of blond hair bobbled with his laughter. He said, "How do you expect me to feel after you stole my girl?"

MacVeagh sat up straight. "Your girl? You mean you're the one that she—"

"We were going to be married. Hadn't sounded out H. A. yet, but it was all set. And first thing I know I read that piece in your paper—"

There was nothing to say. MacVeagh just sat there. He'd been sure it was the contemptible Phil Rogers. His conscience had felt clear. But now, watching the man she should have married . . .

"The worst thing," Johansen added, "is that I like you, MacVeagh. I don't even want to wring your neck for you. But Laura'd better be happy."

"She will be," said MacVeagh flatly. He rose from the table stiffly, made arrangements with the bartender about getting Johansen home, and walked out. There was nothing he could do.

No, he couldn't even be generous and give her back. The scandal of a divorce . . . Magic doesn't work backward. Was this the catch that Molly talked about?

The second thing that happened that night was unimportant. But it makes a good sample of a kind of minor incident that cropped up occasionally on the plateau.

On his way to the office, MacVeagh went past the Lyric. He absently read the marquee and saw that the theater was playing *Rio Rhythm*, Metropolis Pictures' latest well-intentioned contribution to the Good Neighbor Policy. There were no patrons lined up at the box office—no one in the lobby at all save Clara in her cage and Mr. Marcus, looking smaller and unhappier than ever.

He took the usual huge stogie out of his mouth and waved a despondent greeting to MacVeagh. The editor paused. "Poor house tonight?" he asked sympathetically.

"Poor house, he says!" Mr. Marcus replaced the cigar and it joggled with his words. "Mr. MacVeagh, I give you my word, even the ushers won't stay in the auditorium!"

MacVeagh whistled. "That bad?"

"Bad? Mr. MacVeagh, *Rio Rhythm* is colossal, stupendous, and likewise terrific. But it smells, yet."

"I don't get it."

"Stink bombs, Mr. MacVeagh. Stink bombs they throw, yet, into the Lyric. A strictly union house I run, I pay my bills, I got no competitors, and now comes stink bombs. It ain't possible. But it's true."

MacVeagh half guessed the answer even then. He got it in full with Molly's first speech when he reached the office.

"Boss, you've got to look after things better yourself. I don't know how the copy desk let it get by. Of course, that kid you put onto handling movie reviews is green; he doesn't know there's some things you just don't say in a paper, true though they may be. But look!"

MacVeagh looked, knowing what he would see. The movie review, a new department added experimentally since the *Sentinel* had expanded so, stated succinctly: "*Rio Rhythm* stinks."

John MacVeagh was silent for a long count. Then he said wryly, "It's quite a responsibility, isn't it, Molly?"

"Boss," she said, "you're the only man in the world I'd trust with it."

He believed her—not that it was true, but that she thought it was. And that was all the more reason why . . .

"You're kidding yourself, Molly. Not that I don't like to hear it. But this is a power that should never be used for anything but the best. I've tried to use it that way. And tonight I've learned that—well, I'll put in *inadvertently* to salve my conscience—that I'm ruining one man's business and have destroyed another's happiness.

"It's too much power. You can't realize all its ramifications. It's horrible—and yet it's wonderful, too. To know that it's yours—it—it makes you feel like a god, Molly. No, more than that: Like God."

There was an echo in the back of his mind. Something gnawing there, something remembered . . .

Then he heard the words as clearly as though they were spoken in the room. Father Byrne's unfinished sentence: "If you were God—" And Jake Willis' question that had prompted it: "Why doesn't God stop the war?"

Molly watched the light that came on in the boss' eyes. It was almost beautiful, and still it frightened her.

"Well," said John MacVeagh, "why don't I?"

It took a little preparing. For one thing, he hadn't tried anything on such a global scale before. He didn't know if influence outside of Grover would work, though truth should be truth universally.

For another, it took some advance work. He had to concoct an elaborate lie about new censorship regulations received from Washington, so that the tickers were moved into his private office and the foreign news came out to the rewrite staff only over his desk.

And the public had to be built up to it. It couldn't come too suddenly, too unbelievably. He prepared stories of mounting Axis defeats. He built up the internal dissension in Axis countries.

And it worked. Associated Press reports from the battlefields referred to yesterday's great victory which had been born on his typewriter. For one last experiment, he assassinated Goering. The press-association stories were crowded the next day with rumors from neutral countries and denials from Berlin.

And finally the front page of the Grover *Sentinel* bore nothing but two words:

WAR ENDED

MacVeagh had deleted the exclamation point from the proof. There was no need for it.

VI.

Excerpts from the diary of Hank Branson, F.B.I.:

Washington, June 23.

This looks to be the strangest case I've tackled yet. Screwier than that Nazi ring that figured out a way to spread subversive propaganda through a burlesque show.

The chief called me in this morning, and he was plenty worried. "Did you ever hear of a town called Grover?" he asked.

Of course I had. It's where the Hitchcock plant is. So I said sure and waited for him to spill the rest of it. But it took him a while. Almost as though he was embarrassed by what he had to say.

At last he came out with, "Hank, you're going to think I'm crazy. But as best we can figure it out, this is the situation: All this country is at war with the Axis—excepting Grover."

"Since when," I wanted to know, "do city councils have to declare war?"

So he tried to explain. "For two weeks now, the town of Grover has had no part in the war effort. The Hitchcock plant has stopped producing and is retooling for peace production. The Grover draft board hasn't sent in one man of its quota. The Grover merchants have stopped turning in their ration stamps. Even the tin-can collections have stopped. *Grover isn't at war.*"

"But that's nuts," I said.

"I warned you. But that's the case. We've sent them memoranda and warnings and notifications and every other kind of governmental scrap paper you can imagine. Either they don't receive them or they don't read them. No answers, no explanations. We've got to send a man in there to investigate on the spot. And it's got to be from our office. I don't think an Army man could keep his trigger finger steady at the spectacle of a whole community resigning from the war."

"Have you got any ideas?" I asked. "Anything to give me a lead."

The chief frowned. "Like you say, it's nuts. There's no accounting for it. Unless— Look, now you'll really think I'm crazy. But sometimes when I want to relax, I read those science-fiction magazines. You understand?"

"They're cheaper than blondes," I admitted.

"So this is the only thing that strikes me: some kind of a magnetic force field exists around Grover that keeps it out of touch with the rest of the world. Maybe even a temporal field that twists it into a time where there isn't any war. Maybe the whole thing's a new secret weapon of the enemy, and they're trying it out there. Soften up the people for invasion by making them think it's all over. Go ahead. Laugh. But if you think my answer's screwy—*and* it is—just remember: it's up to you to find the right one."

So that's my assignment, and I never had a cockeyeder one: Find out why one town, out of this whole nation, has quit the war flat.

Proutyville, June 24.

At least Proutyville's what it says on the road map, though where I am says just MOTEL and that seems to be about all there is.

I'm the only customer tonight. The motel business isn't what it used to be. I guess that's why the garage next door is already converted into a blacksmith's job.

"People that live around here, they've got to get into town now and then," the old guy that runs it said to me. "So they're pretty well converted back to horses already."

"I've known guys that were converted to horses," I said. "But only partially."

"I mean, converted to the use of horses." There was a funny sort of precise dignity about this correction. "I am pleased to be back at the old work."

He looked old enough to have flourished when blacksmithing was big time. I asked, "What did you do in the meanwhile?"

"All kinds of metal trades. Printing mostly."

And that got us talking about printing and newspapers, which is right up my alley because Pop used to own the paper in Sage Bluffs and I've lately been tied up with most of the department's cases involving seditious publications.

"A paper can do a lot of harm," I insisted. "Oh, I know it's been the style to cry down the power of the press ever since the 1936 and 1940 elections. But a paper still has a lot of influence even though it's hard to separate cause and effect. For instance, do Chicagoans think that way because of the *Tribune*, or is there a *Tribune* because Chicagoans are like that?"

From there on we got practically philosophical. He had a lot of strange ideas, that old boy. Mostly about truth. How truth was relative, which there's nothing new in that idea, though he dressed it up fancy. And something about truth and spheres of influence—how a newspaper, for instance, aimed at printing The Truth, which there is no such thing as, but actually tried, if it was honest, to print the truth (lower case) for its own sphere of influence. Outside the radius of its circulation, truth might, for another editor, be something quite else again. And then he said, to himself like, "I'd like to hear sometime how that wish came out," which didn't mean anything but sort of ended that discussion.

It was then I brought up my own little problem, and that's the only reason I've bothered to write all this down, though there's no telling what a crackpot blacksmith like that meant.

It's hard to get a clear picture of him in my mind now while I'm writing this. He's tall and thin and he has a great beak of a nose. But what I can't remember is does he have a beard? I'd almost swear he does, and still—

Anyway, I told him about Grover, naming no names, and asked him what he thought of that set-up. He liked to speculate; OK, here was a nice ripe subject.

He thought a little and said, "Is it Grover?" I guess some detail in my description of the plant and stuff tipped it off. I didn't answer, but he went on: "Think over what I've said, my boy. When you get to Grover and see what the situation is, remember what we've talked about tonight. Then you'll have your answer."

This prating hasn't any place in my diary. I know that. I feel like a dope writing it down. But there's a certain curious compulsion about it. Not so much because I feel that this is going to help explain whatever is going on in Grover, but because I've got this eerie sensation that that old man is like nothing else I've met in all my life.

It's funny. I keep thinking of my Welsh grandmother and the stories she used to tell me when I was so high. It's twenty years since I've thought of those.

Grover, June 25.

Nothing to record today but long, tiresome driving over deserted highways. I wonder what gas rationing has done to the sales of Burma Shave.

The roads were noticeably more populated as I got nearer Grover, even though it was by then pretty late. Maybe they've abolished that rationing, too.

Too late to do any checking now; I'll get to work tomorrow, with my usual routine of dropping in at the local paper first to gather a picture.

Grover, June 26.

Two of the oddest things in my life with the FBI have happened today. One, the minor one, is that I've somehow mislaid my diary, which is why this entry is written on note paper. The other, and what has really got me worried, is that I've mislaid my job.

Just that. I haven't the slightest idea why I am in Grover.

It's a nice little town. Small and cozy and like a thousand others, only maybe even more pleasant. It's going great guns now, of course, reveling, like everyplace else, in the boom of postwar prosperity.

There's a jiggy, catchy chorus in *The Chocolate Soldier* that goes, "Thank the Lord the war is over, tum-tee-tum tee-tum tee-tover—" Nice, happy little tune; it ought to be the theme song of these times. It seems like only yesterday I was stewing, and all the rest of the department with me, about saboteurs and subversive elements and all the other wartime problems.

Only now I've got something else to stew about, which is why I'm here.

I tried to get at it indirectly with John MacVeagh, a stolid sort of young man with heavy eyebrows and a quiet grin, who edits the Grover *Sentinel*—surprisingly large and prosperous paper for a town this size. Daily, too.

I liked MacVeagh—good guy. Says he didn't serve in the war because a punctured eardrum kept him out, but says he tried his best to see Grover through it on the home front. We settled down to quite a confab, and I deliberately let it slip that I was from the FBI. I hoped that'd cue him into, "Oh, so you're here on the Hungadunga case, huh?" But no go. No reaction at all, but a mild wonder as to what a G-man was doing in Grover.

I didn't tell him.

I tried the same stunt on the chief of police, who kept quoting Bible texts at me and telling me about a murder they had a while back and how he solved it. (Would you believe it? The butler did it! Honest.) Nothing doing on the reaction business. Grover, ever since the famous murder, has had the most crime-free record in the State. Nothing in my line.

Nothing to do but sleep on it and hope tomorrow turns up either my diary or my memory.

Grover, June 27.

I like Grover. Now that the war's over, the department'll be cutting down on its staff. I might do worse than resign and settle down here. I've always wanted to try some pulp writing to show up the guys that write about us. And in a few years Chief Hanby'll be retiring, and if I'm established in the community by then—

And I'm going to have to get out of the department if things go on like this. Had a swell day today—visited the Hitchcock plant and saw their fabulous new work with plastics in consumer goods, had dinner at MacVeagh's and went out to a picture and a bar on a double date with him and his wife—who is the loveliest thing I ever saw, if you like icicles —and a girl from the paper, who's a nice kid.

But I still don't know from nothing.

I sent a wire back to the chief:

WIRE FULL OFFICIAL INSTRUCTIONS AT ONCE MY MISSION LOCAL
POLICE CHIEF WANTS FORMAL OK.

I know, I know. It's a thin story, and it probably won't
work. But I've got to try something.

Grover, June 28.
I got an answer:

YOUR QUOTE MISSION UNQUOTE ALL A MISTAKE. RETURN WASH-
INGTON.

I don't get it. Maybe when I see the chief again—
So now, regretfully, we bid farewell to the sunny, happy
town of Grover, nestling at the foot—

Proutyville, June 29.
As you—whoever you are and whatever you think you're
doing reading other people's diaries—can see, my diary's
turned up again. And that I am, as they say in the classics,
stark, raving mad seems about the only possible answer.

Maybe I thought the chief was crazy. What's he going to
call me?

I read over again what the old guy with—or without—the
beard said. Where he said I'd find the answer. I didn't.

So I went over to see him again, but he wasn't there. There
was a fat man drinking beer out of a quart bottle, and as
soon as he saw me he poured a glassful and handed it over
unasked.

It tasted good, and I said, "Thanks," and meant it. Then
I described the old boy and asked where was he.

The fat man poured himself another glass and said,
"Damfino. He come in here one day and says, 'See you're
setting up to shoe horses. Need an old hand at the business?'
So I says, 'Sure, what's your name?' and he says, 'Wieland,'
leastways that's what I think he says, like that beer out in
California. 'Wieland,' he says. 'I'm a smith,' so he goes to

work. Then just this morning he up and says, 'I'm needed
more elsewhere,' he says, 'I gotta be going,' he says, 'now you
been a swell employer,' he says, 'so if you—'" The fat man
stopped. "So he up and quit me."

"Because you were a swell employer?"

"That? That was just something he says. Some foolishness.
Hey, your glass is empty." The fat man filled my glass and his
own.

The beer was good. It kept me from quite going nuts. I sat
there the most of the evening. It wasn't till late that a kind
of crawly feeling began to hit me. "Look," I said. "I've drunk
beer most places you can name, but I never saw a quart
bottle hold that many glasses."

The fat man poured out some more. "This?" he said, off
hand-like. "Oh, this is just something Wieland give me."

And I suppose I'm writing all this out to keep from thinking about what I'm going to say to the chief. But what can
say? Nothing but this:

Grover isn't at war. And when you're there, it's true.

Washington, June 30.

I'm not going to try to write the scene with the chief. It
still stings, kind of. But he softened up a little toward the
end. I'm not to be fired; just suspended. Farnsworth's taking
the Grover assignment. And I get a rest—

Bide-a-wee Nursing Home, May 1.

VII.

It was hot in the office that June night. John MacVeagh
should have been deep in his studies, but other thoughts kept
distracting him.

These studies had come to occupy more and more of his
time. His responsibilities were such that he could not tolerate
anything less than perfection in his concepts of what was the
desirable truth.

Ending the war had been simple. But now the *Sentinel* had
to print the truth of the postwar adjustments. Domestically
these seemed to be working fine, at the moment. Demobiliza-
tion was being carried out smoothly and gradually, and the
startling technological improvements matured in secrecy dur-
ing wartime were now bursting forth to take up the slack in
peacetime production.

The international scene was more difficult. The willful
nationalism of a few misguided senators threatened to ruin
any possible adjustment. MacVeagh had to keep those men in
check, and even more difficult, he had to learn the right answers to all the problems.

The eventual aim, he felt sure, must be a world state. But
of what nature? He plowed through Clarence Streit and Ely
Culbertson and everything else he could lay hands on, reject-
ing Culbertson's overemphasis on the nation as a unit and
Streit's narrow definition of what constitutes democracy, but
finding in each essential points that had to be fitted into the
whole.

MacVeagh's desk was heavy with books and notes and card
indexes, but he was not thinking of any of these things. He
was thinking of Laura.

The breaking point had come that night they went out with
Golly and the G-man. (Odd episode, that. Why a G-man here
in peaceful Grover? And so secretive about his mission and
so abrupt in his departure.) It might have been the picture
that brought it on, a teary opus in which Bette Davis suffered
nobly.

It was funny that he couldn't remember the words of the
scene. According to all tradition, they should be indelibly en-
graved on the tablets, et cetera. But he didn't remember the
words, just the general pain and torture.

Laura crying, crying with that helpless quiet desperation
that is a woman's way of drowning her sorrows. Himself,
puzzled, hurt, trying to help and comfort her. Laura shuddering away from his touch. Laura talking in little gasps between
her sobs about how he was nice and she liked him and he

was so good to her, but she didn't understand, she never ha
understood how she made up her mind to marry him and sl
would try to be a good wife, she did want to, but—

He remembered those words. They were the only ones th
stayed indelible: "—I just don't love you."

He had quieted her finally and left her red-eyed but slee
ing. He had slept that night, and all the nights since then,
the guest room that some day was to be converted into
nursery.

Was to have been converted.

There's a catch, Molly said. Always a catch. You can mal
your marriage true, but your wife's love—

A man isn't fit to be God. A woman who cannot love yc
is so infinitely more important than the relation of Sovi
Russia to Western Europe.

MacVeagh almost barked at Lucretius Sellers when he can
in. The old printer was a regular visitor at the *Sentinel*. F
wasn't needed any longer, of course, with the new presses ai
the new staff that tended them. But he'd appointed himse
an unofficial member of the *Sentinel*'s forces, and MacVeag
was glad, though sometimes wondering how much of the tru
about the truth Luke Sellers might guess.

Tonight Luke glanced at the laden desk and grinne
"Hard at it, Johnny?" He was sober, and there was worry :
his eyes behind the grin.

MacVeagh snapped his thoughts back from their desola
wanderings. "Quite a job I've got," he said.

"I know. But if you've got a minute, Johnny—"

MacVeagh made a symbolic gesture of pushing books asid
"Sure, Luke. What's on your mind?"

Luke Sellers was silent a little. Then, "I don't like to ta
like this, Johnny. I wouldn't if I wasn't afraid you'd hear
somewheres else. And Molly, even she thinks I ought to te
you. It's getting her. She slapped Mrs. Manson's face at tl
Ladies' Aid last meeting. Not but what that's sensible enoug
but she's generally acting funny. Sometimes I'm almost afra
maybe—"

He bogged down.

"That's a heck of a preamble, Luke. What's it leading up to? Here—want to oil up your larynx?"

"Thanks, Johnny. Haven't had a drink all day—wanted to have my head clear to— But maybe this might help— Well, peace forever! Thanks."

"OK. Now what?"

"It's— Johnny, you're going to kick me out of this office on my tail. But it's about Mrs. MacVeagh."

"Laura?"

"Now, hold on, Johnny. Hold your horses. I know there's nothing in it, Molly knows there's nothing in it, but it's the way people around town are talking. She's been seeing a lot of that manager out at the plant, what's-his-name, Johansen. You work here late at nights, and— Phil Rogers, he saw them out at Cardotti's roadhouse. So did Jake Willis another night. And I just wanted— Well, Johnny, I'd rather you heard it from me than down at Clem's barber shop."

MacVeagh's face was taut. "It's no news to me, Luke. I know she's lonely when I work here. Fact is, I asked Johansen to show her a little fun. He's a good guy. You might tell that to Mrs. Manson and the boys at Clem's."

Luke Sellers stood looking at MacVeagh. Then he took another drink. "I'll spread it around, Johnny."

"Thanks, Luke."

"And I hope I can make it sound more convincing than you did."

He left. John MacVeagh sat silent, and the room was full of voices.

"How does it feel, MacVeagh? What's it like to know that your wife— No, MacVeagh, don't rub your forehead. You'll prick yourself on the horns—"

"Don't listen, MacVeagh. It's just people. People talk. It doesn't mean anything."

"Where there's smoke, MacVeagh— Remember? You didn't think there was any fire in Laura, did you? But where there's smoke there's—"

"You could fix it, you know. You could fix it, the way you fix everything. Something could happen to Johansen."

"Or if you haven't the heart for that, MacVeagh, you could send him away. Have him called to Washington. That'd be a break for him too."

"But it wouldn't solve the problem, would it, MacVeagh? She still wouldn't love you."

"You don't believe it, do you, MacVeagh? She can't help not loving you, but she wouldn't deceive you. You trust her, don't you?"

"MacVeagh."

It was some seconds before John MacVeagh realized that this last voice was not also inside his head. He looked up to see Phil Rogers, the perfect profile as hyperpale as it had been on the night of his aunt's murder. His white hand held an automatic.

"Yes?" MacVeagh asked casually. He tensed his body and calculated positions and distances with his eyes, while he wondered furiously what this meant.

"MacVeagh, I'm going to send you to meet God."

"My. Fancy talk." It was difficult. MacVeagh was hemmed in by files and a table of reference books. It would be next to impossible to move before Phil Rogers could jerk his right index finger. "And just why, Phil, should you take this job on yourself?"

"Maybe I should say because you stole Laura, and now she's making a fool of herself—and you—with that Johansen. I wanted her. I'd have had her, too. H. A. and I had it all fixed up."

It wasn't worth explaining that MacVeagh and Rogers had equally little just claim on Laura. "Noble," said MacVeagh. "All for love. You'd let them stretch your neck for love, too?"

Rogers laughed. "You know me, huh, MacVeagh?"

Play for time, that was the only way. "I know you enough to think there's a stronger motive—stronger for you."

"You're right there is. And you're going to hear it before you go. Go to meet God. Wonder what He'll think—of meeting another god."

This was more startling than the automatic. "What do you mean by that, Phil?"

"I've heard Luke Sellers talking when he was drunk. About General Wigginsby and the butler's confession. Everybody thought he was babbling. But I got it. I don't know how it works, but your paper prints true. What you print happens."

MacVeagh laughed. "Nonsense. Listen to Luke? You must've been tight yourself, Phil. Go home."

"Uh-uh." Rogers shook his head, but his hand didn't move. "That explains it all. All you've done to me. You took Laura. You shoved that softie Johansen into the general manager's job I should have had. You got that sniveling, weak-kneed labor agreement through. You— MacVeagh, I think you ended the war!"

"And you'd hold that against me?"

"Yes. We were doing swell. Now with retooling, new products, trying to crash new markets, everything uncertain— I inherited my aunt's interest in the company. MacVeagh, you did me out of two–three years of profits."

"Do you think anybody'd believe this wild yarn of yours, Phil?"

"No. I don't. I was tight, just tight enough so things made sense. I wouldn't swallow it sober myself. But I know it's true, and that's why I've got to kill you, MacVeagh." His voice rose to a loud, almost soprano cry.

The white hand was very steady. MacVeagh moved his body slowly to one side and watched the nose of the automatic hold its point on him. Then, with the fastest, sharpest movement he'd ever attained in his life, he thrust his chair crashing back and dropped doubled into the kneehole of his desk. The motion was just in time. He heard a bullet thud into the plaster of the wall directly behind where he'd been sitting.

His plans had been unshaped. It was simply that the desk seemed the only armor visible at the moment. And to fire directly into this kneehole would mean coming around and up close where he might possibly grab at Rogers' legs. The wood between him and Rogers now should be thick enough to—

He heard a bullet plunk into that wood. Then he heard it go past his ear and bury itself in more wood. His guess was wrong. He could be shot in here. This bullet had gone past him as knives go past the boy in the Indian basket trick. But Phil Rogers was not a magician slipping knives into safe places, and no amount of contortion could save MacVeagh from eventually meeting one of those bullets.

He heard scuffling noises. Then he heard a thud that was that of a body, not a bullet, and with it another shot.

There was silence for a minute. Then a voice said, "Mac-Veagh? What's become of you?"

MacVeagh crawled out from under the desk. "Undignified posture," he said, "but what would you do if you were hemmed in and this maniac started— Is he hurt?"

It took a while for exchange of information, MacVeagh giving a much-censored version which made it seem that Phil Rogers was suffering a motiveless breakdown of some sort, the other telling how he'd been waiting outside, heard Phil's loud denunciations—though not their words—and then the shots, and decided to intervene. Rogers was so intent on his victim that attack from behind was a snap. The last shot had gone into Rogers' own left shoulder as they struggled. Nothing serious.

"Don't know how I can ever thank you, Johansen," said John MacVeagh.

"Any time," said his wife's lover. "It's a pleasure."

Rogers was on his feet again now. MacVeagh turned to him and said, "Get out. I don't care what you do or how you explain that bullet wound. I'm not bringing any charges. Get out."

Rogers glared at them both. "I'll settle with you, MacVeagh. You too, Johansen."

"Uh-uh. You're having a nervous breakdown. You're going to a sanitarium for a while. When you come out you'll feel fine."

"That's what you say."

"Get out," MacVeagh repeated. And as Rogers left, he

jotted down a note to print the sanitarium trip and the necessary follow-ups on convalescence.

Without a word he handed a bottle to Johansen, then
drank from it himself. "Thanks," he said. "I can't say more
than that."

The tall blond man smiled. "I won't ask questions. I've had
run-ins with Rogers myself. The boss' sister's nephew— But
to tell you the truth, John, I'm sorry I saved your life."

MacVeagh stiffened. "You've still got his gun," he suggested
humorlessly.

"I don't want you to lose your life. But I'm sorry *I* saved
it. Because it makes what I have to say so much harder."

MacVeagh sat on the edge of his desk. "Go on."

"Cold, like this? I don't know how I thought I was going
to manage to say this— I never expected this kind of a
build-up— All right, John, this is it:

"I told you once that Laura had better be happy. Well, she
isn't. I've been seeing her. Probably you know that. I haven't
tried to sneak about it. She doesn't love you, John. She won't
say it, but I think she still loves me. And if I can make her
happy, I'm warning you, I'll take her away from you."

MacVeagh said nothing.

Johansen went on hesitantly. "I know what it would mean.
A scandal that would make Laura a fallen woman in the eyes
of all Grover. A fight with H. A. that would end my job here
and pretty much kill my chances in general. I'll make it clear
to Laura—and I think she'll be as willing to risk it as I am.

"But I'm giving you your chance. If you can make her love
you, make her happy, all right. It's Laura that counts. But if
in another month there's still that haunted emptiness in her
eyes—well, John, then it's up to me."

The two men stood facing each other for a moment. There
were no more words. There was no possibility of words. Ingve
Johansen turned and left the room.

If you can make her love you— Was this the limit to the
power of the god of the *Sentinel?* You can't print EDITOR'S
WIFE LOVES HIM. You can't—or can you?

Numbly MacVeagh groped his way to the typewriter. His fingers fumbled out words.

> "Women have a double task in this new peacetime," Mrs. John MacVeagh, president of the Volunteer Women Workers, stated when interviewed yesterday.
>
> "Like all other citizens, women must take part in the tasks of reconstruction," said the lovely Mrs. MacVeagh, nee Laura Hitchcock. "But woman's prime job in reconstruction is assuring happiness in the home. A man's usefulness to society must depend largely on the love of his wife. I feel that I am doing good work here with the VWW, but I consider the fact that I love my husband my most important contribution to Grover's welfare."

MacVeagh sat back and looked at it. His head ached and his mouth tasted foul. Neither a pipe nor a drink helped. He reread what he'd written. Was this the act of a god—or of a louse?

But it had to be. He knew Laura well enough to know that she'd never stand up under the scandal and ostracism that Johansen proposed, no matter how eagerly she might think she welcomed them. As Ingve had said, it's Laura that counts.

It is so easy to find the most flattering motives for oneself.

He wrote a short item announcing I. L. Johansen's resignation as manager of the Hitchcock plant and congratulating him on his appointment to the planning board of the new OPR, the Office of Peacetime Reconstruction. He was typing the notice of Philip Rogers' departure for a sanitarium, phrased with euphemistic clarity, when Luke Sellers came back.

Luke had been gone an hour. Plenty had happened here in that hour, but more where Luke Sellers had been. The old printer had aged a seeming ten years.

He kept twitching at his little scraggle of white beard, and his eyes didn't focus anywhere. His lips at first had no power to shape words. They twisted hopefully, but what came through them was just sound.

"Molly—" Luke said at last.

John MacVeagh stood up sharply. "What is it? What's wrong?"

"Molly— Told you I was worried about her—"

"She— No! She hasn't! She couldn't!"

"Iodine. Gulped it down. Messy damned way. Doc Quillan hasn't much hope—"

"But why? Why?"

"She can't talk. Vocal cords— It eats, that iodine— Keeps trying to say something. I think it's— Want to come?"

MacVeagh thought he understood a little. He saw things he should have seen before. How Molly felt about him. How, like Johansen with Laura, she could tolerate his marriage if he was happy, but when that marriage was breaking up and her loss became a pointless farce—

"Coming, Johnny?" Luke Sellers repeated.

"No," said MacVeagh. "I've got to work. Molly'd want me to. And she'll pull through all right, Luke. You'll read about it in the *Sentinel*."

It was the first time that this god had exercised the power of life and death.

VIII.

The next morning, Laura looked lovelier than ever at breakfast as she glanced up from the paper and asked, "Did you like my interview?"

MacVeagh reached a hand across the table and touched hers. "What do you think?"

"I'm proud," she said. "Proud to see it there in print. More coffee?"

"Thanks."

She rose and filled his cup at the silver urn. "Isn't it nice to have all the coffee we want again?" As she set the cup back at his place, she leaned over and kissed him. It was a light, tender kiss, and the first she had ever given him unprompted. He caught her hand and held it for a moment.

"Don't stay too late at the office tonight, dear," she said softly.

"Most amazing recovery I ever saw," Doc Quillan mumbled. "Take a while for the throat tissues to heal, but she'll be back at work in no time. Damned near tempted to call it a miracle, MacVeagh."

"I guess this OPR appointment settles my part of what we were talking about," Ingve Johansen said over the phone. "It's a grand break for me—fine work that I'm anxious to do. So I won't be around, but remember—I may come back."

"Gather Phil made a fool of himself last night," said H. A. Hitchcock. "Don't worry. Shan't happen again. Strain, overwork— He'll be all right after a rest."

Father Byrne dropped in that morning, happily flourishing a liberal journal which had nominated Grover as the nation's model town for labor relations.

Chief Hanby dropped in out of pure boredom. The Grover crime rate had become so minute that he feared his occupation was all but gone. "The crooks are all faded," he said. " 'The strangers shall fade away, and be afraid out of their close places.' Psalms, eighteen, forty-five. Grover's the Lord's town now."

John MacVeagh stood alone in his office, hearing the whir of presses and the rushing of feet outside. This was his, the greatest tool of good in the world's history.

"And God saw everything that he had made, and, behold, it was very good." Genesis, as Chief Hanby would say, one, thirty-one.

He did not stay too late at the office that night.

John MacVeagh reached over to the night table for a cigarette. There are times when even a confirmed pipe smoker uses them. In the glow of the match he saw Laura's face, relaxed and perfect.

"Want one?"

"No thanks, dear."

He took in a deep breath of smoke and let it out slowly. "Do you love me?" he asked gently.

"What do you think?" She moved closer and laid her head on his shoulder.

He felt a stirring of discontent, of compunction. "But I— Do you really love me? Not just because of that interview— what I made you say, but—"

Laura laughed. "You didn't make me say it. Except that your being you is what makes me love you, and that's what made me say it. Of course I love you. I know I've been frightfully slow realizing it, but now—"

"I want you to love me. I want you really to love me, of your own self—"

But even as he spoke, he realized the hopelessness of his longing. That could never be now. He had forcibly made her into a thing that loved him, and that "love" was no more like true love than the affection of a female robot or—he shuddered a little—the attentions of the moronic ghost that brought love to Professor Guildea.

He could not even revoke this forced love, unless by figuring some means of printing that she did not love him. And that then would be true, and forbid all possibility of the real love that she might eventually have felt for him.

He was trapped. His power and his ingenuity had made him the only man on earth who had not the slightest chance of ever feeling the true, unfeigned, unforced love of his wife.

It was this that brought it all into focus. MacVeagh understood now the nagging discontent that had been gnawing at him. He looked at everything that he had made, and behold, he felt only annoyance and impatience.

He tried to phrase it once or twice:

"Jake, supposing you knew it was only a trick, this change in your beliefs. It was just a hoax, a bad practical joke played on you."

"How could it be? I used to have crazy ideas. I used to think I was too smart to believe. Now I know different. That's no joke."

"Father Byrne, do you think this labor agreement could have been reached without outside pressure? That men and management really could have got together like this?"

"They did, didn't they, John? I don't understand what you mean about outside pressure—unless," the priest added, smiling, "you think my prayers were a form of undue influence?"

MacVeagh did not try to explain what God had answered those prayers. Even if you could persuade people of the actual state of things, that he and the *Sentinel* had made them what they were, the truth would remain the truth.

He realized that when Molly came back to the office. For Molly knew the whole story and understood. She understood too well. Her first words when they were alone were, "Boss, I'm really dead, aren't I?"

He tried to pretend not to understand. He tried to bluff through it, pass it off as nothing. But she was too sure. She insisted, "I died that night." Her voice was a rough croak. He had forgotten to specify a miraculous recovery of the iodine-eaten vocal cords.

At last he nodded, without a word.

"I suppose I ought to thank you, boss. I don't know if I do— I guess I do, though. Laura came to see me in the hospital and talked. If she loves you, you're happy. And if you're happy, boss, life's worth living."

"Happy—." Then his words began to tumble out. Molly was the first person, the only person that he could talk to about his new discovery: the drawback of omnipotence.

"You see," he tried to make it clear, "truth has a meaning, a value, only because it's outside of us. It's something outside that's real and valid, that we can reckon against. When you make the truth yourself it doesn't have any more meaning. It doesn't feel like truth. It's no truer than an author's characters are to him. Less so, maybe; sometimes they can rebel and lead their own lives. But nothing here in Grover can rebel, or in the world either. But it's worst here. I don't know people any more."

"Especially me," said Molly.

He touched her shoulder gently. "One thing I didn't make up, Molly. That's your friendship for me. I'm grateful for that."

"Thanks, boss." Her voice was even rougher. "Then take some advice from me. Get out of Grover for a while. Let your mind get straightened out. See new people that you've never done anything to except end the war for them. Take a vacation."

"I can't. The paper's such a responsibility that—"

"Nobody but me knows about it, and I promise to be good. If you're away, it'll run just like any other paper. Go on, boss."

"Maybe you're right. I'll try it, Molly. But one thing."

"Yes, boss?"

"Remember: this has got to be the best-proofread paper in the world."

Molly nodded and almost smiled.

For an hour after leaving Grover, John MacVeagh felt jittery. He ought to be back at his desk. He ought to be making sure that the Senate didn't adopt the Smith amendment, that the Army of Occupation in Germany effectively quashed that Hohenzollern Royalist putsch, that nothing serious came of Mr. Hasenberg's accident at the plant—

Then the jitters left him, and he thought, "Let them make out by themselves. They did once."

He spent the night at the Motel in Proutyville and enjoyed the soundest sleep he had known in months. In the morning he went next door to chat with the plump garage proprietor, who'd been good company on other trips.

He found a woman there, who answered his "Where's Ike?"

with "Ain't you heard? He died last week. Too much beer, I guess."

"But Ike lived on beer."

"Sure, only he used to drink only as much as he could afford. Then for a while seems like there wasn't no limit to how much he had, and last week he comes down with this stroke. I'm his daughter-in-law; I'm keeping the joint going. Not that there's any business in times like these."

"What do you mean, in times like these?"

"Mister, where you been? Don't you know there's a war on?"

"No," said John MacVeagh dazedly. The daughter-in-law looked after him, not believing her ears.

MacVeagh hardly believed his, either. Not until he reached the metropolis of Zenith was he fully convinced. He studied newspapers there, talked with soldiers and defense workers.

There was no doubt at all. The world was at war.

He guessed the answer roughly. Something about relative truths and spheres of influence. He could work it out clearly later.

His head was spinning as he got back to his parked car. There was a stocky young man in a plain gray suit standing beside it, staring at the name plate GROVER attached to the license.

As MacVeagh started to get in, the young man accosted him. "You from Grover, Mac?"

MacVeagh nodded automatically, and the man slipped into the seat beside him. "We've got to have a talk, Mac. A long talk."

"And who are you?"

"Kruger. FBI." He flashed a card. "The Bureau is interested in Grover."

"Look," said MacVeagh, "I've got an appointment at the Zenith *Bulletin* in five minutes. After that, I'm at your disposal. You can come along," he added as the G-man hesitated.

"OK, Mac. Start thinking up answers."

Downtown traffic in Zenith was still fairly heavy, even in

vartime. Pedestrian traffic was terrific. MacVeagh pulled his
ar up in the yellow zone in front of the *Bulletin* Building.
He opened his door and stepped out. Kruger did the same.
Then in an instant MacVeagh was back in the driver's seat
nd the car was pulling away.

He had the breaks with him. A hole opened up in the
raffic just long enough to ensure his getaway. He knew there
vere too many bystanders for Kruger to risk a shot. Two
locks away, he deliberately stalled the car in the middle of
n intersection. In the confusion of the resulting pile-up he
nanaged to slip away unnoticed.

The car had to be abandoned anyway. Where could he get
as for it with no ration coupons? The important thing was
▸ get away with his skin.

For he had realized in an instant that one of Kruger's first
uestions would be, "Where's your draft card, Mac?" And
vhatever steps he had to take to solve the magnificent con-
usion which his godhead had created, he could take none of
hem in Federal prison as a draft evader.

Molly stared at the tramp who had forced his way into the
entinel office. "Well," she growled, "what do you want?"

"Molly, don't you know me?"

"Boss!"

The huskies on either side of him reluctantly relaxed their
rips. "You can go, boys," she said. They went, in frowning
umbness.

MacVeagh spoke rapidly. "I can't tell it all to you now,
Molly. It's too long. You won't believe it, but I've had the
eds on my tail. That's why this choice costume, mostly filth.
The rods were the only safe route to Grover. And you thought
should take a vacation—"

"But why—"

"Listen, Molly. I've made a world of truth. All right. But
hat truth holds good only where the *Sentinel* dominates.
There's an imaginary outside to go with it, an outside that

sends me dispatches based on my own statements, that main
tains banking relations with our banks, that feeds peacetim
programs to our radios, and so on, but it's a false outside, ;
world of If. The true outside is what it would be withou
me: a world at war."

For a moment Molly gasped speechlessly. Then she said
"Mr. Johansen!"

"What about him?"

"You sent him to the Office of Peacetime Reconstruction
That's in your world of If. What's become of him?"

"I never thought of that one. But there are problem
enough. It isn't fair to the people here to make them live i:
an unreal world, even if it's better than the real one. Ma:
isn't man all by himself. Man is in and of his time and th
rest of mankind. If he's false to his time, he's false to him
self. Grover's going to rejoin the world."

"But how, boss? Are you going to have to start the war al
over?"

"I never stopped it except in our pretty dream world. Bu
I'm going to do more than that. I'm going to reveal the whol
fake—to call it all a fake *in print*."

"Boss!" Molly gasped. "You . . . you realize this is suicide
Nobody'll ever read the *Sentinel* again. And suicide," sh
added with grim personal humor, "isn't anything I'd recom
mend."

"I don't count beside Grover. I don't count beside men
'For God,' " he quoted wryly, " 'so loved the world—' "

"This is it," said John MacVeagh much later.

That edition of the *Sentinel* had been prepared by a sta
of three. The large, fine new staff of the large, fine nev
Sentinel had frankly decided that its proprietor was mad o
drunk or both. Storming in dressed like a bum and givin
the craziest orders. There had been a mass meeting and
mass refusal to have anything to do with the proposed all-i
lies edition.

Luke Sellers had filled the breach again. He read the copy and nodded. "You never talked much, Johnny, but I had it figured pretty much like this. I was in at the start, so I guess it's right I ought to be in at the end."

This was the end now. This minute a two-sheet edition, its front page one huge headline and its inside pages containing nothing but MacVeagh's confession in large type, was set up and ready to run.

The confession told little. MacVeagh could not expect to make anyone believe in Whalen Smith and wishes and variable truths. It read simply like the story of a colossal and unparalleled hoax.

"There won't be enough rails in town for the guys that'll want to run you out on one, Johnny," Luke Sellers warned.

"I'm taking the chance. Go ahead: print it."

The presses clanked.

There was a moment of complete chaos.

Somewhere in that chaos a part of MacVeagh's mind was thinking, This was what had to happen. You gave your wish an impossible problem: to print that its truth is not truth. Like the old logical riddle about how you cannot say, "I am lying." If you are, it's the truth, and so you're not. Same in reverse. And when the wish meets the impossible—

The wish gave up. It ceased to be. And in the timeless eternity where all magic exists, it ceased ever to have been.

IX.

"All right then, tell me this: If God can do anything—" Jake Willis cleared his throat and paused, preparatory to delivering the real clincher.

The old man with the scraggly beard snorted and took another shot of applejack. "Why doesn't He end the war? I'm getting tired of that, Jake. I wish you'd go back to the weight He can't lift. Father's explained this one before, and I'm willing to admit he makes a good case."

"I don't see it," said Jake stubbornly.

Father Byrne sighed. "Because man must have free will. If men were mere pawns that were pushed around by God, their acts would have no merit in them. They would be unworthy to be the children of God. Your own children you love even when most they rebel. You do not love your chessmen. Man must work out his own salvation; salvation on a silver platter is meaningless."

John MacVeagh stirred restlessly. This idea seemed so familiar. Not from hearing Father Byrne expound it before, but as though he had worked it out for himself, sometime, in a very intimate application.

"But if there is a God—" Jake went on undisturbed.

MacVeagh caught Ingve Johansen's eye and grinned. He was glad Johansen had joined the crackerbarrel club. Glad, too, that Johansen's marriage with Laura Hitchcock was working so well.

The man with the tired face was playing with the black Scottie and trying to think of nothing at all. When he heard footsteps, he looked up sharply. The tiredness was automatically wiped from his face by a grin, which faded as he saw a stranger. "How did you get in here?" he demanded.

The stranger was an old man with a beaked nose. In the dim light it was hard to tell whether or not he wore a beard. He said, "I've been working for you."

The man with the Scottie looked at the defense worker's identification card which said

WHALING, SMITH

He resumed the grin. "Glad to see you. Fine work they've been turning out at your plant. You're a delegate to me?"

"Sort of. But just for me. You see, I'm quitting."

"You can't. Your job's frozen."

"I know. But that don't count. Not for me. But it's thi

way: Since the Army took over the plant, looks like you're my employer. Right?"

The man seemed puzzled as he fitted a cigarette into a long holder. "I guess so. Smoke?"

"No, thanks. Then if you're my employer, you've been a good one. You've got a wish coming to you."

The man with the holder peered at the other. It was hard to make him out. And he'd come in so silently, presumably through the guards.

The grin was crooked as he said, "I don't think you're even here. And since you aren't, there's no harm in playing the game. A wish—" He looked at the globe on the table and at the dispatches beside it. "Yes," he said finally, "I have a wish—"

John MacVeagh paused beside the Gypsy's booth at the Victory Garden Fair. "Want to have your fortune told, Molly?"

Molly shuddered. "Maybe I'm silly. But ever since I was a child I've been scared of anything like magic. There's always a catch."

The Scottie had been trying to gather courage to bark at the stranger. Now he succeeded. "Be quiet, Fala," his owner ordered. "Yes, Whaling, I wish—"

The Ghost of Me

I gave my reflection hell. I was sleepy, of course. And I still didn't know what noise had waked me; but I told it what I thought of mysterious figures that lurked across the room from you and eventually turned out to be your own image. I did a good job, too; I touched depths of my vocabulary that even the complications of the Votruba case hadn't sounded.

Then I was wide awake and gasping. Throughout all my invective, the reflection had not once moved its lips. I groped behind me for the patient's chair and sat down fast. The reflection remained standing.

Now, it was I. There was no doubt of that. Every feature was exactly similar, even down to the scar over my right eyebrow from the time a bunch of us painted Baltimore a mite too thoroughly. But this should have tipped me off from the start: the scar was on the right, not on the left where I've always seen it in a mirror's reversal.

"Who are you?" I asked. It was not precisely a brilliant conversational opening, but it was the one thing I had to know or start baying the moon.

"Who are *you?*" it asked right back.

Maybe you've come across those cockeyed mirrors which, by some trick arrangement of lenses, show you not the reversed mirror image but your actual appearance, as though you were outside and looking at yourself? Well, this was like that—exactly, detailedly me, but facing me rightwayround and unreversed. And it stood when I sat down.

"Look," I protested. "Isn't it enough to be a madhouse mirror? Do you have to be an echo too?"

"Tell me who you are," it insisted quietly. "I think I must be confused."

I hadn't quite plumbed my vocabulary before; I found a couple of fresh words now. "You think *you're* confused? And what in the name of order and reason do you think *I* am?"

"That's what I asked you," it replied. "What are you? Because there must be a mistake somewhere."

"All right," I agreed. "If you want to play games. I'll tell you what I am, if you'll do the same. You chase me and I'll chase you. I'm John Adams. I'm a doctor. I've got a Rockefeller grant to establish a clinic to study occupational disease among Pennsylvania cement workers—"

"—I'm working on a variation of the Zupperheim theory with excellent results, and I'm a registered Democrat but not quite a New Dealer," it concluded, with the gloomiest frown I've ever noted outside a Russian novel.

My own forehead was not parchment-smooth. "That's all true enough. But how do you know it? And now that I've told you I'm John Adams, will you kindly kick through with your half of the bargain?"

"That's just the trouble," it murmured reluctantly. "There must be a terrible mistake somewhere. I've heard of such things, of course, but I certainly never expected it to happen to me."

I don't have all the patience that a medical man really needs. This time when I said *"Who are you?"* it was a wild and ringing shout.

"Well, you see—" it said.

"I hardly know how to put this—" it began again.

"To be blunt about it," it finally blurted out, "I'm the ghost of John Adams."

I was glad I was sitting down. And I understood now why

old Hasenfuss always recommended arms on the patient's chair to give him something to grab when you deliver the verdict. I grabbed now, and grabbed plenty hard.

"You're the—"

"I'm the ghost—"

"—the ghost of—"

"—of John Adams."

"But"—I held onto the chair even tighter—"I *am* John Adams."

"I know," my ghost said. "That's what's so annoying."

I said nothing. That was far too impressive an understatement to bear comment. I groped in the pocket of my dressing gown and found cigarettes. "Do you smoke?" I asked.

"Of course. If John Adams smokes, naturally I do."

I extended the pack.

He shook his head. "I'll have to dematerialize it. Put one on the table."

I obeyed and watched curiously. A hand that was not quite a hand but more a thin pointing shape stretched out and touched the cigarette. It lingered a moment, then came away holding a white cylinder. The cigarette was still on the table.

I lit it and puffed hard. "Tastes just like any other Camel."

"Of course. I took only the nonmaterial part. You wouldn't miss that any more than you miss . . . well, me."

"You mean you're smoking the ghost of a cigarette?"

"You can put it that way."

For the first five puffs it wasn't easy to get the cigarette into my mouth. My hand was more apt to steer it at nose or ear. But with the sixth puff I began to feel as normal and self-possessed as any man talking with his own ghost. I even got argumentative.

"This isn't possible," I protested. "You won't even come into existence until after I'm dead."

"Certainly," my ghost agreed politely. "But you see, you *are* dead."

"Now, look. That's nonsense. Even supernaturally. Because if I were dead . . . well, if I were dead, I'd be my own ghost. I'd be you. There wouldn't be two of us."

"I am glad that I had a clear and logical mind when I was alive. I didn't know but that might have come later; it sometimes does. But this way we can understand each other. What I meant is this: Where I come from, of course I am dead; or if you prefer, you are dead. It means the same thing. Also I am alive and also I am not yet born. You see, I come from outside of time. You follow?"

"I think so. Eternity embraces all time, so when you've gone over from time into eternity, all time coexists for you."

"Not too precise an expression, but I think you grasp the essentials. Then, perhaps you can see what's happened. I've simply come back into time at the wrong point."

"How—"

"Imagine yourself at large in three dimensions, facing a fence with an infinite series of two-dimensional slots. Think how easy it'd be to pick the wrong slot."

I thought a while and nodded. "Could be," I admitted. "But if it's that easy, why doesn't it happen more often?"

"Oh, but it does. You've heard of apparitions of the living? You've heard of *Doppelgänger*? You've even heard of hauntings before the fact? Those are all cases like this—just slipping into the wrong slot. But it's such a damned stupid thing to do. I'm going to take a terrible ribbing for this." My ghost looked more downcast and perplexed than ever.

I started to be consoling. "Look. Don't take it so— Hey!" The implication suddenly hit me. "You said haunting?"

"Yes."

"Is that what you're doing?"

"Well . . . yes."

"But you can't be haunting me?"

"Of course not."

"Then whom are you haunting in my room?"

My ghost played with his ghostly cigarette and looked embarrassed. "It's not a thing we care to talk about. Haunting, I mean. It's not much fun, and it's rather naïve. But after all, it's—well, it's expected of you when you've been murdered."

I could hear the right arm of the chair crack under my clutch. "When you've been—"

"Yes, I know it's ridiculous and childish; but it's such an old, established custom that I haven't the courage to oppose it."

"Then you've been murdered? And that means *I've* been murdered? I mean, that means I'm *going* to be murdered?"

"Oh, yes," he said calmly.

I rose and opened a drawer of the desk. "This," I prescribed, "calls for the internal application of alcoholic stimulants. Damn," I added as the emergency buzzer rang. All I needed was a rush operation now, with my fingers already beginning to jitter.

I opened the door and looked out into star-bright emptiness. "False alarm." I was relieved—and then heard the whiz. I ducked it just in time and got the door closed.

My ghost was curiously contemplating the knife where it stuck quivering in the wall. "Right through me," he observed cheerfully.

It was no sinister and exotic stiletto. Just a plain butcher knife, and all the more chillingly convincing through its very ordinariness. "Your prophecies work fast," I said.

"This wasn't it. It missed. Just wait."

The knife had stopped its shuddering, but mine went on. "Now I really need that stimulant. You drink rye? But of course. I do."

"You don't happen," my ghost asked, "to have any tequila?"

"Tequila? Never tasted it."

"Oh. Then I must have acquired the taste later, before you were murdered."

I was just unscrewing the bottle top, and jumped enough to spill half a jiggerful. "I don't *like* that word."

"You'll get used to it," my ghost assured me. "Don't bother to pour me one. I'll just dematerialize the bottle."

The rye helped. Chatting with your own ghost about your murder seems more natural after a few ounces of whiskey. My ghost seemed to grow more at ease too, and after the third joint bottle tilting the atmosphere was practically normal.

"We've got to approach this rationally," I said at last.

"Whatever you are, that knife's real enough. And I'm fond of life. Let's see what we can do to stave this off."

"But you can't." My ghost was quietly positive. "Because I —or you—well, let's say *we*—already have been murdered."

"But not at this time."

"Not at this time yet, but certainly *in* this time. Look, I know the rules of haunting. I know that nothing could have sent me to this room unless we'd been killed here."

"But when? How? And above all, by whom? Who should want to toss knives at me?"

"It wasn't a knife the real time. I mean, it won't be."

"But why—"

My ghost took another healthy swig of dematerialized rye. "I should prefer tequila," he sighed.

"That's too damned bad," I snapped. "But tell me about my murder."

"Don't get into such a dither. What difference does it make? Nothing you can do can possibly affect the outcome. You have sense enough to understand that. Foreknowledge can never conceivably avert. That's the delusion and snare of all prophecy."

"All right. Grant that. Let's pretend it's just my natural curiosity. But *tell me about my murder*."

"Well—" My ghost was hesitant and sheepish again. "The fact is—" He took a long time to swallow his dematerialized rye, and followed the process with a prolonged dematerialized burp. "To tell you the truth—I don't remember anything about it.

"Now, now!" he added hastily. "Don't blow up. I can't help it. It's dreadfully easy to forget things in eternity. That's what the Greeks meant by the waters of Lethe in the afterworld. Just think how easy it is to forget details in, say, ten years, when the years are happening only one at a time. Then try to imagine how much you could forget in an infinity of years when they're all happening at once."

"But our own murder!" I protested. "You couldn't forget our murder!"

"I have. I know we must have been murdered in this room because here I am haunting it, but I've no idea how or when. Excepting," he added reflectively, "that it must be after we acquired a taste for tequila."

"But you must at least know the murderer. You have to know the guy you're supposed to be haunting. Or do you just haunt a *place*?"

"No. Not in the strict rules. You merely haunt the place because the murderer will return to the scene of the crime and then you confront him and say, '*Thou art the man!*'"

"And supposing he doesn't return to the scene?"

"That's just the trouble. We know the rules, all right. But the murderers don't always. Lots of times they never return at all, and we go on haunting and haunting and getting noplace."

"But look!" I exclaimed. "This one will *have* to return, because he hasn't been here yet. I mean, this isn't the scene of the crime; it's the scene set for a crime that hasn't happened yet. He'll have to come here to . . . to—"

"To murder us," my ghost concluded cheerfully. "Of course. It's ideal. I can't possibly miss him."

"But if you don't know who he is—"

"I'll know him when I see him. You see, we ghosts are psychic."

"Then if you could tip me off when you recognize him—"

"It wouldn't do you any— What was that?"

"Just a rooster. Dawn comes early these summer mornings. But if I knew who he was, then I—"

"Damn!" said my ghost. "Haunting must be so much simpler in winter, with those nice long nights. I've got to be vanishing. See you tonight."

My curiosity stirred again. "Where do you go when you vanish?" But he had already disappeared.

I looked around the empty consulting room. Even the dematerialized rye had vanished. Only the butcher knife remained. I made the natural rye vanish too, and staggered back to bed.

The next morning it all seemed perfectly simple. I had had one hell of a strange vision the night before; but on the consulting-room desk stood an empty pint which had been almost full yesterday. That was enough to account for a wilderness of visions.

Even the knife didn't bother me much. It would be accounted for some way—somebody's screwy idea of a gag. Nobody could want to kill me, I thought, and wasn't worried even when a kid in a back-lot baseball game let off a wild pitch that missed my head by an inch.

I just filed away a minor resolve to climb on the wagon if this sort of thing became a habit, and got through a hard day's work at the clinic with no worries beyond the mildest of hangovers. And when I got the X-rays on Nick Wojcek's girl with her lungs completely healed, and the report that she hadn't coughed for two weeks, I felt so gloriously satisfied that I forgot even the hangover.

"Charlie," I beamed at my X-ray technician, "life is good."

"In Cobbsville?" Charlie asked dourly.

I gloated over those beautiful plates. "Even in Cobbsville."

"Have it your way," said Charlie. "But it'll be better this evening. I'm dropping by your place with a surprise."

"A surprise?"

"Yeah. Friend of mine brought me a present from Mexico."

And even that didn't tip me off. I went on feeling as chipper and confident as ever all through the day's work and dinner at the Greek's, and walked home enjoying the freshness of the evening and fretting over a twist on a new kind of air filter for the factories.

That was why I didn't see the car. I was crossing the street to my house, and my first warning was a bass bellow of "John!" I looked up to see the car a yard away, rolling downhill straight at me. I jumped, stumbled, and sprawled flat in the dust. My knee ached and my nose was bleeding; but the car had missed me, as narrowly as the knife had last night.

I watched it roll on down the hill. There was no driver. It was an old junk heap—just the sort of wreck that would get out of control if carelessly left parked on a steep grade. It was a perfectly plausible accident, and still— The car hit the fence at the bottom of the hill and became literally a junk heap. Nobody showed up to bother about it. I turned to thank Father Svatomir for his shout of warning.

You've seen those little Orthodox churches that are the one spot of curious color in the drab landscape of industrial Pennsylvania? Those plain frame churches that blossom out on top into an exotic bloated spire topped by one of those crosses with an extra slantwise arm?

Father Svatomir was the priest from one of those, and his black garments, his nobly aquiline nose, and his beautifully full and long brown beard made him look as strange and Oriental as his own church. It was always a shock to me to hear his ordinary American accent—he'd been born in Cobbsville and gone to the Near East to study for the priesthood— and to realize that he was only about my age. That's thirty-two, for the record; but Father Svatomir seemed serenely ageless.

He waved away my thanks. "John, my son, I must speak with you. Alone and seriously."

"OK, Father"—and I took him around to the door into my own room. I somehow didn't want to go into the consulting room just yet. I was sure that there was nothing there; but night had fallen by now, and there was no telling.

I sat on the bed, and the priest pulled a chair up close. "John," he began quietly, "do you realize that you are in danger of your life?"

I couldn't help a glance at the door of the consulting room, but I said casually, "Nuts, Father. That little accident out there?"

"Accident? And how many other 'accidents' have befallen you recently?"

I thought of the butcher knife and the wild pitch, but I repeated, "Nuts. That's nonsense. Why should anybody want my life?"

"Because you are doing too much good. No, don't smile, my son. I am not merely indulging in a taste for paradox. I mean this. You are doing too much and you are in danger of your life. Martyrs are not found in the Church alone. Every field has its martyrs, and you are in most grievous danger of becoming a martyr to your splendid clinic."

"Bosh," I snorted, and wished I believed it.

"Bosh it is indeed, but my parishioners are not notably intellectual. They have brought with them from their own countries a mass of malformed and undigested superstitions. In those superstitions there is some small grain of spiritual truth, and that I seek to salvage whenever possible; but in most of those old-country beliefs there is only ignorance and peril."

"But what's all this to me?"

"They think," said Father Svatomir slowly, "that you are working miracles at the clinic."

"I am," I admitted.

He smiled. "As an agnostic, John, you may call them miracles and think no more of it. But my parishioners cannot see matters so simply. If *I*, now, were to work these wonders of healing, they would accept the fact as a manifestation of God's greatness; but when *you* work them— You see, my son, to these poor believing people, all great gifts and all perfect gifts are from above—or from below. Since you, in their sight, are an unbeliever and obviously not an agent of God, why, then, you must be an agent of the devil."

"Does it matter so long as I heal their lungs from the effects of this damned cement dust?"

"It matters very much indeed to them, John. It matters so much that, I repeat, you are in danger of your life."

I got up. "Excuse me a minute, Father . . . something I wanted to check in the consulting room."

It checked, all right. My ghost sat at the desk, large as death. He'd found my copy of *Fanny Hill*, dematerialized it, and settled down to thorough enjoyment.

"I'd forgotten this too," he observed as I came in.

I kept my voice low. "If you can forget our own murder, small wonder you'd forget a book."

"I don't mean the book. I'd forgotten the subject matter. And now it all comes back to me—"

"Look!" I said sharply. "The hell with your memories."

"They're not just mine." He gazed at me with a sort of leering admiration.

"The hell with them anyway. There's a man in the next room warning me that my life's in danger. I'll admit he just saved my life, but that could be a trick. Could he be the man?"

Reluctantly my ghost laid his book aside, came to the door, and peered out. "Uh-uh. We're safe as houses with him."

I breathed. "Stick around. This check-up system's going to be handy."

"You can't prevent what's happened," he said indifferently, and went back to the desk and *Fanny Hill*. As he picked up the book he spoke again, and his voice was wistful. "You haven't got a blonde I could dematerialize?"

I shut the consulting-room door on him and turned back to Father Svatomir. "Everything under control. I've got a notion, Father, that I'm going to prove quite capable of frustrating any attempts to break up my miracle-mongering. Or is it monging?"

"I've talked to them," the priest sighed. "I've tried to make them see the truth that you are indeed God's agent, whatever your own faith. I may yet succeed, but in the meanwhile—" He broke off and stared at the consulting room. "John, my son," he whispered, "what is in that room?"

"Nothing, Father. Just a file that I suddenly remembered needed checking."

"No, John. There's more than that. John, while you were gone, *something* peered at me through that door."

"You're getting jumpy, Father. Stop worrying."

"No. John, there is a spirit in this place."

"Fiddlesticks!"

"Oh, you may not feel affected; but after all, a man of my calling is closer to the spirit world than most."

"Father, your parishioners are corrupting you."

"No. Oh, I have smiled at many of their superstitions. I

have even disbelieved in spirits. I knew that they were doctrinally possible and so to be believed; but I never believed in them personally, as an individual rather than a priest. But now— John, something peered at me."

I swore silently and said aloud, "Calm yourself, Father."

Father Svatomir had risen and was pacing the room, hands clasped like Felix the Cat. "John, my son," he said at last, "you have been a good friend to me and my parish. I have long been grateful to you, and never been able to prove that gratitude. I shall do so now."

"And how?" I asked, with a certain nervous foreboding.

"John," he paused in his pacing and laid a hand on my shoulder, "John, I am going to exorcise the spirit that haunts this place."

"Hey!" I gasped. "No, Father. Please!" Because, I reasoned hastily to myself, exorcising spirits is all very well, but when it's your own spirit and if that gets exorcised—well, what happens to you then? "No," I insisted. "You can't do that."

"I know, John," he went on in his calm, deep voice. "You think that this is more superstition, on a level with the beliefs of my parishioners. But though you do not sense this . . . this *thing* yet, you will in time. I shall save you much pain and discomfort. Wait here, John, while I go fetch some holy water and check up the formula for exorcism. I'm afraid," he added ruefully, "I haven't looked at it since my days in the seminary."

I seized his arm and opened my mouth in protestation too urgent for words.

"John," he said slowly and reproachfully, "are you willfully harboring a spirit?"

A knock on the door cut the scene short and gave me a breathing spell. I like Charlie, but I don't think I've ever before been so relieved to see him.

"Hi," he said, and "Hi," again to Father Svatomir. "That's the advantage of being celibate," he added. "You can grow a beard. I tried to once, but the waitress down at the Greek's didn't like it."

Father Svatomir smiled faintly.

"Three glasses, mine host," Charlie commanded, and produced from under his arm a tall bottle of greenish glass. "Told you I had a surprise."

I fetched three whiskey glasses and set them on the table. Charlie filled them with a flourish. "Noble stuff, this," he announced. "Want to hear what you gentlemen think of it. There's supposed to be a ritual goes with it, but I like it straight. Down the esophagus, boys!"

Was it Shelley who used the phrase "potable gold"? Whoever it was had surely tasted this liquor. It flowed down like some molten metal that had lost the dangerous power to scorch, but still glowed with rich warmth. While the subtle half-perceived flavor still clove to my mouth, I could feel the tingling heat reach my fingertips.

"By Heaven," I cried, "nothing like this has happened to the blood stream since Harvey discovered the circulation. Charlie, my lad, this is henceforth my tipple!"

Father Svatomir beamed and nodded. "I concur heartily. Tell us, Charles, what is this wondrous brew?"

"Tequila," said Charlie, and I dropped my glass.

"What is the trouble, my son? You're pale and trembling."

"Look, Johnny. I know it's high-proof stuff, but it hadn't ought to hit you like that."

I hardly heard them. All I knew was that the onetime barrier separating me from my murder was now removed. I had come to like tequila. I bent over to pick up the glass, and as I did so I saw a hand reach out from the consulting room. It touched the tequila bottle lightly and withdrew clutching a freshly dematerialized fifth.

Charlie refilled the three glasses, "Another one'll put you back on your feet, Johnny. It's swell stuff once you get used to it."

Father Svatomir was still concerned. "John," he insisted, "was it the tequila? Or did you . . . have you sensed what we were speaking of before?"

I gulped the second glass. "I'm all right," I protested. "A couple more of these and I'll— Was that a knock?"

Charlie looked around. "Consulting-room door, I think. Shall I go check?"

I slipped quickly between him and the door. "Never mind. I'll see."

"Had I better go with you?" the priest suggested. "If it were what I warned you of—"

"It's OK. I'll go."

My ghost was lolling back in my chair with his feet propped up on the desk. One hand held *Fanny Hill* and the other the tequila. "I got a good look at the guy that brought this," he volunteered without looking up. "He's all right."

"Fine. Now I have to let in a patient. Could you briefly disappear?"

"Uh-uh. Not till the cock crows."

"Then please hide. Try that cupboard—I think it's big enough."

He started for the cupboard, returned for book and bottle, and went back to shut himself up in comfort. I opened the outer door a very small crack and said, "Who is it?"

"Me, Dr. Adams. Nick Wojcek."

I opened the door without a tremor. Whatever Father Ratomir might say about the other inhabitants of Cobbsville, I knew I had nothing to fear from the man whose daughter was my most startlingly successful cure to date. I could still see the pitiful animal terror in his eyes when he had brought her to me and the pure joy that had glistened in them when I told him she was well.

"Come in, Nick. Sit down and be comfortable."

He obeyed the first half of my injunction, but he fidgeted most uncomfortably. Despite his great height and his grizzled hair, he looked like a painfully uncertain child embarrassed by the presence of strange adults. "My Ljuba," he faltered. "You got those pictures you tell me about?"

"I saw them today. And it's good news, Nick. Your Ljuba is all well again. It's all healed up."

"She stay that way now?"

"I hope to God. But I can't promise. So long as you live

in this dump and breathe cement dust day in and day out,
can't guarantee you a thing. But I think she'll be well nov
Let her marry some nice young man who'll take her awa
from here into the clean air."

.No," he said sullenly.

"But come, Nick," I said gently. It was pleasant to argu
an old man's foibles for a moment instead of fretting ov
your approaching murder. "She has to lead her own life."

"You tell me what do? You go to hell!"

I drew back astounded. There was the sheer venom
hatred in that last phrase. "Nick!" I protested.

He was on his feet now, and in his hand was an ancie
but nonetheless lethal-looking revolver. "You make magic,
he was saying slowly and harshly. "God would let my Ljub
die. You make her live. Black magic. Don't want daught
from magic."

"Nick," I urged as quietly as I could, "don't be a damne
fool. There are people in the next room. Suppose I call f
them?"

"I kill you first," said Nick Wojcek simply.

"But they'll find you here. You can't get away. They
burn you for this, Nick. Then what'll become of Ljuba?"

He hesitated, but the muzzle of the revolver never waver
Now that I was staring my murderer right in the nose, I fe
amazingly calm. I could see, in a clear and detached way, ju
how silly it was to try to avert the future by preknowledg
I had thought my ghost would warn me; but there he was i
the closet, comfortably curled up with a bottle of liquor an
a dirty book, and here I was, staring into Nick Wojcek's r
volver. He'd come out afterward of course, my ghost woul
he'd get in his haunting and go home. While I . . . only the
I'd be my ghost, wouldn't I? I'd go home too—wherever th
was.

"If they get me," said Nick at last, "they get me. I get yo
first."

His grip tightened on the revolver. And at that momer
my tardy ghost reeled out of the closet. He brandished th

empty green tequila bottle in one hand, and his face was carefree and roistering.

My ghost pointed the bottle dramatically at Nick Wojcek and grinned broadly. "*Thou art the man!*" he thundered cheerily.

Nick started, whirled, and fired. For an instant he stood rooted and stared first at the me standing by the desk and then at the me slowly sinking to the floor. Then he flung the revolver away and ran terror-stricken from the room.

I was kneeling at my ghost's side where he lay groaning on the floor. "But what happened?" I gasped. "I don't understand."

"Neither do I," he moaned. "Got a little drunk . . . started haunting too soon—" My ghost's form was becoming indistinct.

"But you're a ghost. That knife went right through you. Nothing can wound you."

"That's what I thought. But he did . . . and here I am—" His voice was trailing away too. "Only one thing . . . could have—" Then there was silence, and I was staring at nothing but the empty floor, with a little glistening piece of light metal on it.

Father Svatomir and Charlie were in the room now, and the silence was rapidly crammed with questions. I scrambled to my feet and tried to show more assurance than I felt. "You were right, Father. It was Nick Wojcek. Went for me with that revolver. Luckily, he missed, got panicky, and ran away."

"I shall find him," said Father Svatomir gravely. "I think that after this fright I may be able to talk some sense into him; then perhaps he can help me convince the others." He paused and looked down at the gleaming metal. "You see, John? I told you they believed you to be a black magician."

"How so?"

"You notice that? A silver bullet. Ordinary lead cannot harm a magician, but the silver bullet can kill anything. Even a spirit." And he hastened off after Nick Wojcek.

Wordlessly, I took the undematerialized tequila bottle from Charlie and paid some serious attention to it. I began to see now. It made sense. My ghost hadn't averted my death—that had been an absurd hope—but he had caused his own. All the confusion came from his faulty memory. He was haunting not mine, but his *own* murderer. It was my ghost himself who had been killed in this room.

That was all right. That was fine. I was safe from murder now, and must have been all along. But what I wanted to know, what I still want to know, what I have to find out and what no one can ever tell me, is this:

What happens after death to a man whose ghost has already been murdered?

FINE SCIENCE FICTION AND FANTASY TITLES AVAILABLE FROM CARROLL & GRAF

- [ ] Aldiss, Brian/NON-STOP — $3.95
- [ ] Amis, Kingsley/THE ALTERATION — $3.50
- [ ] Asimov, Isaac et al/THE MAMMOTH BOOK OF CLASSIC SCIENCE FICTION (1930s) — $8.95
- [ ] Asimov, Isaac et al/THE MAMMOTH BOOK OF GOLDEN AGE SCIENCE FICTION (1940s) — $8.95
- [ ] Ballard, J.G./THE DROWNED WORLD — $3.95
- [ ] Ballard, J.G./THE HIGH RISE — $3.50
- [ ] Ballard, J.G./HELLO AMERICA — $3.95
- [ ] Ballard, J.G./TERMINAL BEACH — $3.50
- [ ] Ballard, J.G./VERMILION SANDS — $3.95
- [ ] Burroughs, Edgar Rice/A PRINCESS OF MARS — $2.95
- [ ] Dick Philip K./DR. BLOODMONEY — $3.95
- [ ] Dick Philip K./CLANS OF THE ALPHANE MOON — $3.95
- [ ] Dick, Philip K./THE PENULTIMATE TRUTH — $3.95
- [ ] Dick, Philip K./TIME OUT OF JOINT — $3.95
- [ ] Disch, Thomas K./CAMP CONCENTRATION — $3.95
- [ ] Disch, Thomas K./ON WINGS OF SONG — $3.95
- [ ] Lovecraft, H. P. & Derleth, A./THE LURKER ON THE THRESHOLD — $3.50
- [ ] Malzberg, Barry/GALAXIES — $2.95
- [ ] Moorcock, Michael/BEHOLD THE MAN — $2.95
- [ ] Moorcock, Michael/FANTASY: THE 100 BEST BOOKS (Cloth) — $15.95
- [ ] Stableford, Brian/THE WALKING SHADOW — $3.95
- [ ] Stoker, Bram/THE JEWEL OF SEVEN STARS — $3.95
- [ ] Sturgeon, Theodore/VENUS PLUS X — $3.95
- [ ] Sturgeon, Theodore/THE GOLDEN HELIX — $3.95

Available from fine bookstores everywhere or use this coupon for ordering.